HIS
SUBSTITUTE BRIDE

Elizabeth Lane

™ MILLS & BOON®

First published in Great Britain 2010
Harlequin Mills & Boon Limited,
Eton House, 18-24 Paradise Road, Richmond, Surrey TW9 1SR

© Elizabeth Lane 2009

ISBN: 978 0 263 87596 6

Harlequin Mills & Boon policy is to use papers that are natural, renewable and recyclable products and made from wood grown in sustainable forests. The logging and manufacturing process conform to the legal environmental regulations of the country of origin.

Printed and bound in Spain
by Litografia Rosés, S.A., Barcelona

For Teresa and Ted
and for San Francisco

Chapter One

San Francisco, April 13, 1906

By the time Quint found the woman, she was dying. She lay faceup on the checkered linoleum, a dollar-size crimson stain oozing through the fabric of her plain white shirtwaist. It appeared she'd been stabbed.

"Virginia!" Quint crouched beside her, clasping her hand. "Can you hear me? It's Quint Seavers!"

The blood-frothed lips moved slightly, but no sound emerged. She was a slight creature, about thirty, he judged, her plain features made plainer by the thick spectacles that lay askew on her nose. Quint was meeting her in person for the first time. But he already knew Virginia Poole to be honest and brave. The man responsible for this was damned well going to pay.

"The letter, Virginia!" His fingers tightened around hers. "Where is it? Can you tell me?"

But she was already gone, slipping away without a sound.

Releasing her hand, Quint cast his eyes around the shabby one-room apartment. The place had been ransacked. Furniture had been toppled, clothes thrown helter-skelter. Kitchen cupboards had been emptied, their contents strewn on the floor. The Murphy bed, which took up one wall, had been lowered, the mattress, quilt and pillow ripped to pieces.

Feathers eddied in the gaslit room, blown by a chilly draft from the open window. Whoever was here hadn't been gone long. They'd probably climbed over the sill when they'd heard Quint pounding on the door. Judging from the mess and the hasty departure, he'd bet good money they hadn't found what they were looking for.

And neither would he.

Quint cursed in frustration. The handwritten letter, linking Supervisor Josiah Rutledge to a crooked scheme involving funds for the city's water system, would provide enough evidence to bring Rutledge down. Even more important, it would alert the public that this critical work wasn't being done.

Quint had written more than a dozen articles for the *San Francisco Chronicle,* stressing the urgent need to repair the city's crumbling network of pipes, aqueducts and cisterns and build a line to pump water out of the bay. Just last week he'd interviewed Dennis Sullivan, the city's longtime fire chief, who'd stated that, given the faulty water system, a major fire could destroy much of the city, with loss of life in the hundreds, if not the thousands.

"This town," Sullivan had declared, "is on an earthquake belt. One of these fine mornings we'll get a shake that will put this little water system out, and then we'll have a fire. What will we do then?"

For a balanced perspective, he'd also interviewed Mayor Eugene Schmitz and Supervisor Rutledge. Both had insisted that repairs were being made in good order.

And pigs could fly, Quint had groused as he left City Hall. Schmitz was almost as crooked as Rutledge. The whole mess stank like rotten fish. But he couldn't just start making accusations. He needed solid proof.

The key to that proof had come yesterday, in the form of a phone call to his desk at the *Chronicle*. Virginia Poole, a clerk on Rutledge's staff, had, by sheer accident, come across the damning letter in a stack of papers she'd been given to file. Knowing what she had, and being a woman of conscience, she'd called Quint and offered to give the letter to him.

He'd arranged to meet her the next evening in a bookshop off Portsmouth Square. When she'd failed to show up, Quint, who'd had the foresight to ask for her home address, had sensed that something was wrong.

Sadly, his instincts had been right.

Sick with dismay, he rose to his feet. At some point, Rutledge must have missed the letter and realized it had been scooped up with the other paperwork. Grilled by her boss, Virginia would have denied seeing it. But she'd probably been too nervous to convince him. One call and the hounds in Rutledge's pay would have been on her trail, with orders to silence her and get the letter back.

It seemed indecent not to cover the poor woman with a sheet, or at least close her eyes. But Quint knew the police would soon be here, alerted by the very thugs who'd committed the crime. If they discovered his presence, he'd be hauled into jail as a murder suspect; and with so many cops in Rutledge's pocket, odds were he wouldn't live long enough to see the inside of a courtroom.

Leaving by the back stairs, Quint slipped into the alley and cut a meandering course down Telegraph Hill to Montgomery Street. The mist-shrouded night was damp and chilly, the lighthouse a great blinking eye in the darkness behind him. Foghorns echoed mournfully across the bay.

Thrusting his hands into his pockets, Quint lengthened his stride. Tomorrow at work he would call in some favors, find out whether Virginia's murder was being investigated or merely hushed up.

He would also make inquiries about her daily routine, talk to her friends, her family if she had any. With luck, maybe he could—

Oh, bloody hell!

Quint halted as if he'd slammed into a brick wall.

Tomorrow morning Clara and Annie would be arriving by train, all the way from Dutchman's Creek, Colorado. Quint had arranged to take the entire week off. He had cleared his calendar of appointments, freeing his time to show them the city.

For weeks he'd looked forward to the visit. Six-year-old Clara was the most important person in Quint's life. Every minute with the little girl was a gift. And Annie Gustavson, her maternal aunt, was always pleasant company. Neither of them had ever been to California. They were eager to experience the marvels of San Francisco.

Now this mess had dropped into Quint's hands, and he had no choice except to deal with it.

It was too late to postpone the visit. Their train would be arriving at the Oakland terminal at 11:00 a.m. tomorrow morning. After such a long trip, he could hardly put them back onboard and send them home. Nor could he walk away from a story so rife with urgency.

What the devil was he going to do?

Quint hailed a cab to take him back to his Jackson Street apartment. Somehow, for the coming week, he would have to be in two places at once. If it meant working early mornings and late nights, or leaving Clara and Annie on their own once in a while, that couldn't be helped. Virginia Poole had given her life to expose Rutledge. Whatever it took, Quint vowed, he would make sure she hadn't died in vain.

"Where's the ocean, Aunt Annie? I want to see it!" Clara bounced with excitement. Her nose smudged the window of the first-class railway car.

"All in good time, Miss Clara Seavers." Annie resettled her weary buttocks against the vibrating seat cushion. She adored her sister Hannah's child, but three days and nights on a rattling train with an active six-year-old had frayed her nerves. She looked forward to a quiet lunch, a lovely hot bath…and Quint. Especially Quint.

Damn his charming, impossible hide!

Maybe after this week, she would finally be over him.

Frank Robinson, who owned the hotel in Dutchman's Creek, had asked Annie to marry him three times. He was decent, kind and passably handsome, with enough money to keep her in comfort for the rest of her days.

Her sister Hannah thought she was crazy for turning Frank down. "You're twenty-three years old, Annie!" she'd fussed. "What are you waiting for, a knight on a white horse?"

The question was wasted breath, and both sisters

knew it. Quint Seavers was no shining knight. But Annie had worshipped him since her teens. That was why she'd turned down Frank Robinson and every other man who'd come courting. To say yes would be to turn her back on Quint—who, in all the years she'd loved him, had barely given her the time of day.

Annie had jumped at his invitation to bring Clara to San Francisco. She'd yearned to experience that great, pulsing city known as the Paris of the West. She was eager, as well, to see the new fashions and copy them for her clients back home. As for Quint…

Annie sighed. She had no illusions about why he'd sent her the ticket. He needed someone to accompany Clara and act as a nanny during the visit. Well, fine. She was determined to have a good time anyway. And she would do her best to see Quint through clear eyes. If she could convince herself the man wasn't worth pining over, maybe she'd be ready to go back home and accept Frank's proposal.

"Will Uncle Quint be there when we get off the train?" Clara asked.

"He said he would."

"Did he promise?"

"In a way, I suppose he did."

"Then he will." Clara nodded happily. "Uncle Quint always keeps his promises! How much longer is it?"

"Not much longer. We should be there in time for lunch." Annie slipped an arm around the little girl.

"What do you suppose your mama and papa are doing without you?"

"I'll bet Papa's taking care of the ranch. And Mama's resting. The doctor says she needs to rest a lot so the new baby won't come before it's s'posed to."

Clara had always been a perceptive child. But Annie was surprised that she understood about Hannah's difficult pregnancy. After a near miscarriage, her doctor had ordered bed rest for the next two months. Her husband, Judd, Quint's older brother, was rightly concerned about her.

"And what about Daniel?" Annie asked, changing the subject. "What do you think he's doing?"

"Being a pest. He's always being a pest," Clara said, dismissing her three-year-old brother. "I hope the new baby pesters him just like he pesters me. It'll serve him right."

"Clara, Clara!" Annie hauled the child onto her lap. "Here, look out the window. We're coming into Oakland now. Soon you'll be able to see San Francisco Bay. It's almost like the ocean!"

"Will we ride on a boat?"

"Yes. We'll be taking the ferry boat across the bay to San Francisco."

"The fairy boat?" Clara's eyes danced. "Will it have fairies on it?"

Annie laughed and hugged her niece. "No, silly, just people."

Thirty minutes later the train pulled into the station. Plastered against the window, Clara scanned the platform. "There he is! There's Uncle Quint! Look, he can see us! He's waving!"

They gathered their things and filed down the aisle to the exit door. Quint was there to greet them, looking tired but unforgivably handsome in a light woolen topcoat and black derby. He helped Annie down the steps, then swept Clara off her feet, waltzing her around until she squealed with laughter.

Watching them, Annie felt the familiar ache. What a breathtaking pair they were, the man and the child. They had the same brown eyes and thick, dark chestnut curls, the same dimpled cheeks and dazzling smiles.

No one with eyes in their head could fail to guess the truth.

Clara was Quint's daughter.

Rounding up a porter to load their bags, Quint ushered his charges toward the ferry terminal. Clara skipped along beside him, keeping up a stream of chatter. Annie, Quint noticed, had scarcely said a word.

He stole sidelong glances at her as they moved along the crowded platform. She'd always been an attractive girl, smaller and more delicately sculpted than her sister Hannah, her hair a deeper, tawnier shade of blond; her eyes darker and more intense, closer to gray than blue.

How old would she be now? Well past twenty, Quint was startled to realize. Why hadn't she married? She was by far the cleverest of the Gustavson girls and almost as pretty as Hannah. She earned a good living, too, with the hats and clothes she fashioned for the ladies of Dutchman's Creek. One would think she'd have men falling at her feet.

Today she wore a smart gabardine traveling suit in a soft russet that brought out the rose in her cheeks. Quint found the dainty hat that perched atop her upswept hair far more flattering than the monstrous creations women were wearing these days. Annie had probably sewn the entire outfit, as well as Clara's navy blue sailor dress, which made her look like a demure little doll.

Clara was growing up too fast, Quint mused as he helped them onto the ferry. And he was missing out on far too much of her life. But that price was his to pay for leaving Hannah with child seven years ago.

They'd been longtime sweethearts, he and Hannah Gustavson. It went without saying that they would marry. But Quint had wanted to see something of the world first. He'd set off for the Klondike gold fields, not knowing that a single fumbling encounter had left Hannah pregnant. When Quint couldn't be reached, his brother Judd had married her to give the baby the Seavers name. Quint had returned eleven months later to find that Hannah and Judd had fallen in love and become husband and wife in every way.

The first time Quint held his baby daughter, his heart had turned over. But even then he'd known what he needed to do. He had walked away, leaving his little girl to be raised in a happy home by the only father she'd ever known.

Much as it stung, Quint knew he'd done the right thing. The ranch was an ideal place to grow up. Judd and Hannah were devoted to their children and to each other. They allowed him to be involved in Clara's life as her beloved, indulgent "uncle."

It was all he could ask—and more than he likely deserved.

Annie's eyes traced the outline of Quint's broad shoulders as he lifted Clara onto a bench next to the rail. His unruly dark hair curled below the brim of his hat, brushing his collar in a way that made her want to reach out and stroke it with her fingertips. Nothing had changed. Quint was as compelling as ever. And she was just as fluttery and tongue-tied as she'd been at fifteen, on the day she'd discovered she loved him.

It had been an April day, she recalled, under a bright Colorado sky. The hillsides were dotted with yellow buttercups and splashes of red Indian paintbrush. Returning birds staked out nesting territory with raucous calls.

With no promise of meat for the stewpot, Annie had loaded an old .22, the only gun her family owned, and set out for the hills to shoot a rabbit. Quint had come by an hour later, on his way home from seeing Hannah. Stopping his horse at a safe distance, he'd watched her plunking away at animals that wouldn't hold still, missing every shot.

"So you're the hunter of the family," he'd teased.

"Somebody's got to do it," Annie had flung back. "Papa's too tired. Mama's too busy. Hannah's too squeamish and Ephraim's too young. That leaves me."

"Not having much luck, are you?" he'd observed.

"That's easy for you to say, Quint Seavers. When your family's out of meat, all they have to do is butcher a steer. For us, it's different. If you're so smart why don't you shoot one of these rabbits?"

"I can do better than that." He'd swung off the horse and walked toward her. "I'll teach you how to shoot one."

And he had taught her—standing beside her, steadying her arm, showing her how to line up the bead in the notch and squeeze the trigger without jerking. His body had been warm through his flannel shirt, his hands soft and tough, like waxed saddle leather. His skin and hair had smelled of store-bought soap. She had breathed him into her senses, as if his essence could permeate every cell in her body.

By the afternoon's end, Annie had shot two rabbits and lost her romantic young heart. Of course, she couldn't let on. Quint was Hannah's beau, and they would likely get married someday. But she could love him in secret, from a distance, like a maiden of old pining for Sir Galahad.

Over time she'd learned that Quint was no Galahad. He'd fathered Clara and broken her sister's heart. She'd expected that would be enough to make her stop loving him. It wasn't.

She was a grown woman now. But a glance from Quint could still turn her into a simpering teenager. On the train she'd felt strong and confident, ready to face him as an equal. Now, after two minutes with the man, her insides had turned to jelly. How was she going to manage a whole week without making a fool of herself?

Clara pressed against the rail, watching the water splash along the side of the ferry. "Is this the ocean?" she asked.

"This is just the bay. We'll see the ocean later, maybe tomorrow." Quint clasped her under the arms to keep her from leaning too far. "For now I have other plans. First we'll stop by my flat to leave the bags and give you girls a chance to freshen up. Then we'll go downtown to have lunch at Delmonico's. How does that sound?"

"Delmonico's?" Annie lifted an eyebrow as the cab began to move. "Goodness, I must say I'm impressed."

"Where else would I go to show off the two loveliest ladies in San Francisco?"

"You were born with a silver tongue in your head, Quint Seavers. Such pretty words!" Did she sound clever or simply waspish?

"I make my living with words—some pretty, some not so pretty, but all true." Quint settled back with one arm around his little girl. "How's your sister?"

"Holding her own. The doctor says the baby's doing fine. But Hannah doesn't take well to bed rest. She's not used to being idle." A smile crept across Annie's lips. "The last time we visited, she was sharing her bed with Daniel and Clara, two puppies, three dolls and a toy train!"

"That sounds like Hannah."

"She's the perfect mother."

"I know—and Judd's the perfect father." Quint glanced down at Clara's beribboned curls. "As for me, I'm doing my best to be a decent uncle."

"You're much more than that. Daniel loves the little trolley car you sent him. Maybe it's time you had a family of your own, Quint."

Quint shifted Clara onto his knee. "That's a fine idea. But first I need to find the right sort of woman."

"And what sort of woman would that be?" The minute she said it she regretted her words.

He hesitated. Her heart sank as she guessed the unspoken answer. Quint had never gotten over his lost love. That was why he'd never married. And that was one reason he was so devoted to Clara. The child was his souvenir, his own little piece of Hannah.

Maybe if she kept reminding herself of that, she could get through the week with her heart intact.

In no time at all they were docking at the ferry building with its impressive clock tower. Quint helped them ashore, saw to their luggage and summoned a horse-drawn cab. Soon they were traveling down Market Street, amid the wonders of San Francisco.

"Look, Uncle Quint! What's that?" Clara pointed as a racing fire wagon, drawn by four horses, rounded the corner ahead of them. Bells clanged as they thundered closer. The cab driver pulled over to let them pass.

"They're on their way to a fire," Quint explained to the wide-eyed Clara. "That big tank on the wagon is the boiler for the steam pump. It helps them spray water to put the fire out."

"Will they put it all out?"

"Let's hope so. Sometimes we have bad fires here because the houses are close together and they're mostly made of wood."

"Is your house made of wood, Uncle Quint?"

He gave her a reassuring hug. "My apartment is in a nice brick building, so don't you worry your pretty head. We'll be fine there."

As they chatted, Annie peered out the cab's open side at the wonders of San Francisco. She'd been in Denver plenty of times to buy fabric and trim, but Denver was a backwater compared to this shining metropolis that throbbed with life and excitement.

Buildings of stone and concrete towered around her like canyon walls. Traffic streamed by in a constant flood—horse-drawn cabs, wagons and buggies, new gasoline-powered autos and electric trolley cars that ran on tracks down the middle of the street.

And the people! Annie had never seen so many or so much variety. Vendors hawked their wares from carts on the sidewalks, everything from cabbages to gold watches and bright bolts of silk. Chinese men in dark, pajamalike garb, their heads crowned by black derby hats, darted among the crowds with burdens slung from poles on their shoulders. A gang of sailors jostled each other as a pretty, foreign-looking girl passed them. Two prosperous-looking businessmen stepped off a trolley and entered a bank.

Traffic sounds made a roar in Annie's weary head. Right now she would gladly have traded lunch at Delmonico's for a nice nap. But she knew Quint had planned the meal as a special treat. She would smile and do her best to enjoy it.

The stop at Quint's apartment was brief, allowing for little more than hauling up the baggage and using the splendid porcelain facilities. They also met the smiling, middle-aged Chinese man called Chao, who worked as Quint's cook and housekeeper.

The two-bedroom apartment was spacious and comfortable, with a brown leather settee and two matching chairs drawn up before the fireplace. The walls were paneled in walnut and sparsely but taste-fully decorated with photographs Quint had taken on his visits to the ranch. There were shots of snow-covered peaks, willows in winter, the house, the barn, the cattle and the wagon loaded with hay. One picture showed Quint's scruffy border collie, Pal, who'd lived into old age and passed on. Another showed a beautifully windblown Hannah on the porch with two-year-old Clara in her arms.

Annie couldn't help wondering how Quint could afford such a place on a reporter's salary. But then she remembered that he'd sold his share of the ranch to Judd and invested the proceeds. He would have all the money he needed. At the very least he could afford to take them to a nice lunch.

The name Delmonico's had been synonymous with glamour and elegance for more than half a cen-tury. The San Francisco version was the most daz-zling place Annie had ever seen. Glittering crystal chandeliers hung above what looked like acres of linen-covered tables decked with fresh flowers. Formally dressed waiters flitted among them, bal-ancing silver trays the size of wagon wheels above the heads of the diners. Seated at a grand piano, a young black man played a tinkling waltz.

The waiter seated them at a table near a window and pulled out the brocade-covered chairs for Annie and Clara. Quint passed on their orders from the à la carte menu—braised chicken for Clara, poached salmon for Annie and a plate of oysters on half shell for himself. Then they waited for their orders, sipping fresh lemonade and nibbling from a platter of tiny crackers, smoked meats, pâtés and cheeses.

Clara's ongoing chatter filled the need for conversation, allowing Annie to observe the diners. Most of the women wore skirts and jackets, beautifully cut and embellished with tucks and lavish embroidery. The fabrics almost made her drool— jewel-toned wools, raw silks, heart-stopping merinos and cashmeres, English tweeds to die for. And the hats! Merciful heaven, such hats! They were veritable museum pieces, piled with clouds of tulle, huge satin bows, artificial birds, sparkling jewels and jutting feathers. Annie had thought her own well-tailored suit and modest chapeau chic enough to wear anywhere. She had, in fact, been one of the most fashionable women on the train. But in this place she felt like a drab little country mouse.

"Why, Quint Seavers! What a surprise!" The speaker was a stunning woman with hair the color of a prairie sunset. She was dressed in a skirt and jacket of emerald silk bombazine, which looked costly enough to feed Annie's mother, brothers and sisters for six months. A forward-curving black plume adorned her hat and framed one jade-colored eye.

"I missed you at the opening of my play," she

cooed. "You aren't angry with me, are you, darling? After that awful scene at the club…"

"Not at all." Quint rose. "Evelyn, I'd like you to meet Miss Annie Gustavson and my niece, Clara. Ladies, this is Evelyn Page, whose acting is the toast of San Francisco."

Annie murmured a polite greeting. Ignoring her, Evelyn focused on Clara. "Your niece? What a delightful surprise! And she's adorable! She looks enough like you to be your daughter!"

"So people say," Quint muttered. "It's good seeing you again, Evelyn. Save me a seat at your next opening night, and I'll write you a nice review."

"You'd better, you naughty man! Ta!" She sashayed toward the door with a flutter of her lace-gloved hand. Quint sighed as he took his seat.

"She's pretty," Clara said. "Are you going to marry her, Uncle Quint?"

"I hardly think Miss Page is the marrying kind," Quint said.

"But she called you *darling*. Doesn't that mean she loves you?"

Quint was saved from answering by the arrival of the waiter with their meals. Annie's poached salmon, cradled on a bed of fresh, steamed kale, looked delicious, not like the lumpy gray-green morsels on Quint's platter of shells. Annie had read about oysters, but she'd never seen them before. They looked downright revolting.

She gave them a tentative sniff and wrinkled her nose. "All I can say is, you've come a long way from Dutchman's Creek, Mr. Seavers," she teased.

Quint appeared not to have heard. He was staring at something—or someone—on the far side of the room. As she watched, his face paled, his eyes went flinty and his mouth hardened into a blade-thin line.

Chapter Two

Quint's attention was riveted to the far side of the crowded restaurant. Only when a tall, swarthy man rose from his place did Annie realize who he was watching.

The man laid a bill on the white linen cloth. Then, strolling across the floor, he cut a path toward their table. A vague unease crept over Annie as she watched him come. He looked to be in his late forties, solidly built, with slick, black hair, an actor's profile and a well-trimmed Vandyke.

His suit of fine gray worsted looked exquisitely expensive. Annie, with her eye for fabric and tailoring, recognized good custom work when she saw it. He carried an ebony walking stick topped by a brass lion's head. Since the stick never touched the floor, Annie judged it to be an ornament, a weapon or maybe both. A large ruby signet ring decorated one finger. A penny-size mole splotched his left cheek.

Reaching their table, the man paused as if he'd just happened upon them. Quint had assumed an air of nonchalance. He made a show of swirling an oyster in the buttery sauce.

At last, with a huff of impatience, the stranger spoke. "Fancy meeting you here, Mr. Seavers. Aren't you going to introduce me to your charming lunch companions?"

Quint finished the oyster and laid the small fork on the plate, taking his time. "Miss Annie Gustavson and her niece, Miss Clara," he said. "Ladies, it gives me no great pleasure to present Mr. Josiah Rutledge, a member of our fair city's board of supervisors."

If Rutledge had caught the slight, he chose to ignore it. "Miss Gustavson, Miss Clara, my pleasure," he murmured, bowing over Annie's extended hand. Clara, she noticed, had slipped out of her chair and moved close to Quint. She shrank against his sleeve as Rutledge smiled at her. Annie had never known her niece to be shy.

Rutledge cleared his throat. "I read your column in the *Chronicle* last week, Seavers. You tread a fine line between speculation and libel. More pieces like that one, and you could find yourself in court."

Quint didn't stir, but Annie sensed the coiled spring tension in him. "I can hardly be sued for writing the truth," he said.

"Truth?" The mole darkened as color flared in Rutledge's face. "You wouldn't know the truth if it bit you in the pants. Do you have any proof?"

Quint speared another oyster with his fork and stirred it in the sauce. A pinpoint of sweat glistened on Rutledge's temple.

"Did you hear me, Seavers? I asked whether you had proof."

Quint paused in his stirring. "Are you saying that proof exists?"

"You don't have a blasted thing, do you?"

Quint shrugged. "Not yet. But give me time. Sooner or later, I'll find a rope to hang you with, Rutledge. When I do, you won't have to ask."

"Ladies, my pleasure." Rutledge turned away with a curt nod and strode toward the exit.

Clara was still clinging to Quint's sleeve. "I don't like that man, Uncle Quint," she piped in her childish voice. "He scares me."

Rutledge froze in his tracks, making it clear he'd heard. Turning slightly, he looked back over his shoulder.

His smile chilled Annie to the soles of her shoes.

They spent the afternoon seeing the city from an open horse-drawn cab. Quint did his best to be a good guide, but Annie could see that he was distracted. At unguarded moments, his features tightened into a worried scowl that was nothing like the rakish, playful Quint she remembered. Something was wrong; and Annie suspected it had to do with the man they'd met at Delmonico's.

The cab took them up Market Street where electric trolley cars clanked along tracks of steel. On either side of the tracks, buggies, wagons and autos crowded the thoroughfare.

Annie gaped at the towering granite-faced Call Building with its wedding-cake top. City Hall, with its massive dome and pillared facade, looked almost as grand as the photographs she had seen of St. Paul's in London.

"The pillars are supposed to be solid marble," Quint said. "That's what our taxes paid for. But I know for a fact they're hollow and filled with gravel. The contractor probably split the difference with the city supervisor who gave him the job." He glanced down at Clara, who'd fallen asleep against his shoulder. "San Francisco's run by a bunch of crooks, from the mayor on down, and one day there's going to be hell to pay for it."

"Is that what you wrote about in your column? The one your friend Rutledge didn't like?"

"My friend?" Quint mouthed a curse. "Rutledge is the worst of the lot. He knows I'm on to his shenanigans. But he's right—I don't have a lick of evidence to pin on him. He keeps his own hands lily-white while his hired thugs do the dirty work."

"And all you can do, as the man said, is tread the

line between speculation and libel. Isn't that dangerous, Quint?" Annie's gaze traced the worried lines on his face, lingering on the shadows beneath his warm brown eyes. It was all she could do to keep from reaching out and brushing back the lock of hair that had strayed from under his hat.

"Dangerous?" His frown deepened. "Maybe. But if I were to disappear, everyone who reads my column in the *Chronicle* would be aware of it. And I've got friends, good friends who know what I know and wouldn't let it rest. That gives me a measure of protection."

Her eyes searched his. Quint's gaze flickered away, just slightly but enough for her to notice. "You're not telling me everything, are you?" she asked.

He sighed. "Little Annie. You always could see right through me."

"You didn't answer my question."

"No, and for your sake, I'm not going to. Just understand that I've stumbled onto a dirty mess. Rutledge is part of it, and things have gone too far for me to back off. I've got to bring him down."

Annie's white-gloved hand crept to her throat. "You *are* in danger! Have you thought of going to the police?"

"No good. Half the force is in Rutledge's pocket."

"Then the federal marshals. Surely—"

"Without solid evidence, they'd laugh in my face. All I can do is use the power of the press to jab at him and hope he breaks. Tomorrow's column should really singe his whiskers."

He reached out, took Annie's hand and cradled it in his palm. "Meanwhile, I have two beautiful ladies to entertain, and I mean to enjoy every minute of their company."

"But we've come at a bad time, haven't we?"

"I'm the one who invited you, remember? Besides, where you and Clara are concerned, there's no such thing as a bad time."

"Spoken like the Quint Seavers I know and love!" Annie reclaimed her hand with a little laugh. Quint's pretty words were lies, of course. He was playing a dangerous game with a dangerous man, and this was no time for distractions. Maybe tonight, when Clara was in bed and they had more time to talk, she would suggest that they cut their visit short.

Clara stirred and opened her eyes. "Can we please get some ice cream, Uncle Quint?"

Laughing, Quint tousled her curls. "Your wish is my command, fair lady. And I know just the place!"

Darkness had fallen, creeping in over the bay like a stealthy black cat. The last trolley car rolled into the barn for the night. Gaslit lamps glowed along the streets. Workmen with their tin lunch pails trudged home to the crowded wooden tenements south of Market Street. The mansions on Nob Hill blazed with light as carriages swept the rich off to parties or to the theater.

In the Jackson Street flat, Quint sat with his feet on the ottoman, gazing into the fire. From the bathroom came the sounds of Annie dressing Clara after her bath. Their girlish giggles resonated like music.

A legal pad and a freshly sharpened pencil lay on the side table. Quint had planned to spend some time jotting down notes for his next column. But tonight his mind was on other things.

The afternoon had been pleasantly spent, driving across the city, seeing the waterfront, the towering new office buildings and the legendary Palace Hotel where Teddy Roosevelt had been a recent guest. They'd laughed as Clara chased pigeons in Union Square and shared dripping ice cream in little sugared waffle cones at a sidewalk café. At the end of the day they'd come home to Chao's savory lamb stew with fresh greens and flaky crescent rolls. Annie had insisted on washing the dishes so that Chao could go home to his family in Chinatown.

Clara had been a delight the whole time. As for Annie...

Quint paused in his thoughts, listening to the muffled sound of her voice through the bathroom door. He'd never given much thought to Hannah's younger sister. The only time he could recall being alone with her was the day he'd taught her to shoot. It was a surprise to find her so intelligent, warm and perceptive. Little Annie Gustavson had grown up to be one fine woman. Any man on earth would be lucky to have her.

The bathroom door swung open and Clara pattered out in her white ruffled nightgown. With her freshly washed curls tumbling around her face, she looked like a six-year-old angel. Quint's heart contracted as she scampered toward him. If he never did anything worthwhile in his life, siring this little girl would make up for it all.

"Would you tuck me in, please, Uncle Quint?" Her chocolate eyes melted him.

"I'll be happy to tuck you in."

"And would you read me *Peter Rabbit* first?" The small book had been a present from Quint two years ago, and she'd brought it along in her bag.

"How many times have you heard that story?" Quint teased. "Do you think it will be any different this time?"

"No. But I like it the way it is." Clara skipped off to get the book. Annie had come out of the bathroom, her sleeves rolled up, her white shirtwaist unbuttoned at the collar. Damp tendrils of hair spilled over her forehead. She looked deliciously soft and mussy.

"While you're reading, I believe I'll take advantage of the warm water and have a bath myself," she said. "We can visit later. Do you mind?"

"Go ahead. And help yourself to my new bathrobe. It's hanging on the back of the door."

She colored slightly. "Oh, really, I—"

"No, try it on. It's cashmere. I paid a king's ransom for it. It'll spoil you silly."

"We'll see." Annie ducked into the bathroom as Clara came bounding back into the parlor with her storybook.

Settling her beside him on the sofa, Quint began to read familiar tale of Peter Rabbit and his mother's stern admonition not to go into Mr. McGregor's garden. By now he knew the words almost by heart—which was a good thing, because his mind had begun to wander forbidden paths. The splashing sounds behind the bathroom door conjured up visions of Annie lying naked in the tub, her small, shapely breasts jutting like pink-crowned islands from a sea of soapy water. He'd never thought of Annie that way before. But damn it, he was thinking of her that way now.

Clara nudged him. "You left something out, Uncle Quint."

"I did? What?"

"The part where Peter feels sick and looks for some parsley."

"Maybe you should read it to me."

"You read it better. But please, pay attention."

Quint forced his concentration back to the trials of poor Peter. He had no business thinking about Annie Gustavson naked, he chastised himself. Unlike most of the women he knew, Annie was every inch a lady. If she knew what was going through his head, she would likely slap him senseless.

Annie eased back in the water, rested her heels on the end of Quint's glorious claw-footed bathtub and closed her eyes. After the long, jarring train ride and the busy afternoon, this was pure heaven.

A bar of soap lay on a shelf next to the tub. Its woodsy, masculine scent recalled the way Quint had smelled when he'd leaned close to her in the cab. She held it under her nose and inhaled deeply, letting the subtle fragrance penetrate her senses. Soaping her hands, she sat up and lathered her skin. An image crept into her mind—Quint, naked in this very tub, rubbing the same soap onto his body. She pictured him massaging the lather into his armpits, down his broad chest and flat belly, between his legs…

Merciful heaven, this wouldn't do! Her self-control was slipping like a broken garter!

The water was getting cool. With a sigh, Annie rinsed herself, pulled the rubber plug and stepped out of the tub. Quint's honey-colored cashmere robe hung on its brass hook. He'd invited her to borrow it. Annie might have refused the invitation, but she'd left her own light flannel dressing gown in the guest bedroom she shared with Clara. It was either put on Quint's robe or get dressed in her clothes again which, since she planned to go to bed soon, struck her as a waste of time.

After toweling herself dry, she lifted the robe off its hook. It felt sensuous and weighty in her hands, like something between velvet and fur. Whispers of scent—Quint's soap, Quint's body—rose from the lush fabric as she wrapped it around her, slid her arms into the sleeves and knotted the thick sash. The softness was heaven on her bare skin. It made her want to purr like a cat.

Clutching the oversize robe around her, she stepped into the hall. Through the open doorway of the guest bedroom, Annie could hear Quint's off-key baritone singing his daughter to sleep. What a shame Quint didn't have children he could claim as his own. The man would make a wonderful father—*if* he could ever bring himself to settle down.

Tiptoeing into the parlor, she curled up on the settee and tucked her bare feet beneath the robe. In the fireplace pine logs popped and crackled. Annie basked in their warmth as she listened to Quint's gruff lullaby. Hannah's photograph, so beautiful, smiled down at her from the wall.

Why should Quint even want to settle down? she mused. He had plenty of money and a comfortable apartment, with a servant to cook and clean. And she'd wager he had his share of women, too, including the flame-haired actress who'd stopped by their table at Delmonico's. As for children, maybe Clara was all the child he needed. He could love and indulge her without the burden of being a father. No ties. No responsibilities. Quint was as free as a bird, and he seemed to like it that way.

Why should she pin her hopes on such a man? It was time she opened her eyes and faced the truth. If she kept her heart set on Quint Seavers, she'd be committing herself to a life of spinsterhood.

"There you are." He came around the back of the settee and settled himself at the opposite end. Reflected flames danced in his warm brown eyes. "Maybe you should keep that robe. You look a lot better in it than I do. How do you like it?"

Annie stirred self-consciously. "It's the most decadent thing I've ever worn. Now, if you'll excuse me, I'll go put on my night clothes and return it to you."

"No, stay." His hand touched her wrist, rousing a tingle of awareness. "Clara's barely asleep. You don't want to wake her. Besides, I've never been alone with a woman wearing nothing but a cashmere bathrobe. Doesn't it make you feel wicked?"

Annie's cheeks flamed hot. He was playing with her, probably laughing at her discomfort.

"Stop teasing me, Quint," she said. "I'm not one of your conquests."

"Oh?" His left eyebrow quirked upward. "Then who are you, pray tell, Miss Annie Gustavson?"

"Hannah's sister. Clara's aunt. And your good friend, as well, I hope."

He leaned closer, his eyes twinkling seductively. "You're all those things. But that's not what I'm asking. I want to know about the woman inside that prim and proper skin of yours. Who is she? Has she ever been in love?"

"I don't think that's any of your business."

He grinned like a naughty schoolboy and settled back into the corner of the settee. "Little Annie. I've known you since you were in pigtails. But right now I feel as if I hardly know you at all."

Annie stared down at her hands. She'd never considered herself shy. With most men, in fact, she could even be clever. But one smile from Quint Seavers was all it took to turn her into a bumbling, tongue-tied schoolgirl.

She forced herself to meet his mocking eyes. "Can't we talk about something else?"

"Whatever you like. You choose."

"All right. Let me think."

Quint studied her as she sat poised in silence. The collar of the cashmere robe framed her throat, lending a glow to her porcelain skin. Dampened by the steamy bath, her hair tumbled around her heart-shaped face, framing her stormy eyes, her elegant cheekbones, her perfect, pillow-soft lips.

Lord, didn't she know how beautiful she was?

He imagined tasting that mouth, nibbling at her lower lip, then crushing her in a long, deep kiss, his hands sliding beneath the cashmere to stroke her satiny skin, loosening the sash to…

"Tell me about you and Josiah Rutledge."

Her words crashed Quint back to earth. His brief fantasy had been delicious. But this was Annie. She was family, and there was a child asleep in the next room. It was time he yanked his thoughts back above his beltline.

Pulling himself together, Quint rose to lay another log on the fire. "Would you like some wine?"

She shook her head. "No, really, I—"

"This isn't Dutchman's Creek, Annie. You're in San Francisco now. Live a little." He took a crystal decanter of merlot from the sideboard and filled two goblets half-full.

"Are you trying to corrupt me, Mr. Seavers?" Her eyebrows arched as he handed her the fragile glass.

"You look like a lady who could use a little corrupting."

She took a tentative sip. "My poor mother would faint if she could see me now. Drinking wine in a man's bachelor flat, wearing nothing but a sinfully expensive bathrobe…" Her eyes flashed at him over the ridge of the wineglass. "So sit down and tell me about your quarrel with Mr. Rutledge. After I've heard you out, we can decide whether Clara and I should stay out the week or go home early."

Quint settled back onto the sofa, wondering how much he should tell her. He didn't want to frighten Annie, or cause her to end the trip too soon. But how could he lie to those clear, intelligent eyes?

He started with the broader issues—the corruption in the city government, the rampant graft and bribery, and the dangerous state of the city's water system. "The mayor and the board may be a bunch of crooks, but our fire department's first-rate. The chief, Dennis Sullivan, has been on the job almost thirty years. He was the one who put me onto the story—said he knew for a fact that money had been paid out to fix the broken pipes and cisterns. But he'd inspected the sites himself, and found that what few repairs had been made were, to quote the good man, nothing but cow dung and feathers. I followed the money trail. It led back to the contractor and to the city supervisor who'd hired him— Josiah Rutledge."

Annie leaned forward, the robe parting enough to reveal a glimpse of creamy skin. Quint willed himself to keep his eyes above her shoulders.

"But you said you didn't have any proof against Rutledge."

"I didn't. It was pure guesswork. At first it didn't matter so much. Getting the water system fixed was more important than nailing Rutledge. I hammered away at him in the paper, trying to make people aware of the problem. That was all I could do—until two days ago. That was when everything changed."

Quint hadn't planned to tell Annie about the incriminating letter. And he definitely hadn't planned to tell her about the murder of Virginia Poole. But her soft, attentive eyes held him captive, spooling the story out of him word by word. By the time he was finished, he felt drained.

He leaned forward, staring into the fire. "I know I shouldn't blame myself. But if Virginia hadn't read my column she wouldn't have contacted me and tried to give me the letter. And she'd probably still be alive."

Annie gazed into her wineglass. "She did the right thing. You did the right thing, too. There's no fault in that."

"But she's the one who paid the price. And now it's up to me. I have to make sure that poor woman didn't lose her life for nothing."

"So you never did find the letter?"

"No. And judging from the way her place was torn apart, Rutledge's hired thugs didn't find it, either. If they had, they'd have stopped looking and left."

"And Rutledge wouldn't have bearded you at Delmonico's. Not unless he suspected you might have it."

"I wish I did have it. That would make things easy. As it is, all I can do is try to bluff the bastard into the open and hope he stumbles."

"So your strategy is to make him think you have the letter, or at least to make him wonder."

Damn, but the lady was sharp. It was a quality Quint found even more intriguing than her beauty.

Annie had set her goblet on the raised hearth. Her hands were clenched in her lap, the fingers interlocked. "I'm frightened for you, Quint. This isn't just another one of your wild adventures. You could be hurt, even killed."

"I'll be fine. Rutledge is a politician. He's too smart to show his hand by coming after me."

She leaned toward the fire, gazing past him into the flames. "If you'd told me all this earlier, I'd have suggested that Clara and I come another time. The last thing you need right now is a woman and child tagging after you."

Quint laid a reassuring hand on her shoulder. Her muscles were knots of tension. His fingers stirred reflexively, massaging the tightness. "There was no way to let you know. By the time it happened, you and Clara were already on the train. But never mind that. I've been looking forward to this visit for weeks, and I don't want it spoiled. I may need to put in some hours at the *Chronicle*—in fact, I'll be there tomorrow morning until about 10:00 a.m. But we should still have plenty of time to enjoy ourselves. All right?"

"Mmm-hmm…" Her shoulders flexed against his palm. Taking it as an invitation, Quint shifted behind her, where he could put both hands into play. "How does that feel?" he asked.

"It's heaven. After all those hours on the train…" Her words dissolved in a moan as his thumbs pressed circles along the edges of her spine. "You really are corrupting me."

"Chao taught me how to do this," he said.

"Chinese magic. Tomorrow, if you and Clara are agreeable, we can take the trolley to Golden Gate Park. There's a fine Japanese garden and a playground with a carousel, and Clara will finally get to see the ocean. How does that sound?"

"Oh…she'll love that." Annie arched her back, surrendering to the spell of Quint's hands. Warmth radiated from his fingertips, easing sore muscles, seeping into tired bones. It would be wonderful just to let go and drift. But she couldn't allow that to happen. For all his bravado, Quint's story had struck cold fear into her heart. The danger to his life was all too real, but in typical male fashion, he was pretending it didn't exist. Somehow she had to talk sense into him.

"Let's take our visit one day at a time, shall we?" she began. "If things get too worrisome, you can put Clara and me on the train."

"Fine." His fingers worked deeper, triggering waves of pleasure that rippled down through her body. Annie felt an exquisite tightening in the deep core of her hips. The voice of common sense shrilled that it was time to call a halt—and she would, she promised herself. Very soon.

"I want to ask one favor of you," she said.

"Granted, as long as it's fun."

The robe's loose collar had slid down onto Annie's shoulders. Quint's hands rested on her bare nape, his strong thumbs working their delicious voodoo at the base of her skull. She closed her eyes. How would it feel to be touched like this in other places? Her breasts? Her hips? She bit back a moan. Things were getting out of control, if only in her mind.

Willing her eyes to open, she glanced toward the wall. Hannah's sunlit face smiled down at her from the simple ebony frame. Annie's forbidden thoughts fled.

"So what's the favor?" Quint's hands had paused.

"Something serious. A promise."

"Then I may need time to think it over. Tell me."

Readjusting the robe, she turned to face him on the settee. "Just this. Rutledge has already had one person killed. We both know you could be next. If the situation gets so threatening that you feel the need to send Clara and me home early…" Annie took a deep breath and plunged ahead.

"This isn't worth your life, Quint. I want your promise that you'll get on that train and go with us."

Chapter Three

Quint cursed his faulty judgment. He should've known better than to tell Annie what was happening with Rutledge. Now she waited for his answer, her mouth determinedly set, her velvet eyes pleading.

The sight of that face was enough to turn his resolve to warm putty. Right then he would have given her almost anything—except the one thing she wanted.

"No. I can't leave here," he said.

"Quint—"

"Don't push this, Annie. You know I can't, and you know why."

She stood, her eyes flashing defiance. "You mean you won't. And, yes, I do know why. It's because you're a man, with more silly male pride than brains. You'd rather be stabbed in some dark alley than walk away and save your own life!"

Rising, Quint opened his mouth to argue, but she stopped him with the touch of a finger to his lips.

"Be still and listen. If Rutledge is as smart as you say he is, he'll find a way to get you without taking the blame. You'll end up as dead as that poor woman. And for what? You said yourself that the whole city government is rotten. You can't fix it by yourself."

"Maybe not. But if I can rouse enough people to action, it might make a difference. That's my job. I can't just turn tail and run."

Annie gazed up at him in despair. His eyes had gone flinty. A muscle twitched along his tightly clenched jaw. The man had closed his ears to reason. He seemed determined to get himself murdered.

"Don't be so blasted noble!" she argued. "Think of the people who care about you—people who'd be devastated to lose you. Clara. Judd and Hannah. Even me…"

"Even you?" The mischief had crept back into his eyes. "Why, little Annie, I didn't know you cared. Maybe I should give this some thought."

"Stop making fun of me!" It was all she could do to keep from slapping the smirk off his face. "Yes, I do care, you big, arrogant, smart-mouthed oaf! You've been my knight in shining armor since I was old enough to tell boys from girls. Even when you were Hannah's beau, I kept you on a pedestal for years. You were my hero, Quint Seavers, and I won't stand back and watch you throw your life away on this…this…"

Her throat went tight, choking off her words. Merciful heaven, what had she just said to him?

Quint was gazing down at her, his eyes glinting amber with reflected flame. Annie's heart lurched as he thumbed her chin upward, bent toward her and captured her mouth with his own.

His lips were velvet and honey, possessing her from the very first touch. As the kiss deepened, Annie went molten in his arms, her blood racing, her skin on fire through the soft cashmere. Her body arched against his. Her hands raked his hair as she kissed him with a ferocity she'd never known she possessed—kissed him with all the dreams and pent-up longing of years. When his tongue glided into her mouth she was startled, but only for the space of a heartbeat. Then she opened to him, gasping as each probing thrust ignited fire bursts in her blood. His strong fingers kneaded her ribs, thumbs tracing the sensitive borders of her breasts.

Her heart was pounding like an Indian drum. She wanted more—his hands on her skin, everywhere, legs tangling, hips pressing close, his splendid body filling hers. He was *making* her want more, she realized. Quint was an expert seducer who knew exactly what he was doing. He didn't love her. He'd made her no promises. He was only taking advantage of a vulnerable moment—taking advantage of *her*.

Alarm bells shrilled in her head as she tore herself away from him. "Enough." She spat out the word. "I'm not your plaything, Quint. I have feelings, even pride. I deserve better than this."

He stepped back, his mouth damp and swollen, his hair tumbling in his eyes. "I didn't know you had so much fire in you, little Annie," he drawled.

She glowered at him, her fury mounting. "There's something I haven't told you. Frank Robinson has asked me to marry him. He'll be meeting my train in Dutchman's Creek, waiting for the answer I promised to give him." Annie drew herself up. "My answer is going to be yes."

Quint stared at her as if she'd slapped him. "Frank Robinson? That prissy old fart who owns the hotel?"

Annie spun away and stalked into the unlit guest room. Before closing the door a final time, she stripped off Quint's cashmere bathrobe, wadded it in her hands and flung it out into the hall.

The latch clicked softly into place. In the silence that followed, Quint walked forward and bent down, gathering up the robe. Annie's scent, mingled with the spicy fragrance of his own soap, rose from its folds. The warmth of her skin still clung to the rich fabric.

He lifted it to his face, inhaling deeply. Little Annie. Lord, what a woman she'd become! First she'd set him aflame with her sweet mouth. Then she'd put him in his place with a bullet to the heart.

Marry Frank Robinson? Hellfire, that would be like hitching a blooded filly to a mule. Not that

Frank was all that bad. But he was nearing forty, and to Quint's way of thinking, he was about as exciting as clabbered milk.

Still, Annie had grown up in a poor immigrant family. A share of her earnings went to help her widowed mother and younger siblings. The stability of a man like Frank Robinson would certainly have some appeal.

But after tasting her passion, Quint couldn't imagine that would be enough for her. The very thought of his beautiful, hot-blooded Annie in bed with that old—

Quint shoved the thought aside. She wasn't *his* Annie, and he'd been way out of line tonight. In fact, without much effort, he'd managed to make a complete ass of himself.

Tomorrow, he vowed, he would work his way back into her good graces. That would include making some rules and following them.

1. He would apologize, on his knees if necessary.
2. He would not lay an unbrotherly hand on the lady for the duration of her visit.
3. He would not call Frank Robinson a prissy old fart or anything else of that nature.
4. While they were together, he would table the issue of Josiah Rutledge and devote himself to having a good time with Clara.

Etching the rules into memory, Quint staggered off to bed. He'd scarcely slept in the past twenty-four hours, and he was punchy with weariness. Tomorrow he would be at work by 7:00 a.m. to draft his next column and look into what the police had done about Virginia Poole's murder. By 10:00 a.m. he'd be back here to take Clara and Annie to Golden Gate Park. Right now what he needed was a few hours between the sheets.

Too bad he couldn't ask Annie to share them.

Annie awoke to bright morning sunlight. Clara's place in the bed was empty. The enticing aromas of bacon and fresh coffee drifted through the open doorway of the guest room.

Flinging her wrapper over her nightgown, she pattered into the kitchen. Quint had mentioned he was going to work early. She could only hope he hadn't changed his mind. After last night's blistering encounter, his was the last face she wanted to see.

Clara was at the kitchen counter with Chao. Still clad in her nightgown, she was perched on a stool, happily engaged in helping him prepare breakfast.

"We're making an omelet, Aunt Annie." Her dark eyes sparkled with excitement. "Chao let me break the eggs and put in the salt and pepper."

Chao gave Annie a good-natured grin. The middle-aged man, who still wore the traditional queue, was using a fork to beat the eggs to an airy froth. If the omelet was half as good as his lamb stew, it was bound to be heavenly.

"Now some butter in the pan," he instructed his eager assistant. "This much, little bit, on your knife." He demonstrated the distance with two fingers. "Then we let it melt."

"Has Quint gone?" Annie's tongue felt as dry as old shoe leather. Maybe she'd drunk more wine than she remembered.

"Uncle Quint went to work." Clara scraped a dab of butter into the frying pan. "When he comes back we're going to ride on a trolley car, all the way to where the ocean is. Can I wear my white pinafore today?"

"If you'll do your best to keep it clean. And you'll need your straw hat, as well. We don't want you getting a sunburn."

The omelet was so light it practically floated out of the pan. Annie enjoyed her share of it at the kitchen table, with bacon, a hot buttered biscuit, orange juice and fresh coffee. A saltwater breeze drifted into the room as Chao opened a window, carrying the sounds of morning traffic from the streets below—the clang of a passing trolley, the clamor of auto horns, the cries of street vendors and the clatter of shod hooves on pavement.

Finishing her breakfast, Annie leaned over the sill. Outside, the awakening city seemed to pulse with life and vitality. So many people, so many divergent lives. So much excitement. No wonder Quint seemed to love this place.

Speaking of Quint… The thought of facing him again made Annie's stomach clench. She'd behaved like a fool last night, first flinging herself at him, then lashing out in blind fury. But the reason for her anger had been sound. Quint didn't love her, never had and never would. He'd seized an opportunity, that was all, and she'd been weak enough to allow it.

Well, it wasn't going to happen again. She'd made sure of that last night. Now that Quint knew she was as good as engaged, he'd be honor bound to behave himself.

Was she as good as engaged? Annie gazed at the thready clouds that drifted above the city skyline. Her memory struggled to bring Frank's long, narrow face into focus. Were his pale eyes blue or hazel? Was that slightly off-colored tooth on the left or right side of his mouth? Even after a few days, she could barely remember. But never mind. She would make her final decision on the train back to Colorado. Right now, she was in San Francisco, maybe for the only time in her life, and she meant to enjoy every minute of it.

By the time Annie had washed, dressed, pinned up her hair and readied Clara for the day, it was nearly 9:00 a.m. While Chao entertained the little girl with a game of dominoes, Annie sat down at Quint's desk and used his typewriter to compose a letter to Hannah and Judd. The machine was new and fascinating. But since she could only type by hunting and pecking, every word was a labor. She managed a few sentences about the train trip and their plans for the day, but little more.

Of course she didn't mention her concern for Quint's safety. The last thing Hannah needed right now was more worries. This trip with Clara had, in part, been scheduled to give her more rest while Rosa, the housekeeper, looked after three-year-old Daniel. At five weeks from full term, Annie's sister could still lose the baby by going into premature labor.

Quint arrived precisely at 10:00 a.m., just as Annie was addressing the letter. Eyes twinkling, arms laden with pink and yellow roses, he burst through the door like a one-man parade. "For you, mademoiselle!" He presented the miniature pink bouquet to a bedazzled Clara, then turned to Annie.

"With my deepest apologies," he muttered, thrusting the wrapped cluster of twelve yellow roses into her hands. They were fresh and beautiful, enhanced with ferns and beaded with morning dew.

"You're shameless, Quint Seavers!" Annie hissed.

"Yes, I know. Will you forgive me for last night?"

Annie rolled her eyes. "Last night never happened. Agreed?"

His dimples deepened irresistibly. "Agreed. And just to seal the bargain I have an added enticement." He reached into his vest and drew out a plain white envelope. "Two tickets for the opera tomorrow night. For you and me. Chao's already agreed to stay here with Clara."

"The Metropolitan Opera?" Annie had seen the posters on the street. The fabled New York company was on tour and playing in San Francisco this week. She'd always dreamed of seeing an opera. But protests were already flocking into her head like black crows. The tickets must have cost Quint a small fortune. And how could she go when she had nothing appropriate to wear?

"Caruso will be here on the seventeenth for their production of *Carmen,*" Quint said. "That show's been sold out for weeks. But before he arrives, they'll be performing something called *The Queen of Sheba.* That one's almost sold out, too, but I called in some favors and got us two of the last box seats." He frowned, noticing her hesitation. "Is something wrong?"

She shook her head. "No, it's a wonderful gesture, Quint. But I know the opera will be a big society event. How can I sit in a box, surrounded by all those elegant women with their jewels and their fancy gowns? You might fit right in, but I don't even own an evening dress."

"Then wear whatever you have. You'll look fine."

Fine. Annie sighed. She'd hoped for a little commiseration, or even a compliment, however insincere. But men just didn't understand. She would go, certainly. This might be her one lifetime chance to see an opera. But she would feel like a leghorn chicken dropped into a pen full of glittering peacocks.

Chao had come with vases for the flowers. Clara handed him her little bouquet, then ran to Quint to tug at his coat. "Can we go now? I want to ride in the trolley car!"

Quint rumpled her curls. "We'll go when your aunt Annie says she's ready."

"I'll just get our straw hats and my reticule," Annie said. "Will we need coats?"

"The day's warming, but the breeze off the water can be brisk. Light jackets should do you fine."

Surrendering the roses to Chao, Annie hurried into the guest room to get the things she'd left on the bed. An image glimpsed in the dresser mirror showed a young woman simply dressed in a high-necked white blouse and khaki walking skirt, her cinched waist marked by a wide leather belt. Her hair was pulled back and twisted into a practical bun that would hold up in a stiff breeze. Her only adornments were tiny pearl ear studs and a simple brooch at her throat.

Sensible, practical Annie. Well, she was who she was. But just once it would be nice to play Cinderella and go to the ball with the handsome prince. Maybe then she could be content with the life that awaited her back in Dutchman's Creek.

"Come on, Aunt Annie, we're ready to go!"

Clara bounded into the room to tug at her skirt. Annie fixed the straw hat on her niece's head, tying the strings under her chin. Then she secured her own hat with a pin, picked up her reticule and the jackets, and let Clara lead her back to the entry where Quint stood waiting. The day's grand adventure was about to begin.

They swung aboard the crowded trolley and managed to find a seat. As the car swayed along the rails, Quint cast furtive glances at Annie. Her color was high, her face glowing. Back in Colorado, she'd been nothing more than Hannah's kid sister. He'd scarcely given her a second look. Now, with every minute they spent together, the attraction grew more compelling.

They'd agreed to forget last night's searing kiss. But for Quint that was easier said than done. In the past twelve hours, he'd relived that kiss a hundred times—not just the kiss, but everything beyond. He'd imagined sliding the robe off her shoulders and stroking the satiny skin beneath, then easing down to cup the ripe moons of her breasts in his hands and kiss the nipples into swollen nubs; then…

But Lord, what was he thinking? Here he was, seated on a trolley with two innocent females, one a precious child, the other a lady who would skewer him with her hatpin if she knew what was going on in his mind. Their transfer stop on Fulton was coming up in a few blocks, and if he didn't keep a sharp eye out they'd end up at the fish market instead of the park.

His three hours at work that morning had been frustrating. There'd been no mention of Virginia Poole in any of the papers. That meant he couldn't afford to show his hand by looking into her death himself. His knowledge of the murder and his presence at the scene would make him a prime suspect, ripe for framing. Rutledge could have paid the police to keep quiet for that very reason. The poor woman's body was probably on the bottom of the bay by now, her flat cleared out and ready to let.

But what had happened to the letter? In all likelihood it was lost. But as long as Rutledge suspected otherwise, there might be a chance of trapping him.

Quint's new column would appear on page two of this morning's *Chronicle.* He'd written it yesterday, in the hope that it might persuade Rutledge to replace the missing funds before certain knowledge came to light. The implication was pure bluff, but Rutledge didn't know that. Maybe, just maybe, the man would rise to the bait.

Quint had weighed the wisdom of showing the column to Annie. But in the spirit of enjoying the day, he'd decided against it. She'd be bound to worry and would surely lecture him about the risk.

Then he would have to argue with her, and the whole outing could be spoiled.

That Annie cared enough to fret over him was something to be pondered. But he had a dangerous task to complete. This was no time for more distractions.

At Fulton Street they caught the trolley that would take them to Golden Gate Park—a vast wonderland of woods, lawns, gardens and cultural amusements, rivaled only by the great parks of New York and Chicago. Laid out in the 1870s on a stretch of barren dunes, it had become the pride of San Francisco. Today the sky was glorious, and Clara was in high spirits. She laughed and chattered all the way, her brown eyes sparkling like sunlit sarsaparilla. He'd be a fool to let his worries keep him from enjoying her, Quint reminded himself. Time passed swiftly. Little girls grew up. And this precious day would never come again.

He swung his daughter off the crowded trolley, and they strolled through the gateway of the park. Quint held Clara's left hand, Annie her right. Anyone watching might have taken them for a young family—father, mother and child. Quint found the notion oddly comfortable. But then, Annie was a comfortable sort of woman—except when she was wrapped in his cashmere robe, her skin dewy with moisture, her gray eyes lit with reflected flame. Last night the sight of her, the scent and feel of her in his arms had driven him wild. Even today, with Clara as a chaperone, it was all he could do to keep from reaching out to touch her waist, her shoulder, her hair.

"I want to see the ocean!" Clara tugged at his hand. "Where is it?"

"The ocean's way at the other end of the park," Quint said. "If we go there first, we'll be too tired for other things. But we'll work our way in that direction and see it before we go home."

"Promise?"

"Promise." Quint gave her hand a squeeze. "First, how would you like to see a real live grizzly bear? His name is Monarch."

As they turned onto the narrow path, Annie dropped behind to give other walkers room to pass. This was Quint's time with Clara, she reminded herself. She was only along to play nanny for the trip.

Would Quint have kissed a woman he thought of as the nanny?

She gave herself a mental slap. Playing these games would only exasperate her. The truth was, Quint Seavers would probably kiss any attractive female who'd give him the time of day. Was that the kind of man she wanted?

Frank Robinson had courted her faithfully for more than a year. Granted, Frank wasn't as exciting as Quint. But he wouldn't go around kissing every woman who came within his reach. He wouldn't leave his poor sweetheart with child to go gallivanting after gold and adventure. And he certainly wouldn't be so reckless as to challenge a crooked politician who'd already shown himself capable of murder!

Annie blinked away a tear of frustration. It was time she faced the truth. Quint wasn't husband material. He was already married—to Hannah's memory and to his freewheeling existence in this glittering town. If he ever did take a wife, the last woman he'd choose would be a drab little country mouse from Dutchman's Creek, Colorado.

"Look, Aunt Annie!" Clara darted back to tug at Annie's skirt. "Over there in that big cage! It's a bear!"

"Oh, my goodness!" Annie had glimpsed bears in the wild, and once she'd seen a dead one on a wagon. But she'd never been close to a live grizzly. Surrounded by thick iron bars that curved inward at the top, the shaggy brown creature was huge, with little pig eyes, a massive snout and paws that would span a dinner plate. According to the information plaque, the creature had been caught full-grown in 1889 for exhibition as a symbol of the park. Now Monarch was getting old and fat, but the years had not dimmed his majesty. In every way, the grizzly was a spectacular animal.

"Hello, Monarch!" Clara bounced up and down, waving. The bear yawned, showing a pink cavern of a mouth lined with jagged yellow teeth. Clara's eyes widened.

"He's probably thinking what a nice little snack you'd make," Quint teased.

"He can't get out, can he, Uncle Quint?"

"Don't worry. Those bars are too strong for him. Besides, if he did get out, I'd wrestle him to the ground and save you!"

Clara giggled. "You're silly! Isn't he silly, Aunt Annie?"

"He's a very silly man," Annie agreed, but she sensed the undertone of truth in Quint's words. If any danger threatened his little girl he would protect her with his life.

In the meadow beyond the bear cage, herds of deer grazed behind an eight-foot wire fence. There were elk and moose, as well, and, in a separate enclosure, some kangaroos, an ostrichlike emu and a pair of zebras. In the children's area there were sheep, goats and piglets, which Clara was allowed to feed and pet. When one baby goat sucked on her finger she squealed with delight.

They strolled through a fairy-tale Victorian greenhouse teeming with ferns, shrubs, vines and flowers from all over the world. Annie was fascinated, but Clara kept racing ahead, eager for the next surprise Quint had promised her.

How like him she was, Annie thought. Restless and brimming with curiosity, unable to resist the call of the mysterious something around the bend. They were two of a kind.

As they left the greenhouse, Quint scooped Clara into his arms. "Close your eyes now," he ordered her. "Promise me you won't open them until I say so."

Clara squeezed her eyes shut. "What if I peek?"

"Then the surprise will be spoiled, and it won't be as much fun. Promise me you won't look. Do it now, before we take another step."

"I promise." She buried her face against the shoulder of his jacket.

"That's my girl. It'll only be for a minute or two."

Above the dark curls, Quint's eyes met Annie's. The tenderness she glimpsed there was so real that it made her throat ache. Clara was far too young to understand the secret of her parentage. For now— and maybe for always—Quint's fatherly love would remain locked away like a hoard of gold coins that could only be parceled out in small amounts. That was the price he'd paid for leaving Hannah.

The path meandered downhill through stands of willow and towering Monterrey cypress. Tangerine butterflies, lost in mating, fluttered against the emerald foliage. Through the trees, Annie glimpsed a children's playground with swings, slides and see-saws. Surrounding the sandy play area was a wide band of concrete where older children and adults circled on roller skates.

Clara squirmed in Quint's arms. "I hear music! Can I look now?"

"Not yet." Quint chuckled mysteriously. "Hang on, we're almost there."

Annie could hear the music, too, a blaring, pumping rendition of what she recognized as the "Blue Danube." By the time they stepped into the cleared area and she saw the flash of swirling color, she'd already guessed what Quint's surprise would be. Clara would be ecstatic when she saw it.

"When I count to three, you can look," Quint said. "Ready? One…two…three!"

Clara opened her eyes, blinked and stared. Her mouth rounded in a little O of amazement.

The carousel was a showpiece. Not only were there horses, but lions, bears, tigers, camels, zebras and swans. They were painted in every hue of the rainbow with glass eyes and gilded trappings. They glided up and down on brass poles as the huge machine revolved beneath its gleaming metal-capped dome, piping out music that sang of circuses and sugar floss and children's laughter.

Savoring her surprise, Quint lowered Clara to the sandy ground. "So which animal do you want to ride?"

Her eyes danced. "Can I ride them all?"

He grinned. "Not at the same time. Choose the one you want to ride first. Then we'll see about another."

"Will you and Aunt Annie ride, too?"

"Certainly we will. First we have to buy tickets. Come on."

While Quint waited in line at the ticket booth, Annie and Clara watched the turning carousel. As it slowed to a stop, the little girl tugged at Annie's skirt and pointed. "That red horse! That's the one I want!"

The horse was riderless for the moment. While Quint rushed up with the tickets, Annie leaped onto the platform and seized the bridle, saving the seat until Quint could clamber after her with Clara. He gave her a wink and a boyish grin. "Good catch, lady," he muttered, lifting the little girl onto the saddle.

In the next moment they began to move. Quint swung onto the black steed that loped alongside Clara's. Annie scrambled for a sidesaddle perch on the charging lion behind them. With music blaring and mounts pumping, they were off.

Clara hung on to the brass pole, her laughter floating back to Annie's ears. Quint glanced over his shoulder. "Uh-oh," he said. "I think that lion back there is following us. Come on, let's ride!" He leaned forward over the black horse's neck. Clara followed his example as Annie growled and roared behind them. The little girl shrieked with delight, laughing so hard that Annie feared she might wet her bloomers.

All too soon the carousel slowed and halted. "I want to ride the lion now," Clara said. "You can ride my red horse, Aunt Annie."

"Are you sure you can handle a lion?" Quint hoisted her onto the golden back. "They can get pretty wild, you know."

Clara gave him a serious look. "I can ride it fine, Uncle Quint. It's only a pretend lion, you know."

Annie had to bite her cheeks to keep from laughing at the expression on Quint's face—first startled, then beaming with fatherly pride. She gave him a smile as he caught her waist and swung her onto the vermilion-painted horse. His hands lingered for an instant as she settled into place. His eyes held hers, triggering a rush of warmth to her cheeks. Then the carousel began to move. Quint remounted and the new chase was on, with Clara roaring and snarling behind them.

By the time the ride ended, Annie was feeling queasy. "You two take another turn if you want," she told Quint. "I need my feet on solid earth. I'll wait for you on those benches by the playground."

While Quint and Clara debated which animal to ride next, Annie tottered over to an empty bench and sank onto the seat. She'd had a problem with motion sickness since she was a little girl. She should have known better than to take that second ride. But it had been so glorious, flying along next to Quint, seeing the boyish merriment in his eyes and the flash of his smile. The memory would stay with her until she forced herself to forget.

Taking deep breaths, she waited for her stomach to settle. On the whirling carousel she caught glimpses of Clara astride a zebra and Quint mounted on a bear. Even the sight made her feel dizzy. Turning away, she glanced around for a distraction.

On the bench beside her, someone had left a neatly refolded newspaper. Annie could see enough of the masthead to recognize it as the *San Francisco Chronicle*—Quint's paper. Curious, she picked it up, opened it to the front page.

The headline story was about a fire in a working-class neighborhood south of Market Street. Ignited by a fallen kerosene lamp, the blaze had consumed two boardinghouses and a dry goods store before the fire department managed to get it under control. An elderly man had perished in the flames.

Annie remembered what Quint had told her about the shortage of water for fighting fires. This time the firemen had stopped the blaze from spreading. Without water the fire would have been unstoppable. Hundreds of people could have died. Many more would have lost their homes and possessions.

She was beginning to understand what drove Quint's crusade against Josiah Rutledge.

Her eyes skimmed the rest of the page. Enrico Caruso, the world's greatest opera singer, had arrived in town and was staying at the Palace Hotel. Mayor Schmitz had announced some new political appointments. A courtroom fight had broken out over a libel suit, resulting in several arrests. Annie turned the page.

There it was at the top of the editorial section—

Quint's new column. With more interest now, she smoothed the page and began to read.

With each line, fear tightened its cold fingers around her throat.

Chapter Four

The San Francisco Chronicle, April 15, 1906
   Yesterday's fire on Folsom Street destroyed
three buildings and, tragically, took one life.
That the damage wasn't worse is a tribute to
San Francisco's magnificent firefighters, who
arrived in time to wet down the blaze and save
the surrounding structures.

Annie glanced toward the carousel where Quint
rode beside his daughter, laughing as if he didn't
have a care in the world. She should have known
he'd use the fire as an excuse to escalate the fight
with Josiah Rutledge. Where danger was concerned, the man had no more common sense than a
fourteen-year-old schoolboy.

   Her fear deepened as she read on.

Yesterday we were lucky. But imagine this scenario if you will. A small accident starts a fire. As the blaze rages, the fire crew arrives with the pumping engine. With their usual efficiency, they connect the hoses to the cistern, start the pump...and no water emerges from the nozzle.

Citizens, our beloved city is a tinderbox. A devastating fire could happen today. It could happen tomorrow. The one certainty is, if we don't update the water system forthwith, it WILL happen.

Three months ago, at the urging of Chief Dennis Sullivan, the Board of Supervisors set aside funds to make the most urgent repairs. The work was to be completed by mid-April. Bank records show that the funds were withdrawn and paid to the contractor. But what have the people of San Francisco received for their hard-earned tax dollars? Let's take a look.

What followed was a detailed list of the needed repairs and the work, if any, that had been completed. Quint's research was meticulous. The conditions he described were shocking and frightening—empty cisterns, faulty valves, cracked pipes that had been dabbed with cheap cement instead of replaced.

So what happened to the money? There are two individuals who can answer that question—the contractor and the board member who arranged to hire him on "agreeable" terms. Sadly, we've grown so accustomed to this kind of chicanery that most of us are inclined to shrug when we hear about it. In this case, however, lives and property are at stake. When certain evidence comes to light, I wouldn't wager a plug nickel on the necks of these two schemers, let alone their jobs and reputations.

Certain evidence… Annie shuddered as the words sank home. Quint had pushed things too far this time. He was playing a deadly game with no winning cards in his hand. Her fingers trembled as they gripped the page, blurring the print before her eyes.

It is this reporter's fervent hope that the responsible parties will experience a reversal of conscience and put the funds to the use for which they were intended. Otherwise it may be too late for them and for their innocent victims—the people of San Francisco.

Annie lowered the paper, dread congealing like cold tallow in the pit of her stomach. Josiah Rutledge's flinty eyes and twisted smile glinted in her memory. The man exuded evil. Quint was tweaking the devil's whiskers.

As she watched the children frolic on the playground, a slow anger began to simmer inside her. Quint had always been a risk-taker—the first boy to test the winter ice on the pond, the first to walk across the railroad trestle—blindfolded. The first to challenge the new bully in town or leap onto an unbroken horse. His thrill-seeking ways had cost him Hannah's love and the right to claim Clara as his own child. But even then, he never seemed to learn his lesson.

Annie's fingers crumpled a corner of the newspaper as she imagined seizing him by the collar and shaking him until his hair tumbled into his mocking brown eyes. Even then, she sensed, Quint would only laugh at her—as he'd been laughing in the face of common sense all his life.

The carousel music had ended. In the silence, the happy shouts of children echoed across the park. Putting the newspaper aside, Annie rose to meet Quint and Clara as they came laughing toward her, so beautiful together, their clasped hands swinging between them.

She would not be so thoughtless as to spoil the day by bracing Quint about his column now, Annie resolved. His time with Clara was too precious for that. But tonight, after the little girl was asleep, he was going to get an earful. He was twenty-eight years old. It was time he stopped behaving like Huckleberry Finn!

Quint glanced at his pocket watch. "How about some lunch? Yesterday it was Delmonico's. Today I want to treat you to the best hot dogs west of Coney Island. The stand is about ten minutes from here."

Annie had read about hot dogs and was eager to try one. Clara, however, hung back, looking as if she were about to cry. "I don't want to eat a dog, Uncle Quint," she said.

Quint chuckled. "It won't be a real dog, sweetheart. Just a sausage on some bread. Come on, you'll like it. I promise."

Clara trailed them to the umbrella-shaded hotdog stand, dragging her feet all the way. When Quint handed her the bun-wrapped sausage slathered in mustard she took a cautious nibble, frowned, then took a bigger bite.

"Do you like it?" Quint asked.

The little girl nodded, her mouth stuffed too full to answer.

"And how about you?" He turned toward Annie, who was trying to maintain a ladylike demeanor while she enjoyed her hot dog. "Do you like it?"

"Mmm-hmm," she muttered.

"You've got a spot that needs wiping. Look at me and hold still." He raised his paper napkin and dabbed at her chin. His warm brown eyes gazed into hers, twinkling with mischief. "Mustard becomes you, Miss Annie," he drawled. "You ought to wear it more often."

Annie swallowed, struggling for composure. Quint would be well aware of his effect on her. For the space of a breath he held eye contact, one brow tilted roguishly upward, as if he could hear her thundering pulse. What an incorrigible flirt the man was! Any woman foolish enough to take him on would have her hands full.

Summoning her will, she tore herself away. "Oh, dear, Clara, you've spattered mustard on your pinafore," she fussed. "I do hope it will wash out." Crimson-faced, she scrubbed furiously at the tiny yellow spot with her napkin. Quint watched her, betraying his amusement with a deepening dimple in his cheek. What a mess she'd made of things. How could she have let down her guard last night, telling him how he'd been her white knight for years? How could she have allowed him to kiss her, taking those intimate liberties with his tongue? The wretched man had probably laughed himself to sleep afterward.

One thing was certain, Annie vowed—it wasn't going to happen again.

They washed down their hot dogs with iced lemonade and shared a shimmering pink cone of the spun sugar treat known as Fairy Floss. Clara giggled as it dissolved into nothing on her tongue. Her lips were pink from the colored sugar.

"I want to see the ocean now," she said.

Quint wiped a dab of mustard off her cheek.

"Then we've got a walk ahead of us. Can you get there without whining to be carried?"

She gave him a scathing look. "I'm not a baby, Uncle Quint. Back home, I walk all around the ranch and never get lost. I can even ride my pony by myself."

"That's putting me in my place!" Quint grinned as he took her hand. "To the ocean, ladies!"

They followed the path toward the west end of the park, passing meadows, small lakes and stands of forest. The air was scented with pine, the grass dotted with spring wildflowers. Annie was getting footsore by the time they stopped to admire a tall Dutch windmill surrounded by a sea of scarlet, pink and yellow tulips. The scene was breathtaking.

"Tired?" Quint glanced down at Annie.

She shook her head. "I'm fine."

"We're almost there. Listen—you, too, Clara. You can hear the sound of the ocean."

Annie held her breath. The sound that reached her ears was a whispered roar, still faint, but more powerful than anything she could imagine.

"I hear it!" Clara danced up and down. "Let's go."

They left the trail and started up a low dune with Quint holding Clara's hand. Impatient, the little girl broke away and raced to the top. "Oh!" she cried. "Oh, look!"

Annie clambered up beside her, halted and stared in stunned silence. She had seen the bay, with its wind-rippled water and bustling ships. She had seen rivers and lakes back in Colorado. But nothing could have prepared her for the ocean. It was wild and fierce and vast beyond imagining. Waves higher than she was tall rolled toward the beach to crest and fall in crashing white foam. Beyond the breakers, the glistening water stretched farther than she could see, all the way to exotic places like China and Japan and the South Sea Islands.

Quint had come up beside her. His hand rested lightly on her shoulder. "So what do you think of it?" he asked.

"It's…unbelievable." Annie blinked away an unexpected tear. "Can we go down to the water?"

He laughed like a boy. "Come on! Oh—but first we'll have to take off our shoes. The only way to walk on the beach is barefoot."

They scrambled down to a level spot at the foot of the dune. The sea wind whipped Annie's hair into unruly tendrils. Loose strands blew across her face as she bent to unhook the tight buttons on her high-topped shoes.

Clara was already barefoot, as was Quint. She tugged at his hand, eager to be off down the beach.

"Go on," Annie said. "I'll catch up."

"No, we'll go together." Quint crouched in the sand and began undoing the tight buttons. "Stay with us, now, Clara, and don't run off. The tide's coming in, and those big waves can sneak up on you."

As he talked, Quint's strong fingers worked, loosening each stubborn fastener from around Annie's ankles and easing the shoes off her feet. Turning modestly away, Annie loosened her garters, rolled her stockings down and kicked them off next to her shoes. Having grown up poor on a farm, she was tough-footed and accustomed to rocks and stickers. But walking on the fine, wet beach sand was like walking on liquid silk. It felt heavenly.

The first time a foamy wave swept up the beach to curl around her bare ankles, Annie jumped and snatched up her skirt. Quint laughed and captured her hand. His other hand caught Clara's. "Come on!" he shouted, plunging into the shallow surf.

"We'll get soaked!" She hung back, resisting.

"Yes we will! Don't be so damned sensible, Annie." He jerked her forward. "Come on!"

Splashing foam, they dashed along the edge of the waves. Clara shrieked with laughter. Annie's hair fell loose to stream behind her in the wind. It was the closest she'd ever come to flying.

Out of breath at last, they collapsed on the dry beach above the waves. Annie's lower legs and the hem of her skirt were caked with wet sand. Her wind-whipped hair fluttered in her face.

Flushed and tousled, Quint sprawled beside her. Turning, he raised himself on one elbow and cupped her chin with his free hand. "You're a beautiful woman, Miss Annie Gustavson," he muttered. "Any man who could see you like this, barefoot and windblown, your eyes shining like a little girl's, would fall down and worship you. So why do you think you have to settle for Frank Robinson?"

Because I can't have you. Annie bit back the words. He was playing with her, giving her tantalizing glimpses of what could never be hers. Why couldn't he just leave her alone?

"What makes you think I'm settling?" she countered. "Maybe I love him."

The sound he made in response was somewhere between a snort and a growl. But then, after the way she'd kissed him last night, Annie could hardly blame him for being contemptuous. She was bracing herself for more questions when Clara came scampering up.

"Look what I found!" She was cradling a shell in her two hands. The shell was as perfect as a baby's ear, pink and rounded like the conch shells Annie had seen in books, only this one was smaller. It was exquisite.

"Can I keep it, Uncle Quint?"

Quint smiled. "Of course you can. It's your own gift from the ocean. Let me show you something."

Taking the shell from her, he cupped it to her ear. "Can you hear anything?"

She listened intently, brown eyes wide with wonder. "A sound. Like whispering."

"It's the sound of the ocean," Quint said. "Wherever you are, even back on the ranch, you can hold that shell to your ear and hear it."

"Really?" Her eyes grew bigger.

"Really. Try it when you get back to my place. You'll see."

She pushed the shell into the pocket of her pinafore. "I'm going to keep it forever."

By the time they were ready to leave the beach they'd filled their pockets with shells and built an enormous sand castle at the edge of the incoming tide. The late afternoon sun hovered low, casting fiery glints across the waves as they trudged up the dune. Quint caught a horse cab for the ride back to his apartment, and Annie was grateful. They were worn out and far too dirty to walk back through the park and catch the trolley.

Clara sat between them on the leather seat. Within minutes she'd nodded off to sleep, her curly head sagging against Quint's arm. Annie glanced down at her with a tired smile. It had been a wonderful day—perhaps the most wonderful day of her life. What a shame it had to end.

Her spirit sank as she thought about Quint's column. For the past few hours she'd managed to put the matter aside. It would be tempting to pretend she hadn't seen it. But Quint had put himself in danger. Somehow she had to convince him to leave town and protect himself. Knowing Quint, he would resist her logic all the way. She was not looking forward to the clash of wills.

Quint sat on the leather sofa before the fireplace, a clipboard propped on his knees. From the bathroom came the faint sound of splashing as Annie took her turn in the bath. Outside, gaslit lamps glowed along the main streets. From the crowded tenements of Chinatown, the aromas of roast duck and burning joss sticks drifted on the evening breeze.

They had arrived home at dusk, tired, damp and hungry. Chao had greeted them with hot noodle soup and fresh biscuits. By the time they'd finished eating, it was Clara's bath and bedtime.

Annie had been unusually quiet on the ride home and at supper. Quint sensed a storm brewing, and he knew the cause of it. His eyes hadn't missed the newspaper she'd left on the park bench. She'd read his column and she wasn't happy about it.

At least she hadn't made a scene in front of Clara. But Quint knew what she was holding back. Now that Clara was in bed and Chao had gone home, the storm was bound to break.

Quint sighed. It was touching that Annie cared enough to worry about him. But she needed to understand that he couldn't turn tail and run from the battle with Rutledge. This was his chosen fight, a matter of honor and duty. There was far more at stake here than his own life.

From the bathroom, he heard the gurgle of water running down the drain and the light creak of a floorboard as she stepped out onto the mat. He willed himself to erase the picture that had formed in his mind—damp ivory skin, rose-tipped nipples, droplets gleaming on the soft curls of her—

Damn!

Chewing on the stub of his pencil, Quint struggled to focus on the task at hand—jotting down new ideas for his next column. But his tired brain refused to obey. It was far easier to remember how Annie had looked on the beach today, her face flushed and happy, her glorious hair streaming in the wind. If they'd been alone, he'd have been tempted to take her in his arms, wrestle her to the sand and show her exactly what she'd be missing if she married Frank Robinson.

He heard the creak of the bathroom door and the patter of her footsteps crossing the hall to the guest room. A few minutes later she appeared, covered to the throat in her high-necked nightgown and plaid flannel wrapper. Her wet hair was loosely braided down her back.

"How's Clara?" he asked as she settled herself at the far end of the sofa.

"Fast asleep with her shell tucked under the pillow. She was worn out, poor little thing. But it was a wonderful day. Thank you."

"Nobody enjoyed it more than I did."

She shifted against the cushions. "I think Clara and I should leave tomorrow," she said.

Quint gazed into the fireplace where the wood had burned down to crumbling coals. He'd expected a lecture, punctuated, perhaps, by tears and angry demands. He hadn't expected this. "So soon?" he asked, feeling as if he'd been cut adrift.

Annie didn't answer.

"You could at least tell me why," he said.

"You shouldn't have to ask. I read your piece in the paper."

He exhaled wearily. "I didn't plan this, Annie. It just happened."

"That doesn't mean you can't walk away."

He shook his head. "I have to see this through. A good woman's dead because she tried to help me. If I don't finish what I started, she'll have died in vain. And what if there's a bad fire later on? What if people lose their lives because of what I failed to do?"

Annie sat silent, firelight casting her pensive face in rose gold. At last she turned toward him, her eyes soft and sad. "Well, then, if you won't leave, the best thing we can do is get out of your way. Having us here is one distraction you don't need."

Quint felt a sudden sinking. "What about the opera tomorrow night? I was looking forward to it."

"I'm sure you can find someone else to go with you. We had a wonderful day. Let's leave it at that."

"Fine." Quint stared into the fire, feeling drained.

He'd been looking forward to this visit for weeks. Now, too soon, it was about to end. But Annie was right. This business with Rutledge had escalated to the danger point. The days ahead were going to demand his undivided attention.

"Oh, damn it, Annie…" Impulsively he reached out and pulled her to his side. She came, warm and unresisting, to sag against his shoulder. Her hair was damp through his shirt. The scent of the soap he kept in his bathroom mingled with her womanly fragrance. Only now did Quint realize how much he would miss Hannah's little sister. Next time he saw her, she could be a married woman. The very thought made him want to grind his teeth.

"Do you have a gun?" Annie's question came out of nowhere, catching him off guard. "You really need to carry some kind of protection."

"There's a pistol locked in my desk. But I really don't think—"

"Be sensible, Quint. Thanks to your column, Rutledge will think you have the letter. He's already killed for it once. What's to stop him from doing it again?"

"Believe me, I've thought of that. But Rutledge is no fool. He'd know I wouldn't have the letter on me. It stands to reason that I'd keep it somewhere safe, most likely with instructions for somebody to publish it if I came to harm."

"But you don't even have the letter!"

"As long as Rutledge thinks I do, that doesn't matter. It's called a bluff, Annie. Poker players do it all the time."

She turned on him, eyes blazing. "This isn't a poker game, Quint. I've known you all my life, and you never change. It's as if you believe you're wearing some kind of invisible armor that will keep you safe. Well, you're not. You can get hurt, just like anybody else."

"I know that, Annie," he said quietly.

"And you can hurt other people, too," she continued as if he hadn't spoken. "You can't imagine what Hannah went through all those months you were gone, not knowing if you were dead or alive."

"I'd say my brother did a pretty good job of consoling her." Quint could have bitten off his tongue. He'd long since gotten past what had happened between Hannah and Judd. But that wasn't how he'd made it sound.

"And you've never forgiven them for it, have you?" Annie retorted. "Are you still in love with Hannah? Is that why you have this death wish?"

Quint groaned inwardly. Now they'd both said too much, and things were spiraling out of control. There was just one way to answer Annie's accusation, and it wasn't with words.

Catching her shoulders he jerked her close and kissed her.

For the first few seconds she fought him, fists

pummeling his chest as she twisted in his arms. Then, as he persisted, her lips went molten. She softened against him with a little moan. Her hands clutched the back of his head, fingers clawing at his hair. Heat slammed through Quint's body, pounding into his loins. Aroused and hungry, he battled for self-control. Would she stop him if he swept her up in his arms and carried her to his bed? Would he want her to?

His hands found the curves of her body through the soft flannel of her gown—her hips, her breasts. Lord, this was crazy. This was Annie, the little pig-tailed girl he'd known forever.

But she didn't feel like a little girl now. She was all woman, warm and sweet and sensual. He deepened the kiss, thrusting with his tongue, wanting more…

"Aunt Annie…" Clara's voice quivered down the hallway. As Annie broke away from him, Quint turned to see his daughter standing in the hallway. Below the tangle of damp curls, her small face was as pale as bread dough.

"Aunt Annie," she whispered, "I think I'm going to…"

Clamping her hand over her mouth, she rushed toward the bathroom.

Chapter Five

Clara was still feeling sick the next morning. The ginger tea that Chao brewed had settled her stomach, but her sparkle was missing. She lay propped against a stack of pillows, her Peter Rabbit book on her lap and her seashell cradled against her ear.

Annie leaned over the bed, one hand testing the small, pale forehead. "No fever," she said. "Probably just too much excitement and strange food. But I'm afraid taking her on the train today will be out of the question."

Quint stood in the doorway, dressed for work. "Do you want me to telephone for a doctor?" he asked.

Annie shook her head. "I'm sure it's just an upset stomach. If I can keep her resting, she should be fine."

"Will you be all right? I've left my office number by the telephone in case you need me."

Annie forced herself to meet his worried brown

eyes. Neither of them had mentioned last night's explosive kiss. It was as if they were both pretending it had never happened.

"Don't worry about us," she said. "I know you have a lot to do at work. Just be careful, please. Do you have your pistol?"

He nodded and touched the slight bulge under his vest. "Not that I expect to need it." He took a step toward the door, then paused. "Since you're going to be here, are we still on for the opera tonight?"

The opera. With so much on her mind, Annie had all but forgotten about it. "I suppose so," she said. "As long as Clara isn't worse by tonight."

"Later, then." He gave Clara a wink. "You get better, sweetheart, hear?"

Clara blew him a kiss, and then he was gone. Annie stood by the front window, watching as he bounded down the steps and strode up the street toward the trolley stop. The memory of his arms and his seeking, demanding mouth swept over her, leaving her weak-kneed. She should have stopped him last night, shoved him away or said something to put him in his place. But where Quint was concerned, she had no more resistance than a moth to a burning candle. If she let him, he would break her heart. But right now that didn't seem to matter.

What if she never saw him again? What if Josiah Rutledge's thugs were waiting outside the *Chronicle* Building? They could easily gun him down as he stepped off the trolley, or drag him into an alleyway, slit his throat and dump him in the bay.

Why had she let him go? She should have wept, fainted, anything to keep him here. Merciful heaven, what if she'd sent him to his death?

By midmorning, Clara had listened to *Peter Rabbit* three times, nibbled a little milk toast and fallen into restful slumber. Annie, who'd been awake most of the night, was on the brink of nervous exhaustion. Too restless to sleep, she prowled the flat, battling the urge to telephone Quint and check on him. He would hate that, she knew.

As the clock struck 11:00 a.m., she gazed morosely out the window. Outside, the sun was shining. Traffic was bustling in the streets. Why not go out? With Clara sleeping peacefully and Chao here to watch over her, there was no reason she shouldn't try a little expedition on her own.

Spirits rising, she smoothed her hair, pinned on her hat and slipped on her jacket. She'd brought a fair amount of cash with her. Maybe she could shop for some new fabrics or find a pretty shawl to wear over her plain blouse at the opera.

"I should be back by 2:00 p.m.," she told Chao. "Is there anything you need me to pick up while I'm out?"

Chao flashed his toothy, good-natured grin. "No, miss. Everything is fine here. If the Little Miss wakes up, I'll make her some lunch. Take your time and enjoy."

"Thank you, Chao. I'll try not to be too long." Annie closed the door and hurried down the steps. She'd studied a city map and was getting a feel for the layout of San Francisco's streets. The Jackson Street trolley would take her to the shopping district where she could wander to her heart's content. If she lost her way, she had only to wave down a cab and give Quint's address to the driver.

She stepped out at a brisk pace, swinging onboard the trolley as she'd seen other people do. Going out was just what she'd needed, she'd told herself. At least it might divert her mind from Quint for a few hours.

Before long Annie had lost herself in a bewitching maze of stores, small shops and pushcarts. Never in her life had she seen so many beautiful things for sale—dazzling silk brocades from China, Spanish shawls, Irish lace, exquisite Manchester woolens, rainbows of airy tulle. Intoxicated by a myriad of colors and textures, she willed herself to make practical choices for her clientele back in Dutchman's Creek—good black silk bombazine for mourning wear, light gabardines for spring jackets and skirts, pretty pastel organdies, edgings and laces, ribbons and buttons. Before she knew it her arms were full of bags and bundles. It was time to leave before she spent herself into the poorhouse.

On the way back to the trolley stop, she paused at a pushcart stand to buy a stuffed velveteen rabbit for

Clara. If she had time, Annie mused, she could make it a little red jacket like Peter's. Clara would love that.

She was just turning away when something in a shop window caught her eye. She took a step closer, then another and another, as if drawn by invisible strings. There, displayed on a dress form behind the glass, was the most elegant ivory silk gown Annie had ever seen.

She studied the dress, trying to analyze why she found it so striking. The gown was almost stark in its simplicity, unadorned by lace or beading. But the way it was cut, the drape of the neckline, the light smocking that shaped the bodice, the curve of the seams from slender waist to slightly flared hem, amounted to absolute perfection.

The next thing she knew, Annie was inside the door of the shop. Maybe if she could try on the gown, she'd be able to see how it was made and duplicate the style at home. Making a copy wouldn't be easy, even for her. The design was, in its subtle way, a work of genius.

The silver-haired woman behind the counter gave her a smile. "May I help you, miss?" she asked in an accented voice that, to Annie's ear, sounded Slavic.

"That gown in the window. It looks to be about my size. May I try it on?"

The woman's black eyes narrowed. "That one's a display model. I can take your measurements and have one made to fit in about two weeks."

"That won't do. I'm leaving town tomorrow, and I need the gown for tonight—for the opera." Now where had that come from? The notion of wearing the gown to the opera hadn't entered Annie's mind until now.

The woman shrugged. "Try it, then. But if you want it, you must take it as it is. No time for alterations before tonight." She went to the window and unbuttoned the back of the gown. The silk whispered seductively as she slipped it off the padded dress form.

"Thank you. I'll be careful with it." Annie carried the gown behind a carved Indian screen and laid it over the back of a chair. Her fingers trembled as she removed her jacket, hat, blouse and skirt. This was silly, she lectured herself. There was no way she could justify buying an expensive dress to be worn just once. She would try it on for just a moment. Then she would give it back, thank the woman and leave.

Lifting the skirt carefully, she slipped the gown over her head. The silk glided down her body like water, as soft as a caress against her skin. The fabric smelled lightly of sandalwood, as if it had been stored in a perfumed box.

Behind her back, her hands fumbled to work the silk-covered buttons through their loops. There was no mirror in the screened enclosure, so she would have to step out into the shop to see herself.

"Let me help you." The shopkeeper had appeared like a jinni behind her. Her strong brown fingers refastened the misaligned buttons and tugged the skirt into place. "The fit is perfect," she murmured. "If you want it, I can give you a good price."

Annie shook her head. "No, really I—"

"Come out and look at yourself." The woman steered Annie toward the mirror. "Close your eyes now, and don't open them until I tell you."

Surrendering, Annie allowed herself to be guided across the wooden floor. Deft fingers loosened her hairpins. She felt the weight of earring hooks.

"Now you can look," the shopkeeper said.

Annie opened her eyes. "Oh…" she whispered.

The woman reflected in the full-length mirror was as elegant as a swan. The draped bodice of the dress set off her long neck and slim shoulders, revealing just a hint of bosom. The tapered waist fit Annie as if it had been sewn on her body, and the silk's creamy hue, set off by the dangling crystal earrings, heightened the color in her eyes and cheeks. Annie had never considered herself more than passably attractive—Hannah had always been the beauty of the family. But dressed in this exquisite gown, she looked and felt absolutely stunning.

The shopkeeper beamed. "See, it was made for you. Don't worry, I will give you a good price, with the earrings as a gift."

"It's perfect, Annie breathed. "But for just one night, I really can't afford—"

"For the opera tonight and for your wedding later, yes? Imagine how it would look with a veil and flowers. A perfect wedding gown to pass on to your daughters, even your granddaughters. Such a treasure would be cheap at any price. How much can you pay? We will arrange it!"

The woman did have a valid argument. A simple, stylish wedding gown could get a lot of use in her family, passed from sister to sister, from mother to daughter. And the thought of strolling into the opera house with Quint at her side...

"I'll take it," Annie heard herself saying. "If we can agree on a reasonable price, of course."

Fifteen minutes later she was staggering out of the shop, balancing the carefully wrapped gown with her other purchases. After buying a pair of long white gloves she had just enough change left in her pocket for trolley fare.

What had she done? Annie battled buyer's remorse as the trolley rattled up Powell Street. She had never made such an extravagant purchase in her entire frugal, sensible life. Just the thought of it made her feel shaky. But then the gown could be reused for family weddings, she reminded herself. And now that she had it, she could study its construction and make other dresses from the same pattern. No doubt it would be a popular style in Dutchman's Creek this summer.

But this was no time for practicalities. Tonight she would be Cinderella, floating on the arm of her handsome, impossible prince. For now, that was enough to justify every penny she'd spent.

Quint's day at work had been uneventful—maddeningly so, in fact. After yesterday's damning column, he'd been braced for fireworks from City Hall or threats of a lawsuit and worse from Rutledge. Nothing of the kind had happened.

The silence was beginning to rattle him. Something was afoot, but what?

After lunch he'd telephoned home to check on Clara. The young lady herself had answered his call. She'd informed him in her miniature grown-up way that she was doing much better, thank you, and that her aunt Annie had gone shopping.

Annie's going out had troubled Quint more than he cared to admit. A pretty woman alone, unaccustomed to city ways, would be easy prey for some unsavory brute bent on mischief. But he was being overprotective, he'd told himself. Annie was a smart lady, accustomed to being on her own. She could take care of herself.

Still, he'd felt a wave of relief when he'd called again later and learned from Chao that she was safely back. He'd declined Chao's offer to call her to the telephone and simply asked him to pass on a message—he'd be working late to cover for another reporter who'd fallen ill, but he'd be home in time for the opera.

Now, as he stepped off the trolley and walked up the darkening street, Quint felt a vague uneasiness. Josiah Rutledge was known for his volatile nature. The column had been written to trigger a reaction. This unexpected silence was like waiting for a dynamite explosion and wondering what had happened to the fuse.

What if Rutledge had recovered the letter by now? If he knew Quint was bluffing, the man could bide his time and wait for his nemesis to trip himself up. It was the one possibility that made sense. But that didn't mean it felt right.

Pausing at the foot of the steps, he turned and gazed back into the deepening dark. Here and there, streetlights were flickering on. Wisps of fog slunk like furtive cats around the lampposts. A lone tradesman's wagon, pulled by a drooping bay, rolled along the street. The plodding rhythm of shod hooves on pavement echoed through the twilight.

Quint studied the shape of each shadow. Was anyone out there watching him? Following him? His hand brushed the cold weight of the pistol beneath his vest.

Maybe it would be wise to stay home tonight. Annie might be disappointed, but she hadn't seemed that excited about the opera in the first place. As he recalled, she'd even argued that she had nothing to wear. Likely as not, the change of plans would come as a relief.

Feeling better, he mounted the stairs to the second floor. Clara welcomed him at the door, dressed in a clean white nightgown and clutching a stuffed velveteen rabbit. She looked rosy and well. One less worry, thank heaven.

She greeted Quint with a hug. "Look what Aunt Annie brought me!" Eyes sparkling, she held up the rabbit for inspection. "His name's Peter. Aunt Annie's going to make him a red jacket."

"Very nice. Where is your aunt Annie?"

"She's in the bedroom, getting ready for the opera."

Quint glanced down the gaslit hallway toward the closed door. "Would you go and ask her to come out? I need to talk to her."

Quint watched his daughter scamper down the hallway and vanish into the guest room, closing the door behind her. A moment later the door opened again and Annie stepped out into the soft light.

Quint's mouth went dry.

She stood poised like a doe, lips parted, eyes wide and wary. A faceted crystal teardrop glittered below her left ear, scattering faint, iridescent dots of light over her cheek. Its mate dangled from her fingertips.

The ivory silk floated around her like a cloud, defining her curves and heightening the glow of her creamy skin. She'd been shopping, Quint remembered. And this gown had been her purchase. She looked ravishing in it.

His heart leaped and plummeted by turns. Annie Gustavson had grown up dirt-poor. What little money she had, she'd earned with her own hands. The dress would have cost her dearly. For all the perceived danger, Quint knew he could not deny her this chance to shine.

"What is it?" she asked. "Is something wrong, Quint?"

Quint shook his head. He had to clear his throat to find his voice. "No. Just wanted you to know I was home. Take your time getting ready. I still need to change."

"That's fine." She turned to go back into the bedroom.

"Annie—"

She stopped, poised like a vision. "Yes?"

"You look beautiful."

The color deepened in her face. "Thank you, Quint," she murmured, and vanished into the guest room.

As the door closed behind her, Quint entered his own room to change into his evening clothes. Carefully he unbuckled the shoulder holster and laid it on the bed, leaving it handy to strap on again.

Tonight he would walk into the Grand Opera House with a queen on his arm.

He would be ready to protect her with his life.

* * *

Bundled in her cloak, Annie sat next to Quint in the hooded carriage. The evening was cool, the air sharp with the iodine smell of the sea. Tendrils of mist crept along the gutters. The mournful sound of foghorns echoed through the darkness.

The Grand Opera House, built when the city was younger, stood a block south of Market Street in what was now the working-class district. The long ride from Quint's Jackson Street flat took them through the main part of town. Leaning forward beneath the carriage hood, Annie could see the majestic buildings that rose on both sides of the street. Lit by electricity, they glittered like star-filled castles in a modern-day fairyland.

Fine buggies, cabs and automobiles moved with them along the street. Their sidelights glowed like fireflies as they funneled toward the glowing beacon of the Grand Opera House.

"What are you thinking, Annie?" Quint's breath stirred her hair as he spoke. Her pulse quickened. She hadn't realized he was so close to her.

"I can see why you love this city," she said. "It's a magical place. There's so much to discover."

"Then stay and discover it. You don't have to leave tomorrow. In fact, I'd much rather you didn't."

Annie willed her resolve not to weaken. "We've already been over this, Quint. Our bags are packed and our traveling clothes are laid out for tomorrow morning. If you insist on staying here, you'll be better off without us."

He sighed and settled back in the seat. "Then what do you say we call it a truce and make the most of tonight? Maybe you can come back here again sometime..." He paused, his arm settling around her shoulders. "That is, if you're not married to Frank Robinson."

Annie gazed down at her gloved hands. Right now the last thing she wanted to think about was being married to Frank. "And what if I am?" she retorted.

"Then I'd call it a tarnal waste of beauty and passion."

Heat flashed in Annie's cheeks. She glanced away to hide her emotions. "You're a fine one to advise me, Quint Seavers. What if I never have another chance?"

"Don't sell yourself short, Annie. The way you look tonight, you could have every eligible man in San Francisco at your feet."

Every man but you.

"You can certainly do better than Frank," he said. "The man spits tobacco and wears sissy-looking trousers that show his socks. Not only that, but he must be closing in on forty, at least."

"Well, I'm twenty-three, and so far he's the only one who's asked me. I want a family. I don't want to be everybody's old maid aunt."

"Then give it time. You're young yet, and you're

a beautiful woman. Wait for a man who'll make you happy."

They were passing the *Chronicle* Building where Quint worked. Annie's gaze traced its towering walls, counting the windows that marked each floor. As the count grew, so did her frustration.

Why had she told Quint how she felt about him? Why had she let him kiss her, not once, but twice—and with his tongue, for heaven's sake? Now he was playing her like a trout on a line, knowing she was vulnerable, knowing she wanted him. It was downright humiliating.

She should have slapped his face the first time he laid an ungentlemanly hand on her!

"Frank's decent and generous, and he isn't poor. Maybe that's all I need to be happy." Annie wanted her words to hurt him, but she knew better. So did Quint.

"Something tells me you'll need more than that, Annie." His arm lay lightly behind her, almost as if by accident, but she could feel the teasing pressure of his fingers through her cloak. She battled the heat of awareness that rippled from the point of contact.

"I'm not a fool," she said. "There was nothing dashing or romantic about my own father, but he gave my mother seven children and worked himself to death taking care of them. I'd settle for that kind of love any day."

"Settle?" His fingers tightened subtly.

"Would I be better off with someone who'd sweep me off to the stars and break my heart?"

Someone like you?

Quint's compelling fingers had stilled. Their carriage had pulled into line outside the Grand Opera House. Annie forgot her argument as her dazzled gaze took in the glowing, pillared facade. Modeled after the great opera houses of Europe, it was one of the finest halls in the Western Hemisphere. Tonight the foremost opera company in the United States would be performing—and she, Annie Gustavson from Dutchman's Creek, would be in the audience. This would be the evening of a lifetime. Nothing, she vowed, was going to spoil it.

Quint paid the driver and offered his arm to help Annie out of the carriage. She held her head high, struggling to hide a sudden attack of nerves. What difference did a pretty new dress make? She didn't belong in a fancy place like this. She was just a country mouse, and everyone would know it.

Quint, on the other hand, looked smashing in his black tie and tails. He was a heartbreakingly handsome man with the self-confidence to fit in anywhere. As the carriage pulled away, Annie noticed a number of women casting furtive glances at him—elegant women glittering with jewels and wrapped in furs against the evening chill. She clutched her dark blue woolen cloak around her shoulders. Everyone here seemed to have money, and this was clearly the place to show it off.

But never mind, Annie lectured herself. She'd come to see an opera, maybe the only one she would ever see in her life. She would do her best to forget discomfort and enjoy it.

She tried not to stare like a bumpkin as Quint escorted her into the cavernous lobby. Never mind the gilt, the grandeur, the gleaming marble and polished mahogany, the velvet draperies and the sumptuously dressed opera-goers. She would behave as if she saw such things every day of the week.

"Let me check your wrap." Quint had stepped behind her. His hands lifted the cloak from her shoulders and whisked it away. "Stay right here," he said. "I don't want to lose track of you. I'll only be a minute."

Annie watched as he made his way toward a built-in counter behind a row of pillars. There was a line of men waiting to check their coats and their tall silk hats. Quint, she surmised, might be more than a minute. But what a chance to study the gowns!

The crowd flowed around her like a river, headed for the main floor seats or the curving staircases on either side that led to the upper landing, the boxes and the balcony. Annie forgot her own unease as her eyes feasted on beaded silks and satins, rich brocades, exquisite Belgian lace, flounces and ruffles and ruching. And the jewels! Ropes and ropes of pearls and glittering diamond brooches; here a stunning emerald necklace with matching earrings, there a ruby choker, probably worth more than Annie earned in a year. One silver-haired matron wore a diamond tiara like a queen. Annie had no doubt that the diamonds were real.

Dazzled by so much finery, Annie failed to see the tall, dark man making his way through the crowd. Not until he was standing squarely in front of her did she look up into the chiseled face of Josiah Rutledge.

Her knees went weak beneath her skirt.

"Miss Gustavson, what a pleasant surprise." He bowed formally over her gloved hand. "I trust you're enjoying your visit to our fair city?"

"Yes, very much." Annie forced herself to meet his gaze. It was like looking into the eyes of a cobra.

"I trust you'll enjoy the opera," he said. "The Metropolitan is always first-rate. Do you have tickets for the *Carmen* opening on the seventeeth?"

"I shan't be here then," Annie said. "In any case, I understand all the performances are sold out."

"What a pity. Caruso's not to be missed." Rutledge smiled, showing a glint of gold tooth. "If you change your mind about leaving, tell your friend Mr. Seavers that I've got a pair of extra tickets. If he'll come around to see me, he can have them— my gift to a lovely lady."

Annie felt the chill all the way down to the heels

of her kidskin slippers. "Thank you, I'll tell him," she said. "But I doubt he'll be taking you up on your offer."

"What a shame." Rutledge's reptilian smile stretched thinner. "Enjoy the performance, Miss Gustavson. Perhaps we'll meet again."

He slithered off toward the stairs, powerful, confident and dangerous. Annie sagged against a marble pillar, her heart pounding. Where in heaven's name was Quint?

Chapter Six

Quint had never cared much for opera. The lighter musicals that played the Columbia or the raucous vaudeville shows at the Orpheum were more to his liking. But tonight's tickets had fallen into his hands, and he'd wanted to show Annie a memorable evening.

Just how memorable remained to be seen.

He had turned from the coat check counter just in time to see Rutledge walking away from where he'd left Annie. By the time he'd reached her side, Rutledge had vanished and Annie was incandescent.

"The nerve of the man!" she'd sputtered. "It wasn't so much what he said as the way he said it. And the way he looked at me—like a snake watching a bird! If I'd had a hatpin, I'd have stabbed him with it! He's plotting something against you, Quint. Something evil."

At first she'd wanted to leave. It had taken Quint

several minutes to calm her down and talk her into staying. Now, an hour into the performance, she sat beside him in the shadows of the small, very private box. Her spine was rigid, her gloved hands clasped in her lap as she watched the white-robed chorus parade around the stage waving peacock-feather fans.

Quint studied her from his chair. The gown was perfection on her, so pure and simple that more lavishly dressed women looked gaudy by comparison. The inexpensive crystal earrings sparkled against her cheeks. They were pretty enough, but for Annie he would have chosen pearls, flawless and glowing like her skin. Given his way, he would drape her naked body in pearls and lay her on a bed of champagne-colored silk with her glorious hair spread on the pillow…

Lord, if Annie knew what he was thinking, she would slap him silly.

His gaze returned to her profile, etched like alabaster against the dark red draperies. Her lips, he noticed, were trembling.

Quint fought the urge to reach out, take her in his arms and kiss away her fears. He already knew how sweet those lips would taste. He imagined tasting them again and again until she melted against him and surrendered to his loving.

The very thought of Annie beneath him flooded Quint's loins with heat. He would love her slowly and skillfully, he thought, taking the time to stroke her small, perfect breasts, letting his mouth feast on her swollen nipples until they throbbed. Then he would take his kisses lower, down along the flat of her belly, skimming the soft gateway to her womanhood, teasing her with his hands and lips until she bucked against him in a fever of need. Still he would force himself to wait. Only when she was slick with her own woman honey would he move between her legs, penetrating silkily and pushing deep, deeper inside….

"Quint—" She nudged his arm, startling him out of his reverie.

"Down there on the main floor," she whispered. "Four rows back, near the center. Do you see him?"

Quint followed the direction of her gaze. Even from behind, Rutledge's dark, pomaded head was unmistakable.

"And that blond-haired woman he's sitting with. Do you know her?"

Quint suppressed a wry smile. "Everybody knows her. That's Delilah Stanhope, one of the richest widows in San Francisco. Her husband made it big in railroad and mining stock before he dropped dead from apoplexy last year. Looks like our friend Rutledge is set on moving up in the world."

"What do you suppose they're doing down there?"

Quint reached out and tucked her gloved hand into his. "They appear to be watching the opera. Why don't we do the same?"

Annie made a visible effort to relax as his fingers

tightened around her hand. He liked having her close. And she looked so beautiful tonight, damn it, he wanted to show her off to the world. He wanted to stand up in the box and shout, *This is my woman! My Annie! Just look at her, you mugs! Look at what you'll never have!*

Hellfire, what was wrong with him?

He remembered that first night in his apartment, how she'd sat there wearing nothing but his bathrobe, and told him how she'd put him on a pedestal, even when he was Hannah's beau. Then, when he'd kissed her, she'd caught fire in his arms, and she'd set him on fire, as well.

Was Annie in love with him?

The question was far from trivial. Annie Gustavson wasn't just any woman. She was extended family—Hannah's sister. If he played with her affections and broke her heart there'd be hell to pay for years to come.

And if he didn't play with her affections, she'd go home and marry Frank Robinson.

Most of the women in Quint's past understood the rules of the game. You enjoyed the thrills, you had a few laughs, and when the novelty wore off you moved on. But those rules weren't Annie's rules. She was the kind of woman who'd only play for keeps.

Was it time he started playing for keeps, too?

The very idea made him break out in cold sweat. Annie was beautiful and smart, spirited and passionate; and she understood him as well as any woman could, except maybe Hannah. In most ways she was perfect for him. But he needed time to think things out. And time was the one thing he didn't have. Annie would be leaving with Clara on the morning train. And when that train pulled into Dutchman's Creek, Frank would be on the platform, waiting for her answer.

Quint swore under his breath.

On the stage below, a buxom soprano draped in gold chains and what appeared to be twenty yards of cheesecloth, was belting out a tempestuous aria with lungs that would do credit to a sea lion. And this was only the second act. He'd had higher hopes for the evening. But Rutledge's appearance had put a scare into Annie. She was doing her best to enjoy the show, but the tension in her hand betrayed her screaming nerves.

She had seen the devil, and she was afraid—not so much for herself as for him, Quint reminded himself. Her concern touched him more deeply than he cared to admit.

The box was dark and secluded. Impulsively Quint circled her shoulders with his arm and drew her against his side. Leaning awkwardly, he brushed a light kiss on her cheek. "It's all right, Annie," he whispered. "There's nothing for you to be afraid of."

"Please, Quint," she pleaded. "Please come with

us when we leave tomorrow. I have this awful feeling—what if I never see you again?"

"Would you care?" His lips brushed the bridge of her nose.

"Don't be silly. We'd all care. If anything were to happen to you, all of us—Clara, Hannah, Judd and little Daniel—the whole family would be devastated."

"I asked about you."

Her eyes flashed into his. "Now you're backing me into a corner. Are you trying to make me say that I love you?"

Her raw honesty struck Quint with the force of a shotgun blast. His throat jerked tight. The next question emerged as a rasp. "Do you, Annie?"

She glared at him, blinking back furious tears. "I've loved you all my life. That's why I haven't married. And that's why I'm going home and saying yes to Frank. I'm tired of hurting all the time. I'm tired of wanting what I can't have."

"Oh, damn it, Annie—" Quint felt something shatter inside him. With a groan he turned his chair and gathered her onto his lap. He'd half expected her to resist, but she came willingly, curling into his arms like a child. Words failing him, he cradled her close.

"Don't you dare say you love me, too," she muttered against his chest. "If you do, I'll know you're lying. But there's one thing I swear. If you're not on that train with us tomorrow, I'm going to find Frank

Robinson and drag him in front of a preacher the very day I get home!"

He groaned, knowing he couldn't let her budge him. "Do that and you'll regret it for the rest of your life."

"Will I?" Annie pushed away from him. As the music rose, she flung the challenge back at him. "Then just see if I don't do it, Quint Seavers! Who are you to tell me what I will or won't re—"

He stopped her words with a brutal kiss that crushed her lips and bent her backward over his arm. For an instant she struggled. Then her arms went hard around him. As the orchestra crescendoed to a cymbal-crashing climax she returned the passion, fire for fire. Stars exploded in Quint's head. His loins ignited like dry tinder. Burning with need, he molded his hand to her breast. Propriety and common sense be damned. He wanted this woman any way he could have her.

The audience broke into a ripple of polite applause as the house lights went up. Act two of the damnedly interminable opera was over.

Annie had flown out of Quint's arms when the lights came on. She sat primly in the chair, arranging the folds of her skirt like a little preening bird. With her face flushed, lips swollen, hair becomingly mussed, she looked more delectable than ever.

The audience was stirring, some people standing up to stretch for the short intermission, some moving up the aisles. Rutledge remained in his seat, chatting with the voluptuous widow Stanhope. So far, the bastard appeared to be up to nothing more sinister than a night at the opera with an attractive and wealthy woman.

Quint tried to make small talk with Annie, but their conversation sounded as if they were reciting lines from a badly written play. They needed to talk about what had just happened—or better yet, do more than talk. But this was neither the time nor the place for it.

"Are you enjoying the opera?" he asked.

"Yes, very much. Are you?"

"Frankly, I expected better from the Met. The papers will be all over them tomorrow. I should've taken you to see *Babes in Toyland* at the Columbia."

"Victor Herbert? I've heard of that one. Clara would have enjoyed it, too. We could've taken her along."

"Stay another night. I'll call in some favors to get tickets."

"Don't make things harder, Quint." Her posture had gone rigid. "My decision's been made. It's final, and you know what it is."

"So you'd go home and marry Frank out of sheer stubbornness?"

"Stop it. Look, the house lights are dimming. Let's just watch the opera."

She settled back as the curtain went up. Quint had lost all interest in the show. He watched her hungrily as she shifted in her chair and fidgeted with her earring. The faceted crystal glinted in the darkness. He wanted nothing more than to be alone with her. But the end of the performance seemed hours away.

The end of the performance.

Quint couldn't explain the vague tingling of his danger sense, but he'd learned not to ignore it. Rutledge was putting himself in plain sight for a reason. Something was going down tonight, and the bastard wanted to make sure he was seen elsewhere.

Quint touched Annie's shoulder. "Let's go," he said.

She hesitated, then simply nodded and took his proffered arm. Neither of them spoke as he led her out onto the landing and down the stairs to the empty lobby, where they picked up their wraps. Bundled against the evening chill, they walked out of the theater into the foggy darkness.

A half-dozen cabs waited along the curb, the horses drowsing, the drivers huddled into their coats. Annie clasped Quint's arm as he walked down the line of them, chose one and helped her onto the leather seat. She waited while he murmured some instructions to the driver, an old man he appeared to know, then climbed up next to Annie and settled himself at her side.

As the carriage began to move, he slipped an

arm behind her shoulders. Fog swirled around them, veiling them from the rest of the world.

Annie laid her head on his shoulder. She loved him. But pinning him down was like trying to lasso the wind. He might knock himself out to keep her from marrying Frank. But he'd let her die an old maid before he'd marry her himself. The only woman he'd ever loved enough to marry was Hannah. Now that he'd lost her, his heart was safely locked away—maybe forever.

"Thank you for leaving with me," he said. "I hope you didn't mind."

She shook her head. "I'd spent enough time in that chair. Besides, judging from what I've read, most operas have sad endings. I don't need a sad ending tonight."

His lips grazed her forehead. "Stay, and maybe we can make it a happier one."

"You know I can't, and you know why."

His arm pulled her closer. "Then it appears we have what's known in poker as a Mexican standoff."

"Do we? You could end it, you know, with a little common sense."

"So could you, if you'd accept the fact that I have a job to do." Quint drew a long, ragged breath. "Promise me one thing. If you decide to marry Frank, make sure it's for the right reasons. Don't just do it to punish me."

Annie struggled to ignore the stabbing sensation

in her chest. "So you can't stand the thought of guilt, is that it?" she bantered.

"Guilt has nothing to do with it. I just don't want you making a hasty choice."

"Frank's been courting me for nearly a year. I'd hardly call that hasty. And who are you to tell me what choice to make, Quint Seavers? I—" She broke off, peering through the fog at the unfamiliar street. "Where are we going?"

"Back to the flat. We're just taking the long way around." Turning in the seat, he laid a finger across her lips. "Let's just be quiet and enjoy the ride, shall we? Talking only seems to get us into trouble."

He eased her close against his side. Lulled by his warmth and the steady *clop-clop* of iron-shod hooves on the pavement, Annie felt herself begin to relax. She lay back against his shoulder, breathing in the cool mist. By now it was late. Most of the buildings were dark. Fog had softened the street-lights to ghostly blurs. Even the driver of their carriage was only a shrouded half-seen presence.

Listening to the distant foghorns, Annie felt a sense of magic, as if they were drifting alone in a world of clouds and darkness. It was like a scene from a romantic novel, except that this story would end with her getting on the train tomorrow and going home to Colorado.

It was quite possible that she would never see Quint again.

She closed her eyes and nestled closer. Her head came to rest against the hard outline of the pistol beneath his vest. She went rigid as a new possibility struck her.

What if Quint had suspected Rutledge's thugs were waiting to ambush him on the way home from the opera? In that light, his leaving early and taking a circuitous route home made perfect sense.

"What's the matter?" he murmured. "You're as tense as a bowstring."

"You told me not to talk."

"Your body's doing the talking for you. What is it?"

"Why did you want to leave the opera early?"

"Because I was bored. And because I wanted to be alone with the most beautiful lady there."

"Balderdash! You wanted to make sure Rutledge wouldn't give you a surprise party on the way home. Why didn't you tell me?"

He stared at her, then broke out in a rough-edged laugh. "What a little worrywart you are! If I were to be gunned down in the street, especially in the company of a lady, the story would be all over the morning papers. Everybody would guess who was behind it. Rutledge wouldn't take such a risk. And in any case, we've outsmarted him, haven't we?"

Annie peered through the fog at the outlined rows of sleeping tenements. A dark-colored cat flashed across the roadway and vanished into an alley. "I certainly hope so," she said.

"Then let's relax and enjoy the ride. And I do mean enjoy."

His knuckle grazed her jaw, nudging her chin toward him. Softly at first, like the brush of a falling petal, his lips skimmed hers. Annie surrendered with a hunger that burned all the way through her body. Her pulse was galloping, her thoughts whirling like painted animals on a carousel. In her wild confusion, only one thing seemed certain. Frank Robinson was going to have to find himself another bride.

He kissed her again with exquisite restraint— nibbling her mouth, her cheeks, her closed eyelids. Annie moaned as heat rippled in the depths of her body, spilling down into her thighs. She twisted toward him on the seat, opening her cloak. Back in the box at the opera he had touched her breast. The waves of sweet sensation had triggered tears. She wanted to feel his touch again...and again.

Maybe tonight was all they would ever have. Maybe she would never marry. No one could predict the future. But something beyond common sense told Annie that if she didn't let Quint make love to her, she'd regret it for the rest of her days.

His arms invaded her cloak, pulling her close as he deepened the kiss. Her frantic fingers guided his hand toward her breast. A whimper shook her body as he cupped her, his thumb stroking her nipple through the thin silk. He answered her with a low growl as her tongue played with his.

His hand fumbled with her draped bodice to cradle the sensitive flesh beneath the silk. She bit back a little cry at the first contact of his fingers. It was as if every cell in her body was opening like a flower. She had never felt more alive or more womanly.

"Don't be afraid to stop me, Annie," he murmured against the curve of her neck. "I don't want you to be sorry."

"I refuse to be…sorry." Her head tipped back, loosening her hair. She arched against him, drowning in the sensual rush of touch and smell and taste. In the limited privacy of the carriage there was only so much they could do. But soon they would be back at Quint's flat. Clara would be asleep and Chao would be leaving. They would be alone. The thought of what could happen triggered a dark throbbing inside her.

Annie's breath caught as his fingers raised the hem of her petticoat and touched the thin cotton stockings beneath. She tensed for a moment, startled as his hand eased gently up her leg to the opening in her drawers. "Shhh…" He kissed her mouth. "I won't hurt you, girl. I only want to pleasure you."

"I know…" she murmured against his lips. "I just—oh…" She gasped as his fingertips found her intimate folds and began a tender exploration. She was so wet that they slid over the tingling surfaces. "Oh…" she whimpered as unimaginable feelings shimmered through her body. "Quint, I—"

His lips stopped her moan as he reached the tender, swollen nub at her center and stroked it with a feather touch. "Shhh…" He whispered with a chuckle. "We don't want to entertain our driver, do we?"

Annie scarcely heard him. She was lost in the savage magic that those teasing fingertips aroused in her. Her legs had fallen open beneath her skirts. Her hips bucked against his hand, seeking more, wanting more, all he could give her. Each thrust heightened the sensation. She felt it mounting, cresting like a wave, higher and higher.

His mouth swallowed her cry as she tumbled over the edge.

By the time Annie had spiraled back to earth, the carriage had stopped in front of Quint's apartment building. While she straightened her skirts, Quint swung to the pavement, paid the driver a generous tip and strode around the carriage to assist her. Face flushed, eyes lowered, Annie accepted his proffered arm. After the intimate thing she'd let him do, she felt inexplicably shy.

As the carriage pulled away, he turned her to face him. "Look at me, Annie," he said.

When she didn't respond he lifted her chin. Tears welled in her eyes as she gazed up at him.

"Lord, but you're beautiful," he said. "You make my heart stand still. Don't you know that?"

She gulped back the tightness in her throat. Next to Hannah's golden beauty, Annie had always felt invisible, especially in Quint's eyes. Now he was saying words she'd hungered to hear. But they were only words. How could she let herself believe them?

"I wouldn't have taken anything from you tonight," he said. "I only wanted to give you pleasure—and to show you the warm, passionate woman you really are."

"To show me why I shouldn't marry Frank?" The words snapped out of her before she could bite them back. Now would be the time to tell him she'd decided not to marry Frank after all. But Quint was behaving as if he'd done her a favor. He hadn't needed her, maybe hadn't even wanted her.

It was all Annie could do to keep from slapping his smug, arrogant face.

He shook his head. "Annie, I didn't mean—"

"Never mind." She stepped back, freeing herself from his grasp. "Let's just go inside. I'm sure Chao will be anxious to get home to his family."

Turning she mounted the stoop and, without waiting for him, opened the front door. His footsteps echoed behind her as they climbed the stairs to the second-floor landing, but Annie didn't look back at him. She couldn't bear the thought of meeting his eyes.

Tonight she had told Quint she loved him. In the carriage she'd surrendered her heart, body and soul.

She'd even been prepared to sacrifice what she could give only once.

And what had Quint given her in return? A blasted demonstration!

Thank goodness she'd be leaving tomorrow morning. After tonight, she didn't care if she ever saw him again.

At the entrance to the flat she paused. The door would be locked, and only Quint had the key. She would have to wait for him here.

He came up onto the landing, fumbling in his pocket. Annie moved aside while he inserted the key in the lock and tried to turn it. "Odd," he muttered, "it doesn't seem to be… Oh, no! Please, God, no!"

Crashing through the unlocked door, Quint plunged into the flat with Annie behind him. The brightly burning gaslights illuminated a nightmare scene. The entire place had been ransacked—drawers dumped, upholstery slashed, rugs torn up, books ripped apart, cabinets and cupboards emptied, with their contents strewn on the floor.

A dark form lay facedown on the threshold of the kitchen, hands stretched forward, motionless. Annie recognized Chao's dark garb and long braided queue.

Clara! Where was Clara? Wild with dread, Annie raced into the guest room.

The bed was empty, the bedclothes torn and flung to one side, the mattress slashed open.

Two objects lay on the carpeted floor next to the

bed. Annie cried out as she recognized them. One was a brown velveteen rabbit. The other was a small pink seashell, as perfect as a baby's ear.

Chapter Seven

Chao whimpered as Quint bent over him. At least the Chinaman was alive—one small spark of hope in a nightmare that was fast spinning out of control.

Annie stood in the doorway of the guest room, her face ashen. Her gloved hands clutched the velveteen rabbit she'd bought Clara earlier that day. "Clara's gone," she said. "There's no sign of her."

"Could she be hiding?" It was a wasted question. Quint knew what had happened and he knew why.

"Everything's torn apart. There's no place left where a little girl could hide." Annie's shattered gaze met his. He knew what she was thinking—the same thing he was. They should have been here tonight.

This was his fault. He'd laughed in the face of danger, telling himself Rutledge didn't dare hurt him. But he'd been wrong. Lord, how wrong he'd been. Rutledge had known exactly where and when to strike.

Quint willed his hands to stop shaking. Falling apart wouldn't help Clara, nor would it help Chao, who lay bleeding and semiconscious on the floor. If ever there was a time to be calm, it was now.

Annie had moved from the doorway and come back down the hall. Putting the toy rabbit aside, she knelt on the other side of Chao's body. She looked like death. Her silk skirt drooped around her like a wilted flower.

"Chao," she murmured, touching his shoulder. "Can you hear me?"

The only answer was a muffled groan.

"We're going to turn you over," Quint said. "Tell us if we start to hurt you." He glanced up, meeting Annie's eyes. "Now."

Together they lifted him, Annie supporting his head and shoulders, Quint his torso and legs. Chao flinched, but didn't cry out as they eased him onto his back. He was a tough little man, all muscle and sinew beneath his dark broadcloth jacket and trousers.

Annie gasped at the sight of Chao's face. The poor man had been beaten unmercifully. His nose was broken, his lips puffed and bloodied, with two teeth missing. His eyes were bruised and swollen shut. An oozing lump distorted the left side of his shaved head. Quint guessed that Rutledge's thugs had clubbed him hard enough to knock him out.

They probably thought they'd killed him. Or maybe they'd left him alive on purpose.

"The poor devil must've put up one hell of a fight," Quint muttered. "Hold him, I'll get some water."

Annie cradled Chao's head in her lap. Her gown was streaked with his blood, but she didn't appear to notice.

Quint rushed to the kitchen and returned with a cup of water and some clean, damp towels. Chao was trying to keep his eyes open, but with the bruises and swelling it was more than he could do. Crouching beside him, Quint tipped the cup to his lips. Chao's throat jerked as he managed a few painful swallows.

"Tell me what you can," Quint said.

Chao's bloodied mouth twisted with effort. "Nine…clock. Two men. Trick me…say you got hurt." His gaze shifted toward the cup and Quint gave him another sip. "They put…Little Miss in a big sack. I fight…" He coughed, spitting up drops of blood. "Something…hit me. Don't remember…"

Quint gazed down at the man he'd come to think of more as a friend than a servant. By right, those awful bruises, broken face bones and missing teeth should be his, not Chao's. While he'd been at the opera enjoying himself with Annie, this man had been here, fighting for Clara with his life.

Sick with self-loathing, Quint willed himself to stay calm. Right now nothing mattered except finding his little girl and getting her back.

"Did the men say anything?" Annie asked gently.

"A letter. They ask, they hit me. Ask, hit." He shook his head. Tears oozed from his swollen eyes. "I don't have…don't know…"

"There…" Annie took a towel from Quint and began sponging the blood from Chao's face. Her hands were shaking. The fingers of her gloves were stained crimson. "You need a doctor," she said to Chao.

Chao shook his head. "Get me home. My wife has good medicine there."

"Did you see them leave?" Quint demanded.

Again Chao shook his head. Quint's gut clenched as he imagined Clara helpless inside the sack, lifted by rough arms and carried outside. Lord, how terrified she must have been.

Fear and rage screamed inside him. He wanted to fling back his head and howl like a wild animal. He wanted to hunt the kidnappers down and tear them to pieces with his own hands. As for Rutledge…

But he was losing control now, and he couldn't let that happen. Get his daughter back—that was all that really mattered.

"The police," Annie said. "We need to call them."

"No good. Half of them are on the take from Rutledge, and the rest are afraid of him."

Her eyes widened. "But we can't get her back alone! How will we—"

Her words were cut off by the sudden jangle of the telephone. The sound jolted through Quint like an electric shock. Kicking aside an overturned wastepaper basket, he lunged toward the desk, seized the shaft and yanked the earpiece off its hook.

"Hello," he rasped.

"Mr. Seavers." The cold, metallic voice sounded Irish. Definitely not Rutledge. "I believe we have something you want."

The fury that surged over Quint threatened to drown his reason. "Where is she, you son of a—"

"Your niece is quite safe for now. But if you want her back alive you'll deliver something *we* want. I believe you know what it is. A certain letter."

Quint willed himself to be calm while his mind flailed for answers. "All right," he said. "Once Clara's safely back, the letter's yours. But it isn't here, as you damn well found out. It's locked away where I can't get to it until tomorrow."

Silence crackled on the other end of the line before the voice returned. "You've got twenty-four hours. Be here tomorrow night. We'll call and tell you where to meet us."

"I want to talk to Clara."

The only response was a click.

Quint hung up the receiver and turned away from the telephone. Annie was staring at him in horror.

"You don't even have that letter! Why didn't you tell them that?"

Knees giving way, Quint sank onto the edge of the desk. "You don't know these people like I do.

As long as they think I have the letter, they'll have a reason to keep Clara alive. Otherwise…"

"But she's just a little girl! Surely they'd let her go…" Annie's voice trailed off as the truth sank home. Quint felt like a monster as he watched her features sag, watched her slowly break and crumble. The truth was cruel. But she needed to know what could happen.

"And if we can find the letter?" The question emerged as a strained whisper.

"That would improve the odds. But it's no guarantee they'll let her go, especially if she can identify them. For now, they've given me twenty-four hours. Our best chance is to keep stalling them while we try to find her."

"Find her!" Annie cried. "How on earth can we find her? They could be holding her anywhere!"

"I will ask my people to help." Chao had pulled himself to a sitting position. Pain twisted his swollen features. "We go many places. No one looks at us, but we see everything."

Gratitude raised a lump in Quint's throat. Chao was right. The members of San Francisco's Chinese community were like one huge extended family. As servants, gardeners, laundry collectors, janitors, cooks, vendors and laborers, they moved through the city like an invisible army, unnoticed as long as they kept to their places. If anybody could discover where a little girl was being held, they could.

"You'd do that for us?" Annie had taken off her gloves. She reached out and gently cradled Chao's bruised hands.

He drew himself up with remarkable dignity. "I am responsible. If I lose Little Miss, I lose face. If I lose face, my people lose face."

"Then let's get you home," Quint said. "I can telephone for a cab."

Chao shook his head. "I can walk. It is not far, and my legs are strong."

"Then I'll walk with you," Quint said. "With that bump on your head, you could pass out on the way."

"You have a picture of Little Miss?"

"Yes. I carry it with me. It's not recent, but it'll be better than nothing." Quint took Chao's arms and helped him stand. Chao tottered on unsteady legs. His eyes were swollen almost shut and he was clearly in a lot of pain, but had too much pride to complain. Thank goodness his home in Chinatown was only a few blocks south of Jackson Street.

As they turned toward the door Quint's gaze met Annie's. Her eyes were wells of anguish. "Bolt the door when we go," he said. "Don't open it for anyone but me, no matter what they tell you. If I need to telephone, I'll ring twice, then hang up and ring again. Otherwise don't answer. Understand?"

"Yes." She spoke as if her voice had been drawn through ground glass. "I understand."

"I won't be gone any longer than I have to."

Her silence shadowed Quint as he guided Chao into the hallway and closed the door behind him. Annie had every reason to blame him for what had happened. He was the one who'd arranged to leave Clara home while they went to the opera. Worse, he'd dismissed her worries about Rutledge as little more than a case of female jitters. But then, he'd been thinking only in terms of his own safety. That the bastard would target Clara had never entered his mind.

What a reckless, arrogant fool he'd been.

How Annie must despise him.

Annie stood at the kitchen window, clutching Clara's velveteen rabbit. Her eyes peered downward through the fog as Quint and Chao emerged from the back door and vanished into the alley. Only when she could no longer see them did she loose the taut rein she'd kept on her emotions.

Legs collapsing beneath her, she slid down the wall to the kitchen floor. Dry sobs racked her body as she clutched the little rabbit close. She'd told herself she wouldn't cry, that she'd be brave for Clara's sake. But now she found herself helpless. Grief and fear shook her to the marrow of her bones.

When she closed her eyes it was Clara she saw— her chestnut curls flying as she raced along the beach, her dark eyes widening with wonder as she held the seashell to her ears, her small face intent as she played dominoes with Chao.

Now Clara was at the mercy of men who'd destroy anything that stood in their way—even a beautiful, innocent little girl. Where was she now? Was she bound with ropes? Was she locked alone in the dark? Was she shivering with cold? Was she in pain? Only one thing was certain. Wherever Clara was, she would be wild with terror. Only a miracle could save her.

Annie shifted forward onto her knees and began to pray as she'd never prayed in her life. Lips moving in silence she begged and pleaded until the tears scalded her face.

Clara meant the world to so many people—to Hannah, to Judd, to Quint and to her. So much love wrapped up in one little girl. If the worst were to happen, her loss would tear the family apart.

Somehow they would find her, Annie told herself. Somehow they would get her back and put this nightmare behind them. Any other outcome would be unthinkable.

Summoning her strength, she took a deep breath and raised her head. Her late father had always said, "Pray as if there were no work, and work as if there were no prayer." Now that she'd done her praying, Annie resolved, it was time she made herself useful.

Her once-lovely silk gown was rumpled, damp and bloodstained. So much for vanity. Maybe if she hadn't bought the dress, she could have talked Quint into staying home tonight. She hadn't been all that keen on the opera. But she'd wanted to look pretty for him. She'd wanted to walk into the theater on his arm and know that he was proud of her.

Quint would blame himself for what had happened to Clara. But she'd had a part in it, too. She should have stuck to her guns and insisted they leave after her encounter with Rutledge. Instead, she'd allowed Quint to dismiss her fear. Worse, she'd been all too easily persuaded. She'd wanted to be seen with him, to sit in the box surrounded by the cream of San Francisco society, like Cinderella at the ball.

If she'd trusted her instincts, they might have arrived back at the flat in time to save Clara.

Disgusted with herself, Annie rose and walked into the guest room. The luggage she'd packed for the train had been dumped, the linings ripped out of the bags. Clothes, shoes, bedding and loose feathers were strewn over the floor. Finding a white shirtwaist and a dark blue walking skirt, she hung them over a bedpost and began the struggle to get out of her ruined gown.

Earlier that evening, Clara had helped her with the long row of buttons up the back, laughing and chattering the whole time. Now, when the buttons proved impossible to undo alone, Annie ripped her way out of the dress. Why should it matter? She would never wear it again.

After she'd changed her clothes and tossed her earrings onto the dressing table, Annie walked through the flat, taking stock of the chaos. In light of all that had happened, cleaning up seemed trivial. But at least it would give her hands something to do while her mind raced in circles.

Rolling up her sleeves, she stirred the coals in the fireplace and laid on fresh wood. Then she started on the parlor, shoving the furniture back into place, stacking the photographs in their shattered frames, gathering books and papers into some semblance of order. Not that any of it mattered. Nothing would matter until Clara was safe.

The alcove that served as Quint's study was in the worst condition of all. Drawers had been dumped out, files emptied and scattered, the type-writer smashed on the floor. Only the telephone had been left in place on the desk, awaiting the planned call to Quint.

That call, Annie remembered, had come within minutes of their walking through the front door. Since she and Quint had left the opera early, some-one must have been watching the flat, waiting to signal the caller that they'd arrived.

Think!

Annie sank into a chair, hands pressed to her throbbing temples. In order to see a visual signal, say, a flickering light, the caller would have to be close by. The kidnappers—and Clara—could be mere minutes away.

But then again, that idea could be wrong. The

person watching for the signal could have relayed a call to another location, anywhere in the city. And since Quint hadn't been allowed to speak with Clara, she may or may not have been with the caller.

Only one truth was evident. Clara's kidnapping had been planned in every detail and carried out by a ruthless team. The odds of finding her and getting her back…

But this wasn't a question of odds, Annie reminded herself. This was a little girl, alone and terrified. A little girl too precious to lose.

Outside, the fog had turned to a misting rain. Drops of moisture peppered the windows and streamed down the glass. Wind whistled under the eaves. Not even the crackling fire could lift the miasma of chill and gloom that hung over the flat.

Rising, Annie crossed the parlor and drifted toward the bank of windows that looked down on Jackson Street. She was on the verge of looking out when she remembered—the eyes that had seen their arrival could still be there, watching. She'd be foolish to show herself.

What would happen, she wondered, if she were to go downstairs to the street and confront the unseen watcher? Maybe she'd be kidnapped, too, and taken to where Clara was being held. That might not be the worst thing. She could comfort her little niece, protect her, and maybe even find a way to help her escape.

She was giving the idea serious thought when the harsh jangle of the telephone cut the silence like a scream. Annie's nerves crawled as the telephone rang again. Rushing to the desk, she counted the seconds. Quint had said he would ring twice, then hang up and ring again. Maybe he had some news.

The third ring followed the second without a break. This wouldn't be Quint on the other end of the line. It could be anybody—an innocent friend, the kidnappers calling back or even Rutledge himself.

The telephone rang again, then again. Her hand crept across the desk. Quint had told her not to answer. But what if something had gone wrong? What if someone had news about Clara?

She lifted the receiver to her ear. "Hello?"

There was no answer. Just the faint sound of static followed by an ominous click. Annie's hand trembled as she hung up the earpiece. Her skin felt clammy. She glanced toward the door to make sure the bolt was fastened. If only Quint would come home.

Forcing herself to move, she found a broom and started on the kitchen. Broken china and spilled canisters of flour, sugar and rice littered the floor, as if the invaders had enjoyed making a mess.

By now she'd changed her mind about letting herself be kidnapped. Having two hostages would give Rutledge even more bargaining power. His thugs could kill one of the captives just to show they meant business. Quint was right—they would keep Clara alive for as long as they thought she was useful. After that…

Annie's fingers whitened on the broom handle as a new thought struck her. Sooner or later Hannah and Judd would have to be told about Clara. The devastating shock could cause Hannah to lose her baby or worse. But how long could they be protected from the truth? The thought of having to tell them made Annie feel sick. Surely the news could wait a few days, until they knew the outcome. But that decision would have to be shared with Quint.

She finished sweeping the floor and, as an afterthought, measured some coffee and set it to brew on the stove. The pot was just beginning to bubble when she heard a rap on the door. She froze, then sagged with relief as she heard Quint's voice.

"It's me. Unfasten the bolt."

Running to the door, she flung it open. He stood in the doorway, his hat gone, his hair and clothes dripping rain. He looked as if he'd just trudged across a battlefield.

Her first impulse was to gather him into her arms, giving and taking what little comfort she could. Then she saw his face. Quint looked as if he'd aged ten years in the past two hours. His blazing, blood-shot eyes warned her to keep her distance.

She stepped back, giving him room to walk past

her into the parlor. Sinking into the leather armchair, he slumped forward. His forearms pressed his thighs as he stared into the flames.

Silence lay heavy between them. Annie turned back to check the coffee, then paused, resolving to speak. "Is Chao all right?"

"He will be. His wife made some poultices for his face."

"And his people will help us?"

He nodded wearily. "I left them Clara's photograph to pass around. But they won't be able to start looking till tomorrow. I could use some of that coffee."

In the kitchen, Annie found the last two unbroken china cups and filled them with steaming black coffee. Carrying them back to the parlor she placed one on a side table for Quint and took a seat in the opposite chair. Quint might not feel like talking, but Clara's life could depend on their working together. Whatever she had to do or say, he was not going to shut her out of this.

She took a careful sip of the scalding coffee. "Tell me what I can do to help," she said.

He scowled at her over the rim of his cup. "You can stay right here and stay out of the way. This is dangerous business. I don't want to waste time worrying about your safety."

Annie exhaled. This wasn't going to be easy. "Clara is my sister's child, my own niece. I was the one who brought her here. You can't expect me to just sit back and do nothing."

"You won't be doing nothing. I need someone here to pass on information in case there's any news."

"And meanwhile, what will you be doing?"

"Dealing with Rutledge. Talking to people who might know something. Maybe trying to locate the letter."

"While I sit here and wring my hands? I'll go out of my mind."

"That's your problem. I don't need the distraction of worrying about you, along with Clara and everything else."

"I see." Annie gazed down into her cup for a moment, then raised her eyes to lock with his. "Have you thought about what to say to Hannah and Judd?"

The cup tilted in his hand, spilling coffee on the rug. "Lord, no," he muttered. "Can't that wait? You know it would damn near kill Hannah."

"Why do you think I'm asking you?"

He exhaled raggedly, shoulders sagging. "I'd say we take our time. Judd would want to come, but he couldn't get here soon enough to be of any help. And with Hannah and the baby…" He trailed off, shaking his head.

"I agree with you," Annie said. "There's no need to tell them until we get Clara back—and we *will* get her back. I refuse to believe otherwise."

Quint didn't reply, but his haunted eyes told her

more than even she wanted to know. He understood who and what they were dealing with, and he was preparing himself for the worst.

The storm outside had settled into a gray drizzle, drumming a steady dirge against the windowpanes. From somewhere in the flat a clock ticked away the leaden seconds. Annie swallowed the urge to scream her denial into the room. This couldn't be happening. Not in real life. Not to them and not to their precious Clara. It was only a bad dream, a nightmare from which she was due to awaken any minute.

She cleared her throat, breaking the silence. "What do you think happened to the letter? Is there any chance we can still find it?"

"I've asked myself the same question. But the thugs who murdered Virginia Poole tore her place apart looking for it. My best guess is that she realized they were trailing her. Rather than be caught with the letter, she threw it away and headed home. I made it to the bookstore right on time and waited nearly an hour. She never showed up."

"Yes, that's what you told me." Annie knew the rest of the story, as well. He'd gone to Virginia's flat on Telegraph Hill and found the poor woman dying.

But what if she hadn't thrown the letter away? What if it was out there somewhere, just waiting to be found?

Quint spoke as if he'd read her thoughts. "Having the letter would at least give us something to bargain with. But we have to assume it's gone. All we can do is go with what we have."

"Which is nothing."

"You think I don't know that?" His eyes were burning coals in his colorless face. "I've racked my brain for some way out of this mess. I still don't know what I'll do if Chao's people haven't found Clara by tomorrow night. How much longer can I stall those bastards?"

His voice broke. He turned away to stare into the flames. Annie watched him, aching to rise and go to him, to wrap him in her arms and cradle his weary head between her breasts. Quint wouldn't want that, she knew. He would push her away, or worse, tolerate her touch while he quivered with resentment the whole time.

Arranging her features into a calm mask, she rose from her chair. "You'll be no good to anyone if you make yourself sick," she said. "You need to get into some dry clothes and get some rest. While you're changing I'll scramble you some eggs to go with the coffee."

He gave her a tired glance, then turned back toward the fire. "Don't fuss over me, Annie. I know you mean well, but right now I just want to be left alone. Get some rest yourself. I'll call you if I hear anything."

He retreated behind a wall of stubborn silence. Annie waited a moment, then turned away, biting back tears of helpless rage. Quint needed her. And she needed him. But if he hadn't chosen to spend time alone with her tonight, Clara would never have been taken.

For that, Annie knew, Quint would not forgive her—or himself.

Chapter Eight

It was early dawn when Quint opened his eyes. Gritty and disoriented, he blinked himself awake. The parlor was chilly, the fire burnt down to coals. Outside, the rain had stopped. Ashen streaks paled the misted skyline.

He'd been dreaming, he realized. He'd been back at the ranch, teaching Clara to ride her new pony—bright red, like the one on the carousel. Leaning on the fence, he'd watched her walk the pony around the corral. Suddenly the animal had begun to run—around and around, faster and faster until it was nothing but a spinning blur. Alarmed, Quint had leaped into the corral, seized the bridle and halted the horse—only to find the saddle empty. Clara was gone.

Stirring in the chair, he discovered that he'd been covered with a patchwork quilt from his bed. Beneath it, his clothes were still damp from last night's storm. His body felt as stiff and sore as an old man's.

Slowly he sat up, bracing against the coming slam of reality. When it hit, the anguish was physical, nearly doubling him over. He wasn't just awakening from a bad dream. Clara was gone, and it was his fault.

Pushing to his feet, he gazed around the shambles of the flat. Annie had done her best to clean up the mess, but the place was a lost cause. And what did it matter, anyway? Without his daughter, what did anything matter?

He stumbled into the bathroom where he emptied his bladder, brushed his teeth and managed to shave without cutting his miserable throat. The reflection staring at him from the mirror was a madman's—red-eyed, gaunt and desperate. He'd been through some rough patches before. But compared to this, the worst of them had been no more than a church picnic.

On his way to change clothes, he passed the open door of the guest room. Annie lay asleep across the foot of the bed, fully clothed, as if she'd tumbled there from sheer exhaustion.

He stepped into the room and stood looking down at her. Her collar was open, her hair falling loose over the rumpled counterpane. The light that filtered through the thin curtains softened her face and deepened the tired shadows beneath her eyes.

Something in him yearned to stretch out beside her and gather her into his arms. They wouldn't have to make love. Just holding her, feeling her womanly warmth against his body, would kindle the courage he needed to face the day.

He remembered last night, telling her to leave him alone. Lord knows, Annie hadn't deserved the way he'd snarled at her. But he'd been too steeped in self-loathing to accept even a small kindness from her hands. Now he realized she'd managed it anyway, bringing the quilt and tucking it around him as he slept.

Annie had told him she loved him. Quint was just beginning to understand what a precious gift that love was. But if they lost Clara, they would also lose each other. Annie would never be able to look at him without remembering what he'd allowed to happen. Her very tenderness would punish him; and even if she forgave him in time, Quint knew he would never forgive himself. Clara's small ghost, so tragically wronged, would stand between them forever.

Forcing the thought aside, Quint went into his own room, stripped down and pawed for clean clothes among the chaos the kidnappers had left behind. Fifteen minutes later he was dressed for the day. He would visit Chao on the way to the paper. Later, on the pretext of an interview, he planned to pay a call on Josiah Rutledge at City Hall and learn whatever he could. Hopefully he could summon enough self-control to keep from killing the bastard with his bare hands.

He would do his best to act calmly and rationally. But every minute of the day a voice inside him would be screaming like a savage—screaming for his child and for the blood of the monsters who'd taken her. If he didn't get Clara safely back, he would hear that voice for the rest of his life.

Right now he needed to get out of the flat. Annie was exhausted and needed rest. He would write her a note and leave without disturbing her. They could communicate by telephone later in the day. He could only hope she'd heed his order to stay put.

Finding a notepad and a pencil, he scribbled a hasty message.

Bolt the door. Stay inside. Will telephone later. Same signal as before. Q.

He would leave the pad on the bed where Annie would see it first thing when she awakened. The door could be locked from the outside, but she would need to slide the sturdy bolt in place herself. He didn't want her to wait too long.

With the pad in one hand he walked back into the guest room. Annie had moved in her sleep. She lay on her back now with one arm flung above her head. Her blouse had come partway unbuttoned, exposing the satiny curve of one breast. Quint's breath caught as he remembered touching her in the carriage, her softness, her little gasp of wonder as his fingers brushed her sweet, forbidden flesh.

How could any woman be so innocent, and yet so wise?

For a moment he battled the urge to touch her again, to lie down beside her, part her legs and bury himself in her tight, wet heat—to thrust hard and deep, forgetting, for a flicker of time, the worry that was eating them both alive.

It was a fleeting impulse. But as he brushed it aside, Quint realized he'd become aroused. He was as hard as a hickory log. He cursed under his breath. Not good timing, either for him or for her. Ignoring the tightness in his crotch, he placed the note near Annie on the quilt. He stopped himself just short of reaching out to stroke her cheek. If he woke her, the temptation might be too much for him.

In the parlor he strapped on the pistol and shrugged into his jacket. Letting himself out the door and locking it behind him, he exited by way of the back stairs, as he and Chao had done last night. Rutledge's hired goons could still be watching the building. Annie would be safer if they didn't know he'd left her there alone.

Quint cut through the alley and emerged farther down Jackson Street. The morning was bleak and chilly, the city blanketed in mist. Behind him, to the northwest, the mansions on Nob Hill rose above the fog like castles in a mythical kingdom. Owned by men who'd made vast fortunes in speculation, trade, real estate, banking and railroad building, they rivaled each other in grandeur and ostentation. On the brow of the hill the newly finished Fairmont Hotel glittered in the dawn.

Josiah Rutledge owned a stately Georgian home below the hill. The house would be fine enough to satisfy most men, but Rutledge clearly had higher ambitions. Judging from what he'd seen at the opera, Quint would bet six months' pay that those ambitions were fixed on Delilah Stanhope's bed.

Marriage to the widow Stanhope would make Rutledge one of the richest men in San Francisco. But Delilah was a woman of spotless reputation, known for her charity work among the poor. One whiff of scandal, and Rutledge would be out the door without a fare-thee-well.

And that explained a lot, Quint mused. The money involved in the water system scheme, though substantial, was hardly the kind of fortune to make a man commit murder—or kidnap a child. Delilah Stanhope, however, was a different matter. Rutledge must be salivating to marry her. But a piece of solid evidence, like the letter, could blow his plans out of the water. Even if he didn't go to prison or lose his office, the comely widow would want nothing more to do with him.

Useful information all of it, and very likely true. But how to use it without endangering Clara—that question gnawed at Quint's gut. Telling Delilah Stanhope what he knew might stop her from marrying Rutledge. But Clara would never make it home alive.

For Quint, crossing Mason Street to enter Chinatown was like stepping into a foreign world. Brick walls rose above the narrow streets, concealing a maze of warrens where fifteen thousand Chinese, forbidden to live elsewhere, crowded into a twelve-block ghetto.

Even at this early hour there was plenty of activity. On the sidewalks, women crouched over tiny charcoal braziers, cooking strips of seasoned meat, sliced vegetables and pots of rice in the fresh air. Vendors hawked pickled cabbage and black-striped eggs, cured by burial in the earth. Featherless duck carcasses, their heads intact, dangled in the meat stalls. Joss sticks, thrust into pots of sand, smoldered outside a temple door, perfuming the air with smoky fragrance. Steam rose from a small courtyard where laundry was being boiled. A crimson wedding banner fluttered from a high window.

As one who paid attention to their problems and treated them fairly in his column, Quint was known and tolerated in the tightly knit community. He could walk the streets without fear of getting a piece of brick or a rotten plum pelted at his back. A few of the men even greeted him in passing. But he knew better than to think he was accepted here. If these people agreed to help look for Clara, it would only be out of regard for Chao, a respected elder in this small domain.

Chao, his wife, their two sons and three daughters lived in two rooms above a tailor's shop. Cramped as it was, the apartment was luxurious by Chinatown standards where every inch of living space was precious.

Dodging a gang of pigtailed children, Quint found his way up the narrow stairs. Chao's middle daughter, a pretty child of twelve, answered his knock and let him in.

The tiny apartment was cool, dimly lit and scrupulously clean. Sleeping mats were rolled and placed against the wall to serve as couches. Dishes sat on an open rack in one corner. The walls were decorated with scrolls of Chinese calligraphy.

A well-used table took up much of the space. Chao sat at one end, sipping tea from a porcelain cup as delicate as an eggshell. His head was bound with a cloth. Blue-black bruises ringed his eyes, and his mouth was badly swollen, but otherwise he appeared bright and alert. His wife, a plain, shy woman who spoke no English, stood in the shadows of the kitchen, crushing something in a wooden bowl.

"Can we offer you tea?" Chao forced each syllable out of his swollen mouth.

Quint shook his head as he took a seat. "Thank you, no. How are you feeling, old friend?"

Lips stretched in a grotesque smile. "Not so bad. I will mend, but maybe not so handsome as before. Do you have news?"

"Nothing. Not since last night. What about your people? Will they help us look?"

"They are looking now." Chao's eyes narrowed. "Forgive me. I told them Little Miss was your daughter."

Quint's breath caught, triggering a jab of pain in his chest. "How did you know that? Did Annie tell you?"

"She told me nothing. I guessed. Anybody with eyes would guess the same."

Including Rutledge, Quint thought, chilling beneath his jacket.

"I can come to work if you need me," Chao offered.

"Heavens, no. Stay here and let your wife take care of you. If you get any news, Annie will be in my flat. You can send word there."

Chao nodded his understanding. "My wife will light joss sticks in the warrior temple for your child."

"Please thank her for me." Quint rose to go. He'd done all he could here. "Later today I plan to call on Rutledge at City Hall. On my way home I'll stop by and see you again."

"Be careful." Chao's warning followed Quint like a benediction as he left his friend and descended the stairs. If prayers and hope could save

Clara she would soon be in his arms. But Quint had never set much store by miracles. The danger was real and terrible; and just one thing was certain. To rescue his little girl, he would sacrifice anything, even his life.

Annie wasn't surprised to find Quint gone when she awoke. She understood his need to be out searching for Clara. But his hastily scribbled note left her seething. How could he go without telling her his plans? And how could he expect her to sit on her hands all day when there was so much to be done?

For the first couple of hours she burned up her nervous energy cleaning and rearranging the kitchen cupboards, making Quint's bed and replacing his clothes in drawers and wardrobes, sweeping the carpets, sorting and refiling the papers that had been dumped out of the desk. While she worked, her brain churned out a maelstrom of thoughts and emotions.

What could she do to help save Clara? She barely knew her way around the city, let alone the places where a child might be hidden. She had no weapon, and she knew better than to let herself be taken prisoner. Quint had forbidden her to leave the flat. She knew it was important to be here in case he telephoned, but she felt so frantic. She felt so useless.

Quint hadn't thought to give her a key. But she'd found a spare while she was putting things back in the desk. At least, if she did go out, she'd be able to lock the door behind her. But why leave, especially when Quint had insisted she stay? What could she hope to accomplish?

She worked her way through the parlor, the bathroom and the hall. Only the guest room remained. Steeling herself for the ordeal, Annie began the task of gathering up Clara's scattered clothes and repacking them. Her heart crumbled as she folded the frilly little nightgowns, the stockings and underthings, Clara's white pinafore, her blue sailor dress and straw hat, her beloved Peter Rabbit book.

On the rug Annie found the pink seashell. As she laid it in the suitcase her self-control shattered. Pressing her hands to her face, she doubled over as if she'd been slammed in the belly. Violent sobs racked her body. Such a sweet, happy, innocent little girl, so precious and so loved. How could this have happened?

At last, drained of tears, she put away her own clothes, made the bed and rinsed off her face. Walking back into the parlor, she sank onto a chair and sat staring at the wall behind the desk, where Quint had thumbtacked his large street map of San Francisco. There had to be something she could do to help.

Virginia Poole had wanted to help, she reminded herself. The good woman's desire to do the right thing had gotten her murdered and triggered the events that led to Clara's kidnapping. If she hadn't found that accursed letter, everything would have turned out differently.

Rising, Annie walked closer to the map. Virginia had worked at City Hall, a fair distance from her flat on Telegraph Hill. Annie could imagine her leaving after work with the letter tucked into her reticule, or maybe concealed in her jacket. Would she have understood the danger? Perhaps not entirely, but surely she would have been nervous. She probably would've glanced over her shoulder as she boarded the Market Street trolley that would take her uptown.

The transfer at Market and Kearny would have carried her north toward home, passing Portsmouth Square on the way. The bookstore where she'd arranged to meet Quint was just off the square. Had Rutledge's men been on the trolley with her? Were they already on her trail?

Quint claimed he'd arrived at the bookstore precisely on time and waited an hour without seeing her.

But Virginia would have been at the mercy of the trolley schedules. What if she'd arrived ahead of him?

Concentrating, Annie tried to put herself in Virginia's shoes. She imagined walking into the bookstore, with its crowded shelves of used volumes. The layout of the shelves must have afforded some concealment. If the entire store had been open to view, she wouldn't have chosen it as a meeting place.

Glancing at the clock, Virginia would have realized she was early. With no sign of Quint, she would have found a secluded spot to wait for him.

So far the story made sense. But why hadn't

Virginia been there when Quint arrived? And what had she done with the letter? Surely she wouldn't just throw it away.

Think!

Sinking onto the chair, Annie closed her eyes and imagined herself as Virginia. She was in the bookstore waiting for Quint to arrive. But something was wrong. Something was making her nervous.

Had she recognized Rutledge's men, perhaps through the window? Had she realized they were following her, or had it been some vague sixth sense that made her uneasy?

Whatever it was, she'd been frightened enough to leave without waiting for Quint. And it stood to reason that she would not have wanted to be caught with the letter.

Annie's pulse slammed as the last piece of the puzzle slid home. Her conclusion made perfect sense. She had nothing to go on but logic and gut instincts. But those instincts told her she was right.

She could guess what had happened to the letter. And she knew where to look for it.

Quint had made the routine interview appointment through Rutledge's secretary. Now, as he mounted the steps of City Hall, he wondered if it had been a bad idea. With his nerves frayed raw and his wits dulled by exhaustion, it would be all he could do to keep from grabbing the oily bastard by the throat and choking him till his eyes bulged out of his head.

In his career as a journalist, Quint had interviewed Rutledge six or seven times, and he knew the man's style. Smooth as a greased rattlesnake, all half-truths and evasions. Today, he sensed, would be no different. Rutledge would admit to nothing. But he would be on watch for signs that Quint was cracking under the strain. Those reptilian eyes would miss nothing.

As he approached the reception desk, Quint almost lost heart. What if he said the wrong thing and gave too much away? Maybe it would be safer not to risk it.

But no, he had to take a chance. Rutledge was human, too. He could easily slip or lose his temper and reveal some vital bit of information. If there was anything to be learned, anything that might make a difference, he couldn't walk away.

The young man at the reception desk recognized Quint and greeted him with a smile. "Supervisor Rutledge is expecting you, Mr. Seavers," he said. "You know the way. Right down that hall."

Walking down the corridor, Quint passed the large room where the typing and filing clerks worked. Their desks were lined up in two long rows, all of them occupied save one. The empty desk had the look of having been cleaned out and wiped down, leaving no trace of the person who'd worked there. It was as if Virginia Poole had never existed.

Quint's jaw tightened as he moved on down the hall. He needed to do this for Virginia, as well as for Clara, he reminded himself. Whatever happened, whatever sacrifice it took, he would crush Josiah Rutledge and bring him to justice.

The door to Rutledge's sumptuous office was open. Rutledge was seated behind a vast marble-topped desk in a tufted leather chair that probably cost more than some San Franciscans made in a year. If he had any paperwork pending, it had been cleared away before Quint's arrival.

"Mr. Seavers." Rutledge rose and extended his hand across the desk. Quint was loath to return the gesture, but showing his true feelings would gain him nothing. He shook Rutledge's cool hand, recoiling inside as if he'd just touched a cobra.

He motioned Quint to take a seat in the straight wooden chair opposite the desk. "I must say I was surprised when you requested an interview. But of course, I'm always happy to oblige the press. Would you like a cigar?" The box he extended to Quint was gold plated and engraved with his initials. The cigars inside were likely Havanas, the finest to be had.

"Thank you, no." Quint fished a notebook out of his pocket, pencil poised to begin the farce that would masquerade as an interview. Rutledge steepled his fingers and leaned back in his chair.

"Didn't you enjoy the opera last night, Mr. Seavers? I noticed that you and the lady left early."

Of course you noticed, you slimy sonofabitch. You were keeping an eye on us while your hired goons kidnapped my daughter!

"Miss Gustavson wasn't feeling well," Quint said in a civil tone. "And if you read the reviews this morning, you'll likely agree that the show wasn't up to expectations, especially for the Met. But that's not why I'm here."

"So I gathered when I noticed you'd made an appointment this morning." He glanced at his gold pocket watch, then placed it on the desk where the hard surface would amplify the ticking. "I can give you fifteen minutes. So ask your questions."

A bead of sweat trickled between Quint's shoulder blades. "You've no doubt read my column in yesterday's *Chronicle*. In the interest of good journalism, I'd be interested in publishing your response."

Rutledge's thick black brows shifted inward in a brief scowl. "Actually I didn't take the trouble to read it. But if it's more of the same drivel, I've only one thing to say. Without evidence to support your insinuations, Mr. Seavers, I'd advise you to go bark up some other tree. You won't find a cat in this one."

It was the kind of answer Quint had expected, and he was ready with a counter. "But as Supervisor over the Department of Public Works, you can't deny that the water system is in deplorable condition."

Rutledge shrugged. "The repairs are being made. But with so much to be done, the work's going to take time. Weeks, even months, I'd say. Meanwhile it's all too easy for busybodies like you and Chief Sullivan to go poking into the wrong places and jumping to conclusions. The money's been appropriated, and the needs have been prioritized. Everything will be done to specification. When that happens, you'll be exposed as the muckraking opportunist you are."

Quint forced his lips into a smile. "Believe me, I've been called worse. But what about the contractor, Seamus O'Toole? Is there any reason to believe he might be misappropriating the funds?"

A twitch of one black eyebrow told Quint he'd struck a nerve. According to Virginia, the missing letter had been meant for O'Toole and would nail both men to the wall if it were published.

"Have you spoken with O'Toole?" Rutledge asked.

"Not yet. I suppose I will, but I like to start at the top."

"In that case, I'll save you some time. I can vouch for O'Toole myself. He's an honorable man who does excellent work. I'd trust him with my life."

"For now I'll take your word for it." Quint had already rejected the idea of talking to O'Toole. In all likelihood, the contractor was just trying to earn a living. But in trafficking with Rutledge, he'd sold his soul to the devil. To come clean now would imperil his life and the lives of his family.

Rutledge's gold watch ticked away the seconds.

Quint jotted down a few notes, cursing in silence. Time was running out and, so far, he'd gotten nowhere.

"So you're telling me everything's being done according to plan."

"That's exactly what I'm saying. And that's exactly what I'm expecting your paper to print."

"Fine." Quint glanced toward the hallway, in the direction of the large staff room. "A question for my benefit, if you don't mind. One of your clerks, a Miss Poole, doesn't appear to be working here anymore. The desk where she used to sit is empty. Do you know how I might get in touch with her?"

Again, that slight twitch of the eyebrow. "Miss Poole, you say? Yes, she left rather abruptly. Something about her mother being sick back east. I'm sorry, but that's all I know." Rutledge scowled. "Why would you want to get in touch with her?"

"Nothing important. She'd asked me about becoming a writer. I lent her a book." Quint was skating a thin edge now. Rutledge would know he was lying, and that the lie veiled a threat. Rutledge's men had almost certainly seen him enter and leave Virginia's flat. Now the murder lay between them, a secret that neither man could admit to knowing.

They were playing a deadly game of bluff. But it was Rutledge who held the high cards. He had proven himself capable of killing. And he had Clara. Quint had nothing to play against him except what he knew.

He had pushed the game as far as he dared.

"I see." Rutledge picked up his watch, glanced at the time and closed the engraved cover with a snap. "It appears our time is up, Mr. Seavers. Give my best to the lovely Miss Gustavson—and also to your little niece. I found her delightful when we met at the restaurant, even though she didn't seem to like me much."

A murderous rage flamed through Quint's body. He shot to his feet, looming above the desk. "I'm warning you, Rutledge," he rasped. "If anything happens to Clara I'll be back, and I'll tear you apart with my bare hands."

Rutledge's only response was a cold-eyed stare. "You must be confused," he said. "I haven't the faintest idea what you're talking about."

Quint walked the eight blocks back to the *Chronicle* Building, seething all the way. He'd wanted to face Rutledge, to let the bastard know he'd be held accountable for his actions. But his frayed nerves and hair-trigger temper had betrayed him. Rutledge had been as nerveless as a reptile, prodding him where it would hurt the most, waiting to see him break.

Sooner or later, Quint knew, Rutledge would arrange to have him murdered. Even without proof, he knew too much. Only Rutledge's belief that he had the letter had kept him alive this long. Once that story unraveled, Clara would be killed, and he'd be fighting for his life. Even Annie would have to be silenced.

He thought of Annie now, alone in the flat, helpless behind the barred door. She was the expendable one, he realized. Rutledge could do away with her anytime, as long as he had Clara. That made her especially vulnerable.

The memory of last night's carriage ride swept over him—Annie in his arms, so sweet and eager, her lips petal-soft, her tongue playing breathless games with his; her heart pounding against his hand as he cradled her breast, her little cry as his fingers brushed between her thighs…

Little Annie. She had always been there, quiet and kind, watching with fathomless eyes as he courted her sister. How could he not have seen her? How could he not have known that she loved him… and that one day he would love her?

Now it could be too late for them.

As Quint neared the *Chronicle* Building, the need to hear Annie's voice and know that she was safe set off alarms in his head. He'd left her that morning with nothing more than a scribbled note— a note that explained nothing. He should have taken the time to wake her and apologize for the way he'd brushed her off last night. And he should have made sure she understood why he wanted her to stay in the flat. Maybe he should have left her the gun, as well. As things stood now, Annie was in more danger than he was.

Cursing under his breath, he shoved his way through the revolving door and, rather than wait for the grindingly slow elevator, sprinted up three flights of stairs and down the corridor to the newsroom. A half dozen urgent strides took him past the empty reception counter to his own cluttered desk.

Out of breath, he seized the telephone, lifted the receiver and gave the operator his home number. An eternity seemed to pass before he heard the first ring.

Heart pounding, he waited for the sound of Annie's voice. The phone rang again, then again and again.

There was no answer.

Chapter Nine

∽∾∾∾∽

Portsmouth Square was no place for a lady. That became clear to Annie as soon as the cab pulled away, leaving her alone on the curb. The patchy grass was littered with cigarette butts, old orange peels and beer bottles. Sailors and vagabonds lounged in the shade of the scraggly trees. Along the south border of the park stood the imposing Hall of Justice with its onion-domed tower. On the other three sides Annie could see nothing but cheap dance halls and bars where painted women leaned over the upstairs windowsills.

There wasn't a bookstore in sight.

Had she come to the wrong place?

Steeling her resolve, Annie marched across the square toward the Hall of Justice. The air was rank with the odors of tobacco and urine. Whistles and catcalls rang out as she passed. She kept her head high, her gaze straight ahead. Quint had said the bookstore was off Portsmouth Square. But how far off, and in which direction? It might be safer to ask someone in the courthouse.

She'd tried to contact Quint before leaving the flat, but he hadn't answered her telephone call, and the switchboard operator hadn't known where to reach him. With time running out, Annie had asked the operator to give him a message, then set off on her own. Never mind that the mission was dangerous. To help Clara she would walk into a den of hungry lions.

Following Quint's example, she'd slipped out the back door and cut through the alley. To make doubly sure she wasn't being followed, she'd circled the block before catching a cab on Washington Street. Annie had seen nothing to arouse her suspicion. But her nerves were on full alert. She was as tense as a mousetrap, hair-triggered and ready to spring at a touch.

After asking several people in the justice hall, Annie found a polite young clerk who knew about the bookstore. It was located on Kearny Street, half a block northeast of the square. "It's a run-down place, but you can find most any old book there if you hunt long enough," he told her. "Good luck, miss. And mind the sidewalks. Folks around here tend not to care where they spit."

Annie thanked the young man for his advice and chose a roundabout way to the bookstore, avoiding the open square. The trolley line, she discovered, would have taken her right past the store. She could have gotten off at the next corner and walked back. That's what Virginia Poole must have done. Poor Virginia, clutching the vital letter, so terrified and so brave. Annie could almost feel the woman's presence beside her, giving her courage, urging her on.

The bookstore, fronted in clapboard and bearing a faded sign that read P. Solomon, Used Books, appeared small from the street. But on stepping through the doorway, Annie discovered that it was narrow and deep, like a long railroad car going back into the middle of the block. The shelves looked as if they'd been set up haphazardly over the years and never rearranged into any kind of order. They formed a shadowed maze of nooks, crannies, passageways and dead ends, every one of them crammed with books. Finding the letter in this place would be like looking for the proverbial needle in a haystack.

Forcing herself to concentrate, Annie tried to imagine Virginia walking in through the door, glancing around for Quint and failing to find him. At some point she would have realized that she'd come early and would have to wait. Not wanting to be seen, she would have searched for a spot where she could stay hidden and still have a clear view of the front door. She might also have checked the rear door in case she needed to make a hasty exit.

Annie checked the rear door herself. It was securely locked, probably to prevent a book thief from slipping out the back way. Heavens, what an awful firetrap this place would make!

What would Virginia have done next? Annie did her best to retrace the woman's steps, trying out one hiding place after another. From the first two, it was impossible to see the front door. The next location would have left her open to the aisle, from where she could be trapped and cornered. The one after that could be seen by the old man at the cash register.

At the end of twenty minutes, she'd narrowed her search down to two hidden spots. She could only hope Virginia had been smart enough to choose one of them—and instinct told Annie that the secretary had been as intelligent as she was brave. When danger—real or perceived—had compelled her to leave, Virginia would have made a desperate decision.

She would have taken the letter out and slipped it into the perfect hiding place—between the pages of a book. No need to wait for Quint or be seen with him. She could hurry home to the safety of her tiny flat, then telephone him the next day and tell him where to go back and look.

It was a clever plan. But which book had she chosen? There were thousands and thousands of them here.

Think!

Virginia wouldn't have wanted to be seen hiding the letter. So the book would have been within easy reach. And since a folded paper would be visible between the pages, the book would likely have been large enough to accommodate a flat piece of writing stationery. That would eliminate most of the popular novels and texts that crowded the shelves. Their dimensions were too small. Still, there were scores, if not hundreds, of books that were the right size and shelved in the right places. There was nothing for Annie to do but look through them all.

She started on the top shelf, pulled down a book of architectural drawings and riffled through the pages. A thin cloud of dust rose to Annie's nostrils, making her sneeze. Heaven save her, these shelves probably hadn't been dusted in years!

Only then did it strike her that there might be an easier way to search. On the books that had been recently handled, the dust would be disturbed. If she could find fresh fingerprints or any other sign that a book had been moved…

Eagerly she began peering at the shelves. But the task was harder than she'd hoped. The top shelves were above her head, and it was hard to make out the dust in the dim light. By the end of the first hour, Annie had gone through all the books in one location without finding the letter. Discouraged, she shifted her search to the other spot, farther back in the store. Maybe she'd been wrong about the letter's hiding place. At the very least, she'd been overconfident. She'd had no idea this was going to be so difficult.

Once more she started with the top shelf and worked her way down, checking every book that was tall enough to hide a sheet of paper. By now her energy had begun to flag, and she'd lost track of the time. Quint was going to be furious with her, but she couldn't give up now. The letter had to be here somewhere.

Help me, Virginia, she pleaded to the unseen presence beside her. *Show me where to find it!*

Just then her toe stubbed against the raised end of a warped floor plank. Pain shot up her leg, throwing her off balance. She staggered, clutching at the shelf. Something teetered. For a horrific instant it seemed she was going to bring the rickety structure crashing down, books and all. She braced her weight against the shelf, reaching up to support the top.

Frozen into place, she felt the teetering stop. It was all right. *She* was all right. But her knees had turned to jelly. They folded beneath her as she sank to the floor. What if the shelf had fallen? The domino effect could have toppled half the shelves in the store. Annie gazed down at her shaking hands. She'd been so sure the letter would be here and that she could locate it. But all she'd accomplished so far was to avert a near disaster.

By now, Quint would be wondering where she was. She could also be missing important news. Maybe it was time to give up and go back to the flat.

She was pushing to her feet when she noticed a

tall, thin book on the bottom shelf. It was battered and cheaply made, its pages dog-eared, its thin brown cover frayed at the corners—the sort of book, few would pick up and no one would buy. Annie could just make out the title on the spine.

RAND MCNALLY ROAD ATLAS: USA, 1895

Lightning flashed in Annie's brain. Her pulse lurched as she eased the book from its place and noticed the freshly smeared dust on the cover. Her hands shook as opened the book to the first page.

Oh, Virginia, you clever, clever lady!

For easy reference, the state maps were presented in alphabetical order. Without bothering to thumb through the book, Annie turned to the last few pages. Texas…Utah…Vermont… Here it was— Virginia! And laid facedown over the map was a single sheet of ivory linen stationery.

Forgetting to breathe, Annie picked up the paper by a single corner. A stronger light would be needed to decipher the tangled script of the message. But even in the shadows, the printed letterhead stood out. It bore the seal of the City of San Francisco and the name of the office holder— Supervisor Josiah Rutledge.

The flat was locked when Quint arrived, but there was no answer to his knock. As he fumbled for his own key, dark imaginings boiled up in his mind— Annie at the mercy of Rutledge's thugs; Annie slashed and beaten, raped, maybe even murdered. Drawing and cocking his pistol, he unlocked the door and came crashing through.

The apartment was silent and in perfect order. The books had been reshelved, the files replaced in their drawers, the photographs cleared of shattered glass and hung back on the walls.

But there was no sign of Annie.

Cursing, he charged from room to room. The woman had clearly worn herself out cleaning. There wasn't so much as a dust speck in the entire flat. Nor was there a note or any other clue to what had happened.

The spare key was missing from the desk. That and the condition of the rooms would suggest she'd left on her own and used it to lock the door behind her.

Damn the woman! Hadn't she seen his note? She must have, since she'd made the bed and cleaned the guest room. So why had she left when he'd expressly told her to stay? Was the stubborn little chit trying to prove he couldn't give her orders?

Seething, he picked up the phone and gave the operator the number of the switchboard desk at the *Chronicle*. An unfamiliar woman's voice answered on the second ring.

"*Chronicle* newsroom."

"This is Quint Seavers. Did anybody leave a message for me earlier today?"

"I'm sorry, Mr. Seavers, but I wouldn't know.

Esther was on duty, and she went home sick an hour ago. This is Florence."

Quint sighed. "This is important, Florence. Can you look around the desk for any message Esther might have jotted down?"

"Let's see…" There was a pause and the sound of static. "Sorry, Mr. Seavers. I even checked the wastebasket, but I don't see a thing."

"Blast." Quint bit back a harsher expletive. "Thanks anyway, Florence. If you hear from a Miss Gustavson, tell her she's to go home and wait for me."

"I'll be happy to." Florence's voice was annoyingly cheerful. Quint hung up the phone and began to pace. What now? Should he stay here and wait for Annie to show up? How could he dash out and search when he didn't have the first idea where to look? Damn the woman! With Clara's life at stake, how could she behave so recklessly?

What he wouldn't say to her when he found her—if he found her…

Refusing to continue the thought, Quint holstered the gun, snatched up his keys and strode toward the door.

Annie stepped out of the bookstore and into the blinding sunlight. One arm clutched her reticule against her side. Beneath it, she sensed the faint crackle of the letter, which she'd slipped into the lining of her jacket. It was a volatile burden, as dangerous as a bomb with a smoldering fuse. A woman had been murdered for it, a little girl brutally stolen. Now it was up to Annie to get it to the right place.

As her eyes adjusted to the brightness, she gazed anxiously up and down Kearny Street. Buggies, autos, wagons and pedestrians bustled in both directions, but there wasn't a cab or trolley in sight.

She had no choice except to keep moving. Even a short wait could make her more visible, more of a target for anyone who might be trailing her. She'd been careful leaving the flat, but she knew better than to feel safe. Josiah Rutledge's men would have orders to watch her. If she hadn't lost them, they would certainly question her visit to a bookstore in such a seedy neighborhood—especially if they knew Virginia had stopped by the same store on the day of her death.

If they suspected she had the letter, her life could be measured in minutes.

Fighting panic, she began to walk faster. Her best chance was to blend in with the crowds. To break into a run or to be caught alone in the open would draw attention. So would climbing into a cab. A trolley car might be safest if she could catch one. If not, she would just keep walking in the direction of Quint's flat. She could only pray that Quint would be there when she arrived.

Turning the corner onto Jackson Street, she ducked into a doorway to catch her breath and get her bearings. Back beyond the way she'd come, the buildings of the downtown district towered against the sky. Through the haze she could make out the *Chronicle* Building with its huge clock tower. Inside the newspaper office she would be safe. She could ask for Quint, perhaps wait at his desk until he came for her.

But the *Chronicle* Building was a far distance off, and Annie's danger senses were screaming. She had learned to trust her instincts, and those instincts told her that if she tried to get to the *Chronicle,* she would never make it.

A block ahead of her lay the boundary of Chinatown. Annie had never been there, but there was no mistaking its dark brick walls, with the pagodalike roof of the temple rising above them. Chao lived in Chinatown. If she could find him, or someone who knew him—

Annie broke into a run. She plunged ahead, dodging pushcarts and jostling shoppers in her haste. Behind her, the sound of heavy footsteps pounded the pavement, echoing a rhythm that matched her own. Fear exploded through her body as she raced toward the sheltering walls.

Shadows closed around her as she passed under the gate. Here the streets were too narrow and crowded for anything wider than a hand cart. Shops spilled their goods out of doorways and onto sidewalks. Laundry dangled from webs of clothesline suspended overhead.

As her eyes adjusted to the dim light, she saw, on her left, what appeared to be a melon seller's stall. With her pursuer seconds behind her, she ducked behind it and crouched in the shadows.

From her hiding place she could see the man who was chasing her. He had paused inside the gate, blinking in the sudden darkness. Bull-necked and burly, he was dressed in a snug-fitting brown suit with a dingy shirt and mustard-stained tie. His ugly prizefighter's face was beaded with sweat.

Annie shrank lower as he began casting around like a bloodhound picking up scent. She stopped breathing as he turned in her direction. Her heart slammed so loudly that she almost expected him to hear it.

He had turned away and was checking in another direction when a middle-aged Chinese women, evidently the melon seller, came around the corner brandishing a bamboo pole. Shrieking like an enraged peahen, she charged. A swinging blow from the long stick caught Annie across the forehead, laying open a finger length of raw flesh. Annie clambered to her feet, shoving over the stall and its contents as she plunged out of range. Melons rolled into the street. Her startled pursuer stumbled backward. In the next minute the woman was upon him, whaling at his shoulders with her stick and screaming curses in Chinese.

Annie didn't wait to see the rest. Knowing the

man would soon be after her again, she wheeled and raced down a side alley.

The narrow passageway took her on a winding course deep into the heart of Chinatown. She passed open courtyards filled with steaming tubs of laundry. She glimpsed a pen of speckled ducks and an old woman plucking birds. She dodged a pair of schoolboys who flung something at her back.

Behind her, she fancied she could hear the thud of boots and the harsh rasp of breathing. By now she was getting tired, her own breath came in gasps. Her legs were getting wobbly and she had a painful stitch beneath her corset.

Maybe it was time to get rid of the letter—hide it someplace, tear it to pieces or thrust it into one of the little charcoal burning stoves she'd seen along the street. No matter what happened, she couldn't let herself be caught with it on her body. Too late, she realized that the letter would have been safer if she'd left it in the bookstore. If only she could have gotten word to Quint—

She veered sideways to avoid a pigtailed toddler, narrowly missing a rack of dried fish. Ahead of her the alleyway opened into a street. She could see lights and hear, faintly, the sound of drums and cymbals.

From somewhere behind her came a crash and the sound of shrill Chinese curses. Her pursuer, it seemed, was less careful than she'd been. But he was still on her trail, relentless as ever.

Bursting into the open, Annie saw a wedding procession bearing down on her. Red—the color of good luck and celebration—was everywhere. Marchers balancing tall scarlet banners led the parade, followed by the musicians and the sedan chairs bearing the bride and groom. Friends and family trailed behind, creating a flowing river of movement and color. Annie allowed herself to be swept along while she scanned for an escape route. Ahead, on the far side of the street, another narrow alley cut off to the left. Struggling through the crowd, she reached it and slipped into the shadows.

Panting in terror, she flattened herself against the damp bricks. She couldn't just keep running. She needed a place to hide and rest. As she crept along the dark wall she came to an ornately carved door. Light glimmered through a sliver-thin crack.

Annie gave the door a cautious push. It creaked open a few inches. A smoky smell drifted into her nostrils. Desperate for refuge, she ducked under the low frame and closed the door behind her.

Through a lamplit haze, a large, square room took shape, its low ceiling supported by carved wooden pillars. Built around the sides were wooden beds, not unlike the ones in the bunkhouse at the Seavers ranch. Men reclined on the cushions, sucking on short-stemmed black pipes and exhaling smoke into the air.

Two youths moved among the beds, refilling the pipes and adjusting the pillows to make their guests more comfortable. One of them glanced toward the door and saw Annie. His eyes widened. Hurrying to her side on padded feet, he muttered something urgent in Chinese, clasped her arm and guided her gently but firmly out the door.

As the fresh air cleared her head, Annie realized she'd stepped inside an opium den. But that was the least of her worries now. The sight of a blocky figure silhouetted against the street told her that she hadn't lost her pursuer. She plunged into the darkness, stumbled over a basket and fell against something solid. Her hands felt the hard surface of a high brick wall.

The cluttered alley was a dead end. She was trapped.

"No word about Clara?" Quint asked anxiously.

"Not yet." Chao shifted on the low couch, adjusting the poultice that covered his left eye. "There is time left in the day. Many people will come from work tonight. Maybe then."

"And what about Annie?" Quint knew it was useless to ask, but he was running out of places to look for her. He was beginning to fear the worst.

"I will ask." Chao's expression said what could not be put into words. There were many young women in San Francisco. To Chinese eyes they all looked much the same. Even if someone had seen Annie, they wouldn't be likely to remember her.

Would it be the same with Clara?

"You should go home," Chao said. "If there is news I will send word. In the morning I will come to work. No—" He waved away Quint's protest. "I am strong enough. You will need me."

Quint thanked his friend and left by the outside stairway. Chao was right. He needed to go home, where he could at least be reached. Maybe Annie would be there waiting for him. Maybe for a little while he could put aside this hellish situation and simply hold her, letting her sweet warmth seep through his body. He needed her in a way that he'd never needed anyone in his miserable life.

Damn the woman, where was she? What gave her the idea that she could run off like that, without a word? If anything had happened to her, so help him—

A commotion in the street below riveted his attention. He could see people rushing down a side alley that led into the next block. They were shouting and gesturing like children flocking toward a schoolyard brawl.

Quint hesitated at the bottom of the steps, then turned away with a shrug. Fights between Chinese were settled within the community. Even when blood was spilled, it didn't make news. In any case, he was in no mood to chase down a story. He would go home and hope to find Annie there. If the flat was empty, then he would endure the hell of waiting alone—waiting for Annie, waiting for news of

Clara, waiting for the callers to demand the letter he didn't have.

How far could he go before Rutledge called his bluff? Far enough to get Clara into sight? And then what? The thought of what could go wrong ate like lye into his gut.

As he turned onto Jackson Street the uproar dimmed behind him. He was headed for the boundary at Mason when he felt an urgent tug at his coat. Startled, he turned to see Chao's young daughter, the one who'd opened the door to him that morning. Flushed and out of breath, she spoke to him in urgent Chinese. Quint couldn't understand her, but no words were needed when he saw what was clutched in her hand.

It was Annie's black beaded reticule.

Sick with dread, Quint followed her. At first he expected the girl to lead him back to Chao's. But she darted down the side street toward the center of the melee. Quint raced after her. Wherever they were going, he could only pray that he wouldn't arrive too late.

Trapped in the alley, with no way out, Annie had clambered atop a high stack of wooden crates. She'd managed to pry loose a narrow board with a half-inch nail protruding from the end. It was the only weapon she had to fend off her attacker.

A lifetime of farm work and a heavy dose of terror lent her surprising strength. So far she'd managed to inflict some nasty wounds on the man's head and arms. His suit was torn and his dirty ginger hair was streaked with blood. But she knew it would only be a matter of time before he pulled the stacked crates down and her with them.

If he'd used a gun or thrown a knife, he could have killed her outright. But it dawned on Annie that he was supposed to take her alive. Not that it would make much difference. Once Rutledge got his hands on the letter both she and Clara would be as good as dead.

With every movement the letter rustled against her side. She should have destroyed it while she had the chance, or at least thrown her jacket away. Now she was in trouble and it was too late.

Fighting for her life, Annie was barely aware of the crowd that had gathered. After decades of harsh discrimination, few Chinese would interfere in a fight between Westerners. For most residents of Chinatown, the spectacle would be nothing more than entertainment.

As a hand seized her ankle, she hacked downward with her makeshift club. The blow cracked against the man's arm. He staggered backward, clutching his sleeve and fouling the air with curses. Recovering, he lunged at her again. The stacked crates shuddered and began to tip. Annie scrambled like a cat on a breaking limb, but it was no use. The entire pile began to topple, taking her with it.

She struggled to stay upright on the tumbling crates. But her boots lost their footing. The stick flew out of her flailing hands and vanished into the shadows. Annie found herself on the ground, exhausted and weaponless, with the enemy closing in.

Gulping back panic, she willed herself to be strong.

Chapter Ten

The man loomed above Annie. His tongue flicked a drop of spittle off his lower lip. "Now I gotcha, you hellcat. And now you're gonna pay!" Catching her wrist, he yanked her to her feet and twisted her arm behind her back. Annie clenched her teeth to keep from crying out. To show fear or pain would only egg him on.

Somehow she had to stay calm. Whatever happened, she couldn't let him find the letter.

"Come on, gal," he snarled. "You and me's gonna find someplace nice and private. The boss wants you alive, but he didn't tell me I couldn't have a little fun afore I brung you in."

"Let her go, McCarthy!" Quint's voice rang off the walls of the narrow alley. The crowd parted as he stepped forward, pistol in hand. Annie's legs went watery beneath her.

The man had drawn a knife, maybe the same knife that had killed Virginia Poole. Annie froze as she felt the razor-sharp blade against her throat. "The devil I will!" he snarled. "One step closer, Seavers, and I'll slit her gullet."

The pistol didn't waver. "Harm one hair on her head and I'll deliver you to Rutledge on a meat hook. You know I can do it. Now put that knife down and let her go. All I want from you is a few answers."

"You go to hell, Seavers. Now get out of my way. Me an' this pretty lady's takin' a walk."

Annie willed herself to think clearly. The man called McCarthy had threatened to kill her. But he must know that by the time the knife drew blood Quint would have a bullet in him. Even if he got away, he would have to answer to Rutledge for her death.

She couldn't let him take her away from here. She couldn't let him find the letter. She had to take a chance.

"Please," she whispered, closing her eyes. "I feel faint. I— Oh…"

Annie sagged, willing her body to go completely limp. She felt the blade's edge slide along her skin, felt the trickle of wetness as she fell. Then the roar of Quint's pistol filled the narrow space. McCarthy reeled backward. Twisting on the ground, Annie saw blood streaming from a shoulder wound.

She also saw something she hadn't noticed before—a ladder propped against a wall, leading to the flat roof of the building next door. McCarthy saw it, too. In the next instant he was clambering upward, pulling himself with his good arm.

"Are you all right?" Quint was beside her, pressing his handkerchief to the cut on her neck. It stung, but didn't feel deep.

"I'll be fine," she said. "Go!"

"Wait here. Don't move." He was gone in a flash, springing up the ladder to follow the blood trail. Quint was a crack shot, but he hadn't aimed to kill, Annie knew. He'd only wanted to bring the man down and make him talk. McCarthy could be his one best hope of finding Clara.

A young Chinese girl dropped something into Annie's lap and vanished into the crowd. Annie glanced down to discover her reticule, which she hadn't had time to miss. She called out her thanks but no one paid her any heed. All attention was fixed upward, toward the drama unfolding on the roof.

Still pressing the handkerchief to her neck, Annie staggered to her feet. She couldn't see what was happening, but she could hear running footsteps and Quint's shouting voice.

"Where is she, you butcher? Where's my little girl? Tell me, damn it, before I shoot your legs off!"

Annie heard the whine of a bullet and the sound of shattering glass, followed by more footsteps, running, stumbling. Time seemed to freeze as McCarthy appeared above the roof, his back to the edge, his eyes fixed on Quint.

Someone screamed—only later would Annie realize the voice had been her own. There was a shout from Quint. "No, you fool! No!" Then, arms flailing, McCarthy pitched slowly backward and toppled into space.

The roof was not high, and if he'd landed cleanly, he might have survived with broken bones. But what waited below was a vegetable stand covered by a canvas awning. The awning was supported by two sharp bamboo poles. One of them caught McCarthy's back and penetrated like a lance to emerge through his chest.

A gasp of horror swept like wind through the watching crowd. They backed away as the man hung there, impaled and dying.

Cursing, Quint sprang down the ladder and raced to his side. "Where's Clara?" He seized McCarthy's shoulders in a frenzied grip. "Where is she, damn you? Tell me!"

But it was already too late. The ugly head sagged to one side. The eyes glazed over. Quint released him, still swearing under his breath.

Numb with shock, Annie made her way toward him. He gripped her arm and turned her away from the sight. "Don't look," he muttered. "Let's get the hell out of here."

* * *

They caught a cab on Mason for the short ride home. Quint sat in rigid silence, gazing straight ahead. Annie huddled beside him, a quivering bundle of anguish. The letter was still there, tucked into the lining of her jacket. But how could she tell him about it now when he seemed determined not to speak to her?

She couldn't blame him for being angry. If she'd stayed in the flat, as he'd ordered, none of this debacle would have happened. She could have waited for his call and told him she knew where the letter was hidden. They could have gone to the bookstore together, or he could have gone alone. Instead, driven in part by the need to prove herself, she'd flung common sense aside. Now a man was dead—an evil man to be sure, but one who might have led them to Clara.

Quint paid the driver and ushered Annie upstairs to the flat. His silence was the silence of a powder keg waiting to explode. Once they were safely inside, the explosion was bound to come. She braced herself as he turned the key in the lock.

"Wait." He drew his pistol and stepped through the door ahead of her. Only when he'd checked all the rooms did he beckon her inside and close the door.

"Sit, Annie." He motioned toward one of the leather armchairs. While she settled herself, he slipped off his jacket, opened a cabinet and poured two shot glasses from a decanter of brandy. "Drink it," he ordered, thrusting one glass toward her.

Annie shook her head. She rarely drank spirits and was in no mood to do it now.

"Drink it. You're shaking. It'll calm your nerves."

She glanced down. Her fingers were quivering. Steadying the tiny glass with both hands, she emptied it in a single swallow. It burned down her throat like medicine. She closed her eyes.

"More?" He lifted the glass from her hands. She shook her head. She could feel the heat flowing through her body. The trembling had stopped.

"Are you all right?" he asked.

"Yes, I think so."

"Then tell me what in bloody hell you thought you were doing!" Quint's voice cracked like a whip. Fury glinted in his eyes as he loomed above her. "I told you to stay here! There were reasons for that! So why in blazes did you leave?"

Annie rose to stand toe to toe with him. Keeping her gaze locked with his, she reached into her jacket. Her fingers found the ripped seam in the lining and drew out the letter. "For this," she said, thrusting it into his face. "I left for this."

Quint's throat jerked as he saw what Annie was holding. He snatched the paper from her hand and stared at it in the fading light—the city letterhead, the familiar scrawl of Josiah Rutledge's hand.

Without taking time to decipher every word, he took in the gist of the letter. It instructed Seamus O'Toole, the contractor, to deposit the funds for the water system in a secret account at the Bank of Italy, from which Rutledge would withdraw a small share to pay him for the work. The account number was clearly written.

The letter was pure dynamite. If the money could be traced, the evidence would be enough to derail Rutledge's grandiose plans and probably land him in prison.

But would it be enough to free Clara?

Euphoria and terror warred in Quint's gut. He felt vaguely dizzy.

Annie was staring up at him, her cheek smudged, her forehead scraped, her hair hanging around her face in strings. She had nearly died for this letter. What would he have done if he'd lost her?

"How did you get this?" he managed to ask.

"I put myself in Virginia's place and tried to imagine what she would have done." The story spilled out of her, how she'd tried to telephone him, how she'd left a message, then set out for the bookstore and used reasoning to find the letter. Quint listened to her narrative without interruption until she came to the part where she realized she was being followed.

"You could've left the letter where you found it," he growled. "Why in heaven's name didn't you do that?"

Her eyes widened, but she held her ground. "Yes, I could have left it. I *should* have left it. That was my mistake. But it wouldn't have stopped that awful man from following me. It wouldn't have changed what happened."

Quint opened a desk drawer and laid the letter safely inside. "Nothing would've happened if you'd done what I told you and stayed here." Lord, didn't she know how worried he'd been? Didn't it matter to her, how close she'd come to dying? "Why didn't you wait for me?" he demanded. "We could've gone after the letter together."

"You needed it by tonight. I didn't know how soon I'd see you or how late the bookstore would be open." Tears glistened in her stormy eyes. "I wanted to help Clara. I thought you'd be relieved. I thought you'd be grateful."

She stood a handbreadth away, her words cutting into him like razors. The weight of the past twenty-four hours pressed down on him, threatening to shatter his heart. He'd battled his way through the day and ended up no closer to finding Clara than he'd started. At least Annie had accomplished something.

But he'd come within a hairbreadth of losing her.

Quint's frayed nerves strained and snapped. "Damn it, you little fool, you almost got yourself killed! What do I have to do to keep you safe, rope you like a heifer and hogtie you to the bed?"

She drew herself up. "You don't own me, Quint

Seavers. It's going to take both of us to get Clara back. If you won't work with me, then I'll work alone! Either way, I'm through letting you push me around!"

His irritation rose. "So what if you're out there playing Calamity Jane, and I have to choose between saving you and saving Clara?"

"You save Clara, of course! How can you even ask such a question?" She spun away from him and stalked toward the guest room.

With a lightning lunge he caught her wrist and whipped her against him. Cupping the back of her head with his free hand, he ground his lips against hers in a long, savage, bruising kiss. Caught off guard, she struggled. Then her arms went around him hard. Her hands clawed the back of his shirt, almost ripping through the fabric in their frenzy.

She whimpered as he kissed her cheeks, her eyes, and the thin red knife trail that crossed her throat. His hand jerked her blouse open at the collar. Buttons clattered to the floor as he buried his face between her breasts. His senses drank in her sweat-dampened softness and the salty taste of her skin. He wanted more, a lot more, and he knew she wanted it, too. This wasn't the time he would have chosen to make love to Annie, but he needed her. Lord, how he needed her. With the world falling apart around him, this strong, tender woman was all the anchor he had.

Her fingers tangled in his hair, pressing his face

deeper into her warm cleavage. She smelled like heaven—no, more like home, like Colorado air and spring wildflowers and fresh-cut hay, like everything he remembered and loved.

Dear, sensible little Annie who'd always been there. How could it have taken so long for him to see the wonderful woman she was?

His hands roamed down her back, molding her hips to his. She arched into him, her breath coming in little gasps as she pushed her belly against his arousal. Bracing his legs, he lifted her. Her skirt ruched above her knees as she wrapped him with her legs. He held her close, rocking her against him, feeling the sharp little jut of her pubic bone through layers of cloth. The pressure along his shaft ignited a bonfire, blazing heat through his body.

It was nowhere near enough. He wanted her skin to skin, her lovely body open to the most intimate touch. He wanted to feel her tight and wet around him, fitting him like a satin glove as he thrust hard and deep. He was ready for her now, his crotch strained to bursting.

"Annie…" His lips moved against her bare shoulder.

"Shhh." She stopped his mouth with a fingertip. "Don't spoil this with talk, Quint. Just know that whatever you were about to say, my answer is yes."

With a groan, he shifted her in his arms and carried her into his bedroom.

* * *

Annie's pulse thundered as he lowered her to the bed and stepped back to yank off his collar and tie. For as long as she'd known the facts of life, she'd wanted it to be Quint who made love to her. But now that it was about to happen, her head swam with fear of the unknown. What did she know about pleasing a man? What if he thought she was too thin or too small-breasted?

An image of Hannah's womanly curves flickered in her mind. Annie willed it away. She couldn't change the past and she couldn't change who she was. But if Quint needed her, even if it was just this once, she would give herself completely.

He leaned over her, his shirt unbuttoned to the waist, his eyes glazed with desire. Hands trembling, she reached for his brass belt buckle, unfastened the leather strip and let it drop. Next she tried the top trouser button. Her shaking fingers struggled to work it through the hole.

With a growl of impatience, Quint caught her hand and brushed it to his lips. "That can wait," he muttered, "but not for long."

Lowering himself to the bed he caught her in his arms again. His tongue invaded her mouth, skimming delicate surfaces, meeting her own tongue in a sensuous thrust and parry that ignited her senses like flame to tinder. As his hand cradled her breast through her blouse, the flame became a bonfire, burning away her fear until there was nothing left but need.

His expert fingers worked their way down the front of her blouse and unhooked the stiffened busk of her corset. Annie felt no shame as her clothes peeled away, only a yearning to be touched and caressed. She arched upward as his lips devoured her breasts, moaning softly as he sucked her nipples, laving them to tingling nubs. Waves of liquid heat shimmered down through her body. She felt the clenching between her thighs, hard and deep and hungry, demanding to be filled.

Wild with need, she fumbled to get her skirt, petticoat and drawers down her legs. It became easier when he helped her, nibbling a path along her bare belly, kissing her navel, skimming the nest of hair until she clutched his head and pulled him against her in a silent plea for more. He shifted between her legs, his tongue brushing along her cleft, then probing to find the tingling nub at its center. His touch was the devil's own magic. Annie had never imagined a man could do this to a woman or that anything could feel so exquisite. Her hands clawed his shoulders as the tremors took her, ripping through her body with an intensity that was almost unbearable.

"Wait." Rising, he stood over her, his shirt gone, his underwear and trousers shoved down around his hips. His hands fumbled with the last buttons, releasing his clothes to fall to the floor. The sight of him, in the fading light that slanted through the blinds, took her breath away.

Naked, Quint was all man, broad-shouldered, hard-muscled and magnificent. His chest was darkened by a mat of chestnut curls that left a narrowing trail down his flat belly to frame the gleaming column of his shaft. Looking at the size of him, Annie felt her stomach flutter. How…?

The question evaporated as he lowered himself to the bed and drew her close. The feel of his skin against hers, the roughness of hair, the hard bulk of him against her legs drove everything from her mind but wanting him. She returned his hungry kisses, rubbing her body against him until his breathing roughened.

"I want you, Annie," he rasped, "and I don't think I can wait."

His hand parted her thighs, fingers testing her wetness. Then, opening her legs wider he moved on top of her and pushed inside.

Annie felt his moisture-slicked tip penetrate her flesh, then the hard thrust of his shaft. There was a slight tearing sensation; then the pure wonder of Quint—Quint inside her, filling the most intimate part of her body.

Her mouth opened in a small, silent O as he began to move, pushing deeper, gliding out almost to the point of leaving her, then thrusting in hard, again and again, sending bursts of fire rocketing through her body. Her hands clutched his buttocks as he drove into her, fingers working his firm flesh. She cried out as the spasms shook her. Her legs tightened, pulling him deeper, to a shuddering release.

He groaned, exhaled, and it was over. Spent, he lay between her legs, looking down at her with clear brown eyes.

"You're beautiful, Annie." He brushed a kiss across her mouth. "Next time I won't be in such a hurry."

Wrapped in a warm haze of love, Annie caressed him with her eyes. Those words, she knew, were the best she was going to get. Quint didn't love her. But he'd needed her, and she'd been here for him. She would never be sorry for what had happened.

With a long sigh, he rolled off her and lay on his back, cradling her in the crook of his arm. Annie recalled an overheard conversation between Hannah and Rosita, her married housekeeper, about how quickly men returned to "business as usual" after lovemaking. At least she'd been forewarned about what to expect.

"What are we going to do now, Annie?" He stared up at the ceiling, and she knew his thoughts had returned to Clara. She lay quietly, letting him reason things out.

"We've got the letter," he continued, thinking aloud. "At least that puts us in a better bargaining position. But we can't just hand it over and expect

Rutledge to cooperate. I've seen the letter. You've seen it. We have the bank account number. And who knows what Clara's seen and heard or who she can identify."

"What are you saying?" Annie felt a sudden chill.

"I'm saying that Rutledge won't feel safe until all three of us are silenced." Quint swung his legs over the side of the bed, stood and began pulling on his clothes. "We need a way to get Clara back and get the two of you out of San Francisco. After that, Rutledge will be my problem."

Sitting up, Annie pulled the sheet around her quivering body. Everything Quint had said was true. The letter was no guarantee of anyone's safety. They had to come up with an alternate plan.

Her heart lurched as another thought struck her. "The man who telephoned you—he said he'd call back tonight. Could that have been McCarthy, the one who died?"

"The caller sounded Irish. But I'd have recognized McCarthy's voice. It wasn't him." Quint tucked his shirttail into his trousers. The bed sagged as he sat to pull on his stockings. "McCarthy was probably working with the other man. Sooner or later he'll be missed."

"What about his body?"

"The Chinese don't like police coming into their neighborhood. They'll wait for dark, then haul it beyond the boundary and dump it in some alley. I hated leaving them with that dirty job, but there wasn't much choice."

"So what do we do now?"

He focused his attention on a stubborn shoelace knot. "For now we do the hardest thing of all—we wait. We wait for news from Chao, wait for the bastards to telephone again, or whatever else is supposed to happen. And while we wait, we try to figure some way out of this mess." He glanced toward Annie where she sat huddled in the sheet. "You'll want to get dressed. If something happens later on, you'll need to be ready."

"Yes, of course." Annie's modesty had returned with his change in manner. Clutching the sheet around her, she rose, gathered up her things and headed for the guest room.

A few minutes later she emerged in a clean white waist and dark green skirt, her face splashed, her hair freshly combed and pinned. She found Quint seated at his desk staring at the telephone.

Outside, the twilight was deepening. Streetlamps, blurred by incoming fog, flickered to life like awakening fireflies. In the mansions that crowned Nob Hill and the stately homes along Van Ness Avenue, men and women would be dressing for the cultural event of the year—the appearance of the great Italian tenor, Enrico Caruso, singing the role of Don José in *Carmen*. Women would be lacing their bodies into wasp-waisted corsets, donning their most dazzling gowns, draping themselves in jewels and ermine. An hour from now, elegant carriages, bearing the cream of San Francisco society, would be parading along the streets toward the Grand Opera House.

Annie remembered last night's performance and the thrill of arriving on Quint's arm. How could the world change so much in twenty-four hours? How could anything as trivial as an evening at the opera have seemed so important to her?

Quint glanced up as she walked into the parlor. Annie ached to move to his side and smooth the rumpled curls back from his forehead. But she knew better. He had the look of a man who'd withdrawn into guilt, anger and worry. Even though they'd just made love, he would not welcome tenderness.

It would be like Quint to blame himself for Clara's disappearance. Every moment she was missing was bound to be torture for him. Even lovemaking had been little more than a respite, a release of the tension that, for him, had become unbearable.

"No news?" she asked needlessly.

"Nothing yet," he said.

"It's early. If you're hungry I can fix you something to eat."

He shook his head. "Don't bother. But some coffee might be good."

Grateful for something to do, Annie measured coffee and water into the percolator and set it over the flame on the gas stove. Although there was no milk, they did have sugar. She even managed to find a tin of rock-hard oatmeal cookies that the invaders had missed. Maybe dunked in hot coffee they'd be soft enough to eat.

She returned to the parlor a few minutes later with a tray. Quint was leaning back in his chair, studying the large map on the wall.

Annie laid the tray on the desk. "Where do you think they're keeping her?" she asked gently.

Quint picked up a coffee cup and took a careful sip. "Somewhere close. It wouldn't make sense to take her very far. A hotel room, maybe. Someplace where they could come and go without raising questions."

"What about Rutledge's house? Where is it from here?"

"Not far. Maybe six or seven blocks." He used a yardstick to point to the exact spot on the map. "But it's not like Rutledge to mess with this kind of dirty work. He likes to keep his distance. And he wouldn't want the scum he hires to be seen coming and going from his house."

"Then Clara could be almost anywhere. Maybe it's time we called the police. A kidnapped child— surely some of them would help."

"No. That would be too dangerous for Clara. If the kidnappers knew the police were getting close, they might decide to get rid of her."

The unspoken thought hung in the silence between

them. A terrified little girl wouldn't be easy to keep quiet. It was possible that Clara was already dead.

Annie spooned sugar into her coffee. It was, at best, a way to occupy her hands. "So do you have a plan?"

"Not a good one. I could play it straight, show up where they tell me to, with the letter, and hope to make a trade. But I know it wouldn't be that easy."

"What about the letter?" Annie asked. "You and I know it's real. But how would the kidnappers know they weren't getting a faked copy?"

Quint's finger drummed the desk top. "They wouldn't. Only Rutledge would know for sure."

"Then wouldn't Rutledge have to be close by, to see the letter for himself before he let Clara go?"

"Probably. But Josiah Rutledge is as treacherous as a shark. I wouldn't even venture to guess what he'd do." He glanced up at her. "You're going somewhere with this. What is it you're thinking?"

The idea fell together as Annie spoke. "Get me a gun, Quint—a rifle if there's one to be had. I can shoot. You know I can, you taught me yourself. If I can sneak around from behind and get a bead on Rutledge, get him to let Clara go—"

"No."

His answer stung. "Why not?" Annie demanded. "Having me there could make all the difference."

"And it could get us all killed. I taught you to plunk at tin cans and bring down rabbits with a twenty-two.

Aiming at a man, pulling the trigger if you have to, is different. So is being arrested for murder."

"I'd do it for Clara. You know I would."

Quint shook his head. "No, Annie. Even if you could, I wouldn't let you. I'm responsible for this mess, and I'll take care of it myself—alone."

Annie spun away from the desk and stalked across the parlor. "Of all the muleheaded—"

The telephone jangled, cutting off the rest of her words.

Chapter Eleven

Quint lurched to his feet and snatched the receiver off its cradle. The sound of breathing crackled through the earpiece.

"Hello?" He rasped out the word. Annie had turned and was staring at him with frightened eyes.

An eternity seemed to pass before he heard the answering voice.

"Seavers?"

"Yes."

"You've got the letter?"

"I've got it. But I'm not parting with it until you give me Clara."

There was a maddening pause, as if the speaker were checking with someone else in the room. "Ten o'clock tonight. Pier Number Four. Come alone if you know what's good for the little lady."

"I understand. I'll be there. Now let me talk to Clara."

There was an abrupt click. The line went dead.

Quint's hand shook as he hung up the receiver. "You heard that?" he asked Annie.

"Yes."

"Damn it, I don't even know if she's alive!" He glared at the telephone, fighting tears of helpless rage. "So help me, if those bastards have hurt her…"

His throat choked off the rest of the words. He hadn't wept since the day his father died. At the time, he'd been six years old, just Clara's age. He wasn't about to weep again, Quint vowed. Not as long as there was a shred of hope.

But Lord, she was so small and innocent, his Clara. What she must be going through. How terrified she must be.

Something warm pressed his back. Annie had come up behind him. Her arms slid around his waist, holding him with tender ferocity. Reaching down, Quint found her hand, raised it and buried his lips in her palm. Once, in a world that no longer existed, he'd prided himself on his independence. He'd believed he could stand alone, without needing anyone. What a proud, blind fool he'd been.

A shudder passed through Annie's body. Easing away, Quint turned and gathered her into his arms. They stood holding each other in the silent room. Their heartbeats measured the passing seconds, each one more precious than the last. Before the night ended, he could die, Quint thought. Clara could die. And, with no one to protect her from Rutledge, Annie might lose her life, too.

"Promise me you'll do what I tell you," he said. "Stay here and bar the door. Shove something heavy in front of it if you can. If I'm not back with Clara by first light, telephone for a cab, take it to the ferry and catch the train home."

She pulled away, her eyes reflecting shock. "How can I do that—just leave, not knowing?"

"Listen to me. If the worst happens, Rutledge is bound to send somebody after you. I want to know that you'll be safe."

"Don't even talk like that! I won't hear it!"

"Promise me, Annie!" He gripped her shoulders. "I'm not just thinking of you. I'm thinking of Hannah and Judd and who'll have to tell them. Promise me!"

Her head sagged against his chest. Quint could feel her trembling. "All right," she murmured. "But your chances would be better if you'd let me come with you."

"They said come alone."

"I know." Her arms tightened around him.

His hands massaged her back, feeling the bones of her light corset beneath his palm. "We have to believe it'll be all right, that they'll show up with Clara and give her back."

Annie didn't answer. Quint knew better than to think she believed him.

Glancing past her, he checked the mantel clock. "It's a little past seven-thirty," he said. "What do you say we put our feet up and try to get some rest? Maybe we'll hear some news from Chao in the next couple of hours."

"And if we do?" She gazed up at him. Hope flickered in the depths of her storm-colored eyes.

"That depends on the news. For now all we can do is make ourselves comfortable." He gave her shoulder a squeeze, forcing himself to sound cheerful. "It's chilly in here. Why don't you get a quilt while I light the fireplace?"

"You're sure you wouldn't like something to eat?"

"I wouldn't be able to get it down. How about you?"

"The same, I'm afraid." She turned away and vanished into the guest room.

Safely out of his sight, Annie pressed her hands to her face and allowed the world to come crashing in on her. Her shoulders slumped. Her body shook with dry sobs.

In the past twenty-four hours, life had become a waking nightmare. Clara was missing, possibly dead. Quint could end up dying, as well. And she was helpless to do anything about it. She imagined herself arriving in Dutchman's Creek, stepping off the train to deliver the terrible news. Hannah would be wild with shock and grief, even more so if she lost her baby. And Judd, whose gruff manner hid the tenderest of hearts, would be destroyed. The family would never be the same again.

That she'd just given her virginity to a man who didn't love her seemed a petty thing in light of all that was happening. She would ponder that later. For now she would keep uppermost what was really important—both she and Quint loved Clara. And nothing mattered more than getting her back.

Lowering her hands, Annie began pulling a patchwork quilt off the bed. No tears, she told herself. It wouldn't do to let Quint see her cry. For now she would be the soul of strength and common sense. She would bend, but not break. That was the best she could do for Quint and for the little girl who was the center of his universe—just as he was the center of her own.

Bundling the quilt in her arms, she walked back into the parlor. Quint had the fire going and had pulled the settee close to the heat. The crackling blaze was cheerful in the gloom.

Outside, the fog had crept over the city like a cottony blanket. Far through the mist, the light on Telegraph Hill blinked in and out of sight. Carriages moved like shrouded ghosts through the streets.

Quint had settled with his arm along the back of the settee. Reflected firelight glinted in his eyes.

"Come here," he said, patting the space next to him. "You look dead on your feet."

"I'd say we both do. We should take care not to fall asleep."

"I couldn't fall asleep if I tried. But it might be a good thing for you. Come on."

Annie sank onto the leather cushions and let him pull her against his shoulder. Between the two of them, they tugged the quilt over their legs.

"See, isn't this better?" He eased her back against his chest, circling her with his arm. His behavior toward her was tender, almost brotherly. Was this the same man who'd carried her to the bed, stripped off her clothes and made wild, desperate love to her?

She relaxed against him, both of them struggling to act as if nothing were wrong. If only the world could be as safe and warm as the circle of Quint's arms, Annie thought. If only she could stay like this, cloaked in his masculine aroma, his heartbeat strong and steady against her ear.

As the fire's heat diffused into the room, Annie's eyelids began to droop. She hadn't planned on sleeping, but she was exhausted, and her head fit so comfortably into the hollow of Quint's shoulder. Lulled by the cadence of his breathing, she began to drift. Her mind misted like the darkness outside the window, like the blanketed city. As the fog closed over her thoughts, she sank into slumber.

* * *

Quint brushed a kiss along Annie's hairline, lightly so as not to wake her. Under different conditions he wouldn't have minded carrying her back to bed, crawling in beside her and continuing from where they'd left off before. But right now what he needed was just to feel her in his arms—to hold her close and let her sweet, calm strength seep into him.

Under different circumstances he would look into her eyes and tell her he loved her. But that wouldn't be fair—not when he was setting off on such a dangerous errand. Better he leave her with the words unsaid. Then, if he didn't return, she could go home, marry someone else and have a happy life with no regrets to hold her back.

He could only hope she'd do better than prissy old Frank Robinson!

Her hair was like spun silk against his face. He inhaled, filling his senses with her fragrance. Lord, but she smelled good. He would gladly wake up to that smell, and to the sight of her beautiful face on the pillow beside him, every morning of his life.

But what was he thinking? He'd thrown away his right to happiness when he'd allowed Clara to be taken. In his hubris, he'd believed that Rutledge couldn't harm him. He'd pushed to the edge, tempting fate until it was too late. His precious little girl was gone.

His gaze wandered to the wall, where Annie had rehung his photographs. The portrait of Clara and her mother smiled down at him from the wall next to the fireplace—Hannah with her wheaten hair blowing loose in the spring wind, snuggling a two-year-old Clara in her shawl. He loved that photograph. He was no longer in love with Hannah—she belonged heart and soul to Judd. But Quint cared for her as a brother would, and they shared a special bond in Clara.

If he didn't get Clara back, Hannah would be shattered. He would rather be in his grave, Quint thought, than face the horror in those gentle blue eyes.

And what about Judd? He loved Clara, too. So did Annie.

He had been responsible for Clara's safety. In losing her, he had failed all the people who loved her.

Annie stirred, whimpered and settled back into sleep. In his arms, she looked as innocent and trusting as a child. Touched by her helplessness, he brushed his thumb down her cheek, tracing the edge of her lower lip. His whisper was little more than a breath.

"I love you, Annie. If I can get us all through this mess, I'm coming back and asking you to be my wife. So don't be in too big of a hurry to find somebody else…"

His throat tightened around the rest of his words. Gulping back a surge of emotion, he slipped free, eased her onto the pillows and covered her with the quilt. For a moment he stood looking down at her, eyes tracing the contours of her sleeping face. Then, forcing himself to move, he turned away and walked to the front window.

Was anybody watching? Looking down through the fog he could see the glow of a streetlamp and the outline of a passing freight wagon. By now it was after eight. In the Grand Opera House the curtain would be going up on *Carmen*. Would Josiah Rutledge be in the audience with the toothsome widow Stanhope on his arm? Or would he be out there somewhere, lurking like a spider, waiting for Quint to walk into his web?

Something wasn't right. Quint could feel it in his bones. But since there'd been no word from Chao, what choice did he have except to go ahead?

Moving to the desk, he sat down, took the letter out of the drawer and copied the text onto a notepad. Even if he had the skill to do it, reproducing the letter and trying to pass it off as original would be too dangerous. But at least he could keep a record of the content.

Folding the letter, Quint put it in a plain envelope, tucked the flap and slipped it inside his inner vest pocket. The letter had been dearly bought. Virginia Poole had paid for it with her life. Annie had nearly died for it, as well. But nothing was worth risking Clara. Nothing could be put ahead of getting her back—not even bringing down Josiah Rutledge.

He glanced at the clock once more. Eight-thirty. He had less than an hour to wait before setting out for the docks. It wouldn't hurt to go early. But he needed to wait here, in case of any last-minute word from Chao.

While he waited he would spend his time thinking about what lay ahead and how he could best protect Clara and himself.

Pier Four was off Folsom Street, toward the south end of the waterfront. Quint knew the dock area well. But he couldn't predict where the kidnappers would be. If they had Clara, the operative word would be caution. If not, all bets would be off. He would be fighting for his own life, doing whatever he could to survive.

The revolver lay on the desk. Opening a drawer, he found the box of bullets he kept there. He had fired two shots at McCarthy. Now he replaced them in the cylinder, giving it a spin to make sure it was fully loaded. That done, he clicked the cylinder back into place and slid the gun back into its holster. He didn't plan to kill anyone, but if he could catch one of the bastards alive and make him talk…

Quint's jaw clenched as he buckled on the shoulder harness over his vest. Hannah smiled at him from the photograph. Such a forgiving smile. He'd let her down once. He couldn't let her down again.

* * *

Annie stirred to a light touch on her cheek. Quint was leaning over her, wearing something dark. "Wake up, sleepyhead," he said softly. "It's time for me to go."

She shuddered to full awareness, eyes jerking wide-open. It was night, the parlor lit by the glow from the fireplace. Quint was wearing a navy blue pea coat. She recognized it as the one he'd worn seven years ago, when he'd returned to Dutchman's Creek after an eleven-month absence. Annie had been almost seventeen by then, and her heart had leapt at the sight of him. But he'd paid her no attention. He'd only had eyes for Hannah.

"How…long was I asleep?" She sat up, still disoriented.

"More than an hour. You looked like you needed the rest. There's hot coffee in the kitchen. I can bring you a fresh cup."

"No thanks, I'm all right. Any word from Chao?"

He shook his head. "If there'd been a message, I'd have awakened you. It's almost nine-fifteen. I don't dare wait any longer."

It hit her then, like a sudden blast of winter, that Quint was truly leaving, maybe never to walk through the door of the flat again. She stumbled to her feet. How could she have fallen asleep and lost the past hour with him?

Picking up a knitted sailor's cap, he pulled it

over his hair and ears. On the docks, he would look like a seaman returning to his ship after an evening ashore. And should he need to keep out of sight, the dark colors would help him blend with the shadows. The odds of his returning safe and whole with Clara in his arms were fearfully slim. But Annie had to keep hoping. Otherwise how could she let him go?

She was trembling, fighting tears as he started for the door. *Let him leave,* she told herself. *No good-byes, no emotion. It's better this way.*

Abruptly he paused, swung back and strode toward her. Annie willed herself not to shatter as he took her in his arms. "Remember what I told you," he said. "Block the door. If I'm not back by first light, leave for the ferry."

"You'll be back." She wrapped her arms around him, binding him against her for a few precious seconds. "I've got to believe you'll be back—with Clara."

He brushed a kiss across her forehead. "Then I'll make it so. Whatever it takes, I'll get her back, Hannah. I promise."

In the next instant he was gone, striding to the door and closing it behind him.

His footsteps died into silence down the back hall. Only then, as she was bolting the door, did Annie realize that Quint had called her by her sister's name.

* * *

In a burst of nervous energy, Annie made up the bed where she'd lain naked in Quint's arms. Never again, she told herself. Quint had probably been thinking of Hannah the whole time he was making love to her.

But she couldn't let that bother her now. The only thing that mattered was getting Clara back safely. If heaven would grant that miracle, she would take her niece home to Dutchman's Creek, accept Frank's proposal and try to forget everything she knew about Quint Seavers.

In the kitchen, she poured a full mug of coffee and gulped it down as fast as its heat would allow. It was stronger than she liked and bitter enough to pucker her mouth. But it shocked her drowsy brain into full alert. Now maybe she could think with a clear head.

Refilling the coffee mug, she returned to the parlor, sat down at Quint's desk and leaned back to study the large wall map. The docks extended like a long row of piano keys along the edge of the bay, all the way from the foot of Telegraph Hill to the southern limits of the city. Since they weren't labeled on the map, Annie had no way of knowing where Quint was headed. But the waterfront was a good distance from the Jackson Street flat. He would surely have taken a cab to get there.

She'd seen the waterfront by day, but she could only imagine it by night. There would be dark corners, mountains of cargo, looming ships, scurrying rats and shadowy people. And there would be no end of places where a weighted body could be dropped into the bay to disappear forever. Surely Quint, of all people, would be aware of those dangers. She had to believe he'd know what to do.

The very thought of the place, and what could happen there, made Annie's flesh crawl. She glanced at the clock. It was a quarter to ten. What would he find when he arrived? Dared she hope that the kidnappers would be there with Clara, ready to exchange her for the letter? Or would Quint be lured close and killed, as Virginia Poole had been? And what about Josiah Rutledge? Would he be there?

Annie pressed her hands to her face, her mind groping for answers that were just out of reach. If there was to be an exchange, Rutledge would want to be nearby to verify that the letter was real before giving up Clara. But if he'd given orders to murder Quint and take the letter, Rutledge would want to be somewhere else—most likely at the opera where plenty of people would see him. That would rule him out as a suspect in Quint's death—or more likely Quint's disappearance, since the body would never be found.

And there was another possibility. The thought of it sent a cold spasm through Annie's body. The kidnappers could use Clara as bait to lure Quint close, maybe even trick him into giving up the letter. Then they could kill them both.

Growing more frantic by the minute, Annie rummaged in the desk drawer for something she'd put away when she cleaned—a telephone directory for the city of San Francisco. Her hands riffled through the pages and down the columns to find one name—Josiah Rutledge.

Heart pounding, she picked up the telephone and gave the number to the operator. The connection clicked through. The telephone rang on the other end, once, twice.

"Mr. Rutledge's residence." The male voice was young with a touch of snobbishness. A butler or valet, Annie surmised.

"Is Mr. Josiah Rutledge there?" The urgency in her voice was real. "I must speak with him! Please, this is an emergency!"

"I'm sorry, but Mr. Rutledge isn't at home."

"Is there any way I could reach him?"

"I'm afraid that's not possible. He'll be at the opera until half-past eleven. After that he'll be attending a party for the cast."

"Can you tell me where?"

"I'm not at liberty to say. But if you'd care to leave a message…" His voice trailed off expectantly. Annie replied with the first thing that came into her head.

"Just tell him Virginia Poole called." She hung up

without waiting for his response. She'd learned what she wanted to know. Josiah Rutledge would not be at the dock. While his thugs dispatched Quint, the supervisor would be on public display, with the cream of San Francisco society to vouch for his innocence.

At this very moment Quint would be walking into a trap.

Quint took the cab as far as Front Street and elected to walk the rest of the way to the docks. He needed to clear his head. He also wanted to come onto the pier without drawing attention to himself.

Tendrils of mist swirled around him as he ambled along the boardwalk. This was a rough part of town, crowded with bars, brothels and cheap rooming houses that catered to seamen and dock workers. At this hour the street was dark, but the saloons were doing a brisk business. From behind rickety doors, kerosene lamps cast fingers of light onto the pavement. The muffled sounds of carousing mingled with tobacco smoke to drift on the cool night air. From somewhere down the street, a player piano belted out a tinny rendition of "Hot Time In the Old Town Tonight."

Quint maneuvered around a drunk who'd passed out on the sidewalk. From the nearby docks, he could hear the lap of low tide against the pilings. Foghorns moaned in the darkness, echoing across the bay. He'd covered stories here in his early reporting days. Stabbings, muggings and robberies were common in this part of town. That the kidnappers had chosen to meet him here wasn't a good sign. He would need to be on hair-trigger alert every second.

A rat scampered across his boot as he passed under the gate and stepped onto the pier. A single lantern hung from a post at the far end served as the only light. Otherwise the pier was a maze of sheds, cranes, barrels, boxes, nets and rope coils—everything cloaked in fog and darkness. It was the perfect place for an ambush.

Quint moved gingerly through the shadows, testing each step against any loose board that might creak and give him away. By now his eyes had adjusted to the darkness and he had no trouble finding his way. On his right was a tall shed with an open loft. The height might give him a bird's-eye view of the pier, or at least what he could see of it through the fog.

The shed was unlocked and empty except for a scattering of broken crates. In one corner, a ladder leaned against a hatchway to the loft. Alert to every sound, Quint climbed the ladder and stepped through the opening.

The view from the loft was even more promising than he'd hoped. Dropping to the floor, he belly-crawled to the edge; from there he could see much of the fog-shrouded pier. His eyes probed the shadows. Below him, nothing moved except a pale cat, tearing at the remains of a fish. Tilting his watch to the meager light, Quint checked the time. Ten o'clock straight up. If anything was going to happen, it would happen soon.

Nerves screaming, he checked the pistol in its holster. From here, if he saw the kidnappers coming, he could shoot them down on sight. But that, Quint knew, wasn't likely to happen. If they had Clara with them, he wouldn't want to risk hitting her. And if they didn't, it was essential that he take at least one of them alive.

As he inched forward for a better view, a movement caught his eye. Two husky men in hats and overcoats had appeared around the corner of a storage building. As they emerged through the fog, Quint could see that one of them had a large sea bag slung over his shoulder.

Something inside the bag was moving.

"Seavers!" The taller of the two men spoke. Quint recognized the voice he'd heard on the telephone. "We know you're here. Show yourself, and we'll talk."

"Nothing to talk about." Quint remained where he was, his pistol drawn and cocked. "You give me the girl, and I give you the letter. No one gets hurt, and everybody goes home happy."

"Sounds fine to me." The man had moved close to his partner, who carried the sea bag. The bag shielded them both from Quint's firing position. "Come on down from your perch. Let's do business."

"First I want to see Clara. Open that bag."

"Show us the letter, and we will. We gave her something to calm her down. She'll be sleepy, but otherwise she's fine."

Quint held his position. Cold sweat beaded his body. His hand was clammy around the butt of the pistol. Would he find Clara's lifeless body in the sea bag? But no, he told himself, he'd seen the bag move. It was moving now, something shifting beneath the dark blue canvas. He thought of Clara, helpless and trapped in the dark.

"All right, I'm coming down," he said.

Keeping low, he moved back to the hatch and climbed down the ladder. He'd seen no sign of Rutledge. It made sense that the bastard wouldn't show himself. Even so, something was off. Quint felt it all the way to his bones. But if Clara was in that bag, he would do whatever it took to get her back.

And if it wasn't Clara?

But he couldn't answer that question now. He couldn't take a chance on being wrong.

Through a narrow opening in the door he could see the two men. Neither of them was holding a gun. But then, gunfire might draw a crowd. If they meant to kill him, it would likely be with knives. For that, they would need to get him close.

It registered, as well, that they weren't wearing disguises or masks. Clearly they weren't worried about his identifying them later.

All the signs were bad. If he valued his life, Quint knew this would be the time to find another exit to the shed and vanish into the night. But the sack was moving again, and now, mingled with the night sounds, he heard a distinct whimper.

Sliding the pistol back into its holster, he swung the door open and stepped into full view.

"We know you're armed, Mr. Seavers." The tall man stood partway behind his companion, both of them shielded by the sea bag. "Put your gun down. You wouldn't want to shoot the young lady by accident, would you?"

When Quint hesitated, the stockier man, who carried the bag over his shoulder, drew a wide-bladed hunting knife from under his coat. Grinning, he pressed the tip against the canvas bag. This time the whimper was a sob of fear. Something jerked tight around Quint's heart.

"My friend here would enjoy a little creative carving before we return your niece," the tall man said. "Now put the gun down and kick it over here."

The man who held the knife grinned. His little pig eyes glittered with something akin to madness. Quint had no doubt the threat was real. A bead of sweat trickled down his cheek as he drew the pistol from its holster.

"No tricks now," the tall man barked. "Lay it on the dock and kick it over here."

Quint lowered the pistol to the wet planking and

nudged it with his boot. It spun toward the two thugs, stopping a few feet short. The taller man scowled. "You say you brought the letter."

"I did. But you're not getting a look at it until I see Clara."

The man with the knife grinned. The knife blade pierced the light canvas, probing deeper. From inside the bag came a muffled scream of pain and terror.

Something about the voice—the pitch, the undertone... Suddenly Quint knew.

It wasn't Clara.

It wasn't his precious daughter. But it was a child. A child who couldn't be left to die.

"No, wait! I'll get it for you!" Quint reached into his vest pocket, his mind churning. As his fingers found the flap of the envelope, a daring plan flashed into place. There was no time to think things through. He would have to act now, while surprise was on his side.

His groping fingers maneuvered the folded paper out of the envelope. Leaving the letter inside his pocket, he withdrew the empty envelope and crumpled it in his fist.

"Here! Catch!" He flung the ball of paper over the heads of the two kidnappers. It disappeared into the foggy darkness.

The diversion lasted seconds at most. But it gave Quint time to slam his body into the man with the sea bag. He was as solid as a brick wall, but Quint had the advantage of speed and surprise. The shock of impact knocked the thug off balance. His feet scrambled for purchase on the slippery planks. By the time he regained his footing, Quint had seized the bag in his arms and was sprinting for the side of the pier.

The knife whizzed through the darkness. Quint felt the razor sharp blade sink into the back of his left shoulder. As he stumbled forward, his momentum carried him over the edge.

Still clutching the bag, he plummeted down, down into the cold water of the bay.

Chapter Twelve

The blade burned through the muscles and tendons of Quint's shoulder, rendering his left arm all but useless. But the injury was the least of his worries now. If he couldn't get the bag open, the struggling child in his arms could drown.

Treading water with his legs, he tugged at the water-soaked knot. Beneath the canvas, small shoes kicked frantically against his wrist. Quint swore as he realized the child had been thrust into the bag headfirst. His curses turned to prayers as he inverted the bag and heard a labored gasp.

Gripping the precious burden, he used his legs to propel his body through the water. Behind him, pistol shots rang through the fog. Bullets whined as they ricocheted off the surface. Judging from their aim, the shooters couldn't see, but they could hear him moving; and there was always the danger of a lucky shot. Quint redoubled his efforts. His left arm had gone numb, and the icy bay was sapping his energy. Much longer, and he wouldn't be strong enough to stay afloat.

The child lay quietly over his right shoulder. Had the poor little mite simply stopped struggling, or had a young life ended inside that dark bag? Before anything else, Quint knew he needed to get the youngster out of the water and get the bag open.

The gunshots had ceased. Either the two thugs had run out of bullets and gone or they were walking along the waterfront, waiting for him to come ashore. He could swim under one of the wharves and hide among the pilings, or even try to make it to an anchored boat. But he was tiring fast. Within minutes the cold water would pull him down, and the child with him.

Ahead, through the fog, he could see a floating platform tethered to one of the piers. The top of it rose about eighteen inches above the lapping waves. With the last of his strength, Quint made for it. He might not be able to drag himself up and over the edge. But at least he'd have a place to lay the child while he tried to open the bag.

Gasping, he reached the platform. The muscles in his right arm screamed as he hoisted the bag. The small body inside began to thrash as he heaved the bag onto the boards. A wave of relief swept over Quint as he tugged the strings around to hang over the edge, where he could work on the knot.

By now his legs had gone numb and his hands barely worked. His stiff, cold fingers picked at the knot. An eternity seemed to pass before the wet drawstrings parted and the bag fell open.

For an agonizing moment nothing happened. Then something stirred and began to squirm. A dripping, bedraggled little Chinese boy crept out of the bag. He looked to be about Clara's age, dressed in typical black broadcloth, his hair pulled back and braided in a tiny pigtail. In all likelihood, the kidnappers had simply grabbed him off the street. Quint had expected the child to be gagged and bound. But it appeared that terror had been enough to keep him still.

Teeth chattering, the boy crawled to the edge of the platform. For the space of a long breath his frightened almond eyes gazed down at Quint. Then, without a word, he scrambled to his feet and fled into the fog.

Quint was getting light-headed. Fighting to stay conscious, he made his way around the side of the platform. If he didn't get out of the water soon, he would drown or die of cold and blood loss.

At last he found something that might work—a heavy cargo net flung over a cast-iron bollard that was bolted to the platform. If enough of the net lay around the bollard, it might catch on the ends and support his weight.

The edge of the net hung in the water. Seizing it

with both hands Quint gave it a firm tug. Miraculously, it held fast.

Willing strength into his arms, Quint clasped the net and started dragging himself upward. The knife was still in place, its haft protruding from his shoulder. Pain flashed outward from the blade, shooting up his arm and down his back. He clenched his jaw to keep from screaming as he worked his way toward the edge of the platform. Seconds crawled past. His head had begun to swim. He could feel his grip weakening. He imagined himself passing out, sliding into the black water…

No! He had to keep fighting for Clara and for Annie. One inch, then another. With his last ounce of strength, Quint dragged himself over the edge of the platform and collapsed on the net.

As the world spun into darkness, the last thing he remembered was Annie's face.

The mantel clock chimed the half hour. Annie paused in her nervous pacing to glance at the time. Ten-thirty, and no word. Not a telephone call. Not a knock at the door. What in heaven's name could be happening?

It was early, she reminded herself. Quint could still be waiting for the kidnappers to show up—but no, she knew better than to believe that. Rutledge had gone to the opera and sent his hired butchers to lie in wait for Quint, murder him and take the letter.

With each passing minute the certainty grew that they'd succeeded.

The worst of it was, there was nothing she could do but stare at the clock, pace the rug and pray. All her instincts urged her to fly out the door and search for him. But she didn't know the docks. She wouldn't know where to begin looking or what to do if she found him in danger. And Quint had told her to stay here. He needed to know she was safe. And she needed to be here in case he telephoned or sent word.

Whatever it takes, I'll get her back, Hannah. I promise.

The memory of his last words stung like lye in a wound. Certainly it had been an honest mistake. Quint had been preoccupied and likely unaware that he'd called her by the wrong name. But the mistake told Annie where his true heart lay. Quint might flatter her with pretty words. He might carry her to bed and satisfy his lust. But he was still in love with her beautiful sister, the mother of his child.

Jealousy was an ugly emotion. No one as sweet and loving as Hannah deserved to be its object. But all her life, until she'd started sewing her own clothes, Annie had accepted Hannah's hand-me-downs as her due. Just once, Annie thought, she would like to come first. Especially with Quint.

But what difference did it make? Even now, Quint could be lying dead on some dark pier, and Clara could be lost forever.

Pausing at the front window, she stared out into the foggy night. She'd left the lights off in the flat. Only the fire, long since burned down to coals, cast enough of a glow for her to see her way around the parlor.

In the Grand Opera House on Mission Street, the tragedy on stage would be nearing its final act. Soon the velvet curtain would drop to thunderous applause. Carriages would be lining up at the curb, ready to whisk their owners off to midnight suppers. People would be laughing, drinking champagne and feasting on delicacies fit for a king's table while they discussed Caruso's performance.

Annie turned away from the window, her nerves stripped raw. Would there ever be an end to this nightmare of helpless waiting?

A sound. She froze, listening. Light footsteps padded along the hall from the direction of the back entrance. An instant later she heard three soft taps.

Annie pressed her ear to the door. "Who's there?" she demanded.

"Let me in, miss. I have something to show you."

Her fingers fumbled with the bolt and the latch. The door opened wide enough for Chao to step inside. For a man who'd been beaten nearly to death the night before he looked remarkably fit. His face was bruised, his cut lips scabbed over, and he moved with extra care. But the worst of the swelling was gone from around his eyes.

Except for fear of hurting him, Annie would have flung her arms around the dignified man.

"Mr. Seavers is not here?"

Annie shook her head. "He went to meet with the kidnappers. I'll tell you more in a minute. You said you had something."

Chao reached inside his jacket and drew out something small and white. Annie seized it from him.

It was a finger-length fragment of cotton lace, torn and dirty. Bits of green were tangled in the loose threads. Even in the dim light, Annie recognized it at once. She had sewn it into place herself.

It had come from the hem of Clara's nightgown.

"Where did you get this?" Her heart was pounding.

"My cousin brought it to me. He sweeps Mr. Rutledge's carriage house and hauls the manure away. This was caught on a nail by the stairs."

Annie's knees gave way. She sank onto an ottoman. "The stairs. Where do they go?"

"To a place under the roof. My cousin says they store chairs and things up there."

"Has he heard anything? Any unusual sounds?"

"He says no."

Annie pushed to her feet. "She could still be there. I have to go and find out."

Chao nodded. "I will go with you."

"No. Somebody needs to find Quint." Talking fast, she poured out the story of the telephone call, the kidnapper's demands, her phone call to Rutledge's home and her fears for Quint's safety. "Something's gone wrong," she said. "You know the city and the docks, Chao. Find him if it's not too late. Bring him home."

Chao hesitated. His beaten face creased into a scowl. "I understand. But how can you go alone? So much danger for a woman at night—"

"I'll do whatever I have to." Annie turned away to get her coat.

"Wait!" Chao strode into the kitchen and opened a bottom drawer. There, neatly folded, was a plain black jacket and trousers like the ones he wore when he came to work. "I keep clean clothes here to change if I get dirty. You put them on with a hat. I will show you how to walk. No man will pay attention."

"Show me now. Then you can leave."

Chao's instruction was brief. What he showed Annie was a caricature of Chinese behavior. But at least it might keep her out of trouble. She practiced the small, shuffling steps, the downcast gaze, the hands tucked into her sleeves for warmth. "Keep to the right, close to the edge of the sidewalk," he said. "Don't look at anybody. Remember, you are invisible."

"I understand." Annie reached for her reticule and snatched out a handful of bills. "Here, take this for cab fare. You have your own key?"

"Yes, and thank you. I will do my best for him. May our ancestors be with us all."

"Go! Hurry!" Annie all but shoved him out into the hall. She stood listening as his footsteps faded away. Then, locking the door, she raced into the guest room to change.

Chao was close to Annie's size. His clothes were a comfortable fit on her. Annie knotted the drawstring waist of the trousers and fastened the frog loops down the front of the jacket. The costume would be especially helpful if she needed to hide, run or climb. But she still needed to do something about her blond hair.

Conscious of the need to hurry, she rummaged in her suitcase for a pair of thin black stockings. Stretching out the top of one, she slid it on like a cap, covering everything but her face, then crowned her head with Quint's black derby. The disguise was far from perfect, but at least it might work in the dark.

Carrying her reticule was out of the question. Unfastening the top of the jacket, Annie wrapped a few bills in a handkerchief and stuffed it down the front of her corset. The key could go there, too, once she'd locked the door. In the kitchen she found a sharp paring knife, which she slid into the top of her boot. It might come in handy for cutting through ropes or defending herself.

What did she think she was doing? Could she really break into Rutledge's carriage house, find Clara, if she was there, and rescue her from a gang of murderers?

But there was only one answer to that question. She could do it—she *would* do it—because she had to.

It was time to leave. But there was one last thing she wanted. It would be of no use except to give her courage. But courage was what she needed most of all.

Back in the guest room she unfastened Clara's suitcase and reached inside. Her fingers found the little seashell, so fragile and yet so strong. Annie clasped it in her hand as she walked back into the parlor.

Hannah—serene face smiled from the photograph on the wall. Of all the people who would suffer from Clara's loss, Annie knew that her sister's pain would be the most wrenching of all.

"I'll get her back, Hannah," she whispered. "Whatever I have to do, so help me, I'll bring her back to you."

In her own promise, Annie heard the ring of Quint's. Suddenly she understood. His words hadn't been for her or even for Hannah. His promise had been for the family, for Hannah and Judd and their children, for her, for himself and the circle of love that bound them all together.

Tears blurred her eyes. "You come back, Quint," she whispered into the silence. "Come back for all of us. And I'll come back, too—with Clara."

Slipping the seashell into her pocket, she hurried out the door.

* * *

Rutledge's residence was easy enough to find. Annie had checked the address in the telephone directory and traced the route from Jackson Street on Quint's map. Despite Chao's warning to stay invisible, she had covered most of the seven-block distance at a run. Out of breath now she crouched in the shrubbery at the end of the drive. Her ribs heaved beneath the rigid stays of her corset. If only she'd thought to loosen the laces. But that was the least of her concerns now.

The imposing two-story stucco home was surrounded by trees, shrubbery and a six-foot iron fence. The gate to the drive was fastened, but not locked—probably because Rutledge hadn't returned from his evening out. Getting inside wouldn't be a problem. But what could be waiting beyond that fence? Armed guards? Dogs? Annie was just beginning to realize how dangerous her mission was.

Groping under a clump of privet, she found a fist-sized rock. Rising onto her knees, she lobbed it over the fence. It landed on the lawn with a thud.

Flattening her body on the ground, Annie counted the seconds. Time crawled past. No dogs. No voices. She forced herself to wait a full minute. Then she cast around for an even larger rock. Years of farm life had given her strong arms and plenty of practice. The second rock flew long and true, crashing through the limbs of a cypress before thudding onto the grass below.

Again she held her breath and waited. Only when she was satisfied that no one was coming did she creep to the gate, slip through and close the latch behind her.

Finding the carriage house was no problem. All she needed to do was follow the broad, concrete drive. Beyond the house a well-worn strip of gravel branched off to the left. At the far end of it, Annie could see the carriage house rising above a tangle of ailanthus trees. Its walls were sooty, time-weathered brick. The low, slanting roof was crowned by a cupola that looked newer than the rest of the structure. At one end, a brick chimney towered above the roof. Years ago the place might have been a home, gutted and converted when the present house was built. Tonight, seen through swirls of drifting fog, it looked ancient and forbidding. Clara would be wild with terror in such a place.

Quint had believed that Rutledge would never hide Clara on his own property. But Rutledge must have thought it too risky to hide her anywhere else. Now the question was, would Clara still be here?

Keeping to the shadows, Annie crept toward the carriage house. The wide, barn-style doors fronting the building were closed. When she tried to open them, she found both doors bolted and securely padlocked.

She gazed up under the long eave. It jutted out from the wall, sheltering a colony of swallows' nests. There appeared to be no windows on the upper floor, just a low space under the roof. Even by day it would be pitch-dark in that space. There would be spiders, rats and mice, even bats if they had a way in and out. What a horrible place to keep a child.

But she was wasting time. Circling the building, she found one more entrance, a narrow door on the end nearest the house. But it was locked, as well, with a cylinder bolt requiring a key. There appeared to be no other way in. She could only hope that the carriage had yet to arrive, and that she'd be able to sneak inside while the driver wasn't looking. For now, all she could do was hide and wait.

She chose a patch of deep shadow under a low-hanging willow tree, with a view of the drive. Untended weeds grew around the base of the trunk, tall enough to provide a screen. Hollowing out a flat spot, she sat down cross-legged to wait.

The night was chilly and Annie was lightly dressed. Before long she was shivering. She wrapped her arms around her ribs, trying to stay warm. Crickets shrilled in the grass around her. A barn owl screeched in the darkness.

She'd resolved to think about some contingency plans for getting Clara and herself to safety. But it was Quint who kept stealing into her thoughts—his face, his voice, the smell of his skin, his firm, naked buttocks, the line of dark hair that trailed down his belly… A few hours ago she'd been in his arms. He'd been inside her, where she'd ached so long for him to be, thrilling her with each deep thrust of his body.

She'd never felt more alive, or more womanly, than during their lovemaking. If she died tonight, she would want her last thoughts to be of Quint, his skin pressed to hers, his body shuddering with the hot spill of his seed. Of all her memories, that was the one she would choose to carry with her.

Annie was fighting sleep by the time she heard the snort of a horse and the jingle of harness brass. Seconds later she saw the carriage lights. Then the horses and carriage emerged out of the fog. The passenger seat was empty. But of course Rutledge would have gotten off at the house. Hopefully the driver would be eager to put away the carriage and horses and hurry off to bed.

Annie waited until the carriage had passed her hiding place. Then she straightened her cramped legs, rose out of the weeds and crept forward.

Chao had told her what little he knew about the building. The side on her left had been converted to a stable with bins for feed and stalls for the two carriage horses. The other side housed the carriage, spare parts and tools. The stairway to the attic was on the carriage side.

The driver, a lanky fellow with scruffy blond whiskers, reined in the team and climbed down from the seat. By the dim light of the carriage lamps, he drew a key ring out of his trouser pocket, unlocked both doors and swung them open. Guiding the team, he backed the carriage into place, snuffed out the side lamps, unhitched the horses and led them to their stalls.

Now was the time. Keeping low, Annie darted in through the open door and ducked behind the carriage. In the back corner, a narrow stairway led upward into the darkness. Climbing it now would be too risky. But some boxes stacked underneath offered a hiding place. Creeping under the stairs, she squeezed her way back to the wall. But the space behind the boxes was too narrow for her to crouch. She would have to move the boxes out a few inches and pray the driver wouldn't notice.

Holding her breath, she braced the stack and used her feet to inch it away from the wall. Only then did she notice the half-empty beer bottle someone had left on top. Before she could stop it, the bottle tipped and crashed to the concrete floor. The odor of stale beer permeated the air.

"Who's there?" A lantern flickered as Annie shrank behind the boxes. She held her breath as the light scanned each corner and came to rest on the broken bottle. The driver cursed. "Damned rats," he muttered and turned away.

Annie exhaled, praying the man wouldn't return with a broom to clean up the mess. She went limp with relief when, at last, he walked outside, swung the wide doors shut and slid the bolts into place. Waiting in the dark, she heard the faint click of padlocks snapping shut. Her heart dropped. She'd managed to get into the carriage house. But what about getting out?

Staying hidden, she forced herself to count nerve-fraying seconds. Then, carefully, she shifted the boxes and moved toward the stairs. The carriage house was dark, but her eyes had adjusted enough to make out shapes. Using her hands, and what little vision she had, she found her way to the foot of the steps and began to climb.

There was no door at the top, just a three-foot opening cut in the attic floor. That might explain why the carriage house, which most thieves would ignore, had been securely locked. There had to be something—or someone—in that attic that Rutledge wanted to keep hidden. Annie could only pray that it was Clara.

The darkness deepened as Annie groped her way upward. A light would be a godsend. But touch and hearing would have to serve in place of sight.

As she gained the attic floor, something furry scampered across her shoe. Growing up on a farm, she'd dealt with rats and mice aplenty. She wasn't afraid of them. But the dark air was rank with the odor of droppings. What if the rats had harmed Clara? What if the fetid smell of the place had made her sick? The thought made Annie shudder.

Feeling her way with her feet, she moved away from the opening toward the far end of the attic, where a sliver of night glinted between the wall and the roof. As her eyes adjusted, she could make out black shapes that she guessed to be old furniture.

"Clara?" Annie's voice quivered in the stillness. "Clara, it's Aunt Annie. Can you hear me?"

In the silence that followed, Annie could hear her own shallow breathing. Something rustled in the far corner.

"Clara, is that you?" She held her breath, listening.

"Clara?" There was a thrashing sound, a furious thumping from behind a wall of furniture. Annie flung herself toward the sound, bruising herself against sharp corners as she fought her way to the narrow mattress that lay against the wall. On the mattress, just discernible in the darkness, lay a small white form. Moving. Alive.

With a little cry, Annie flung herself onto the mattress and gathered the little girl in her arms. Clara was bound hand and foot, her mouth gagged with a dirty bandanna. Annie fumbled in her tangled curls to find the knot. When Clara's mouth was uncovered, she began to sob.

"It's all right, love," Annie murmured, cradling her close. "Here, hold still and let me cut these ropes." She found the paring knife and used it to cut through the rough strands of hemp. Clara's wrists and ankles were chafed raw. Her hands and feet were swollen. Annie rubbed them to restore the circulation as Clara struggled to find her voice.

"Bad men…they tied me up and put me in the dark. I want to go home, Aunt Annie. I want Uncle Quint and Mama and Papa."

"Hush." Annie cradled her close, rocking the little girl in her arms. "I'm going to try to get us out of here. You'll need to be brave a little longer, all right?"

"All right." Clara nodded. The poor child had been terribly brave already, Annie thought. Now it was up to her to get Clara to safety. She could only pray that Quint would be waiting when they arrived back at the flat.

"Let's go," Annie said. "Can you walk a little?"

"I think so." Clara pulled herself up. "But I don't have any shoes."

"It's all right. You'll have to follow me down the steps, but once we're outside I can carry you. Come on."

Feeling their way, they crept toward the staircase. Annie moved ahead, keeping Clara behind her. At least there was a little more light below. She could see the way down, and she could make out the narrow door near the foot of the stairs. That door was their one hope of getting out—if only it could be opened from the inside. In a moment she would know.

"Why are you dressed up like Chao?" Clara asked.

"Chao lent me these clothes so I'd be harder to see," Annie said. "I'm very thankful he did."

"Where's Uncle Quint?"

The question tore at Annie but she forced herself to sound cheerful. "He went off to find the men who took you. He'll be happy to know you're all right."

To her relief, Clara seemed satisfied with the answer. Annie took the small hand in hers as they reached the bottom of the stairs. "Stay close to me," she said. "I need to open this door."

It was too dark to see the workings of the lock. Annie would have to depend on her fingers and her memory. She had seen the lock from the outside—a cylinder bolt with a keyhole. But anyone working in the carriage house would need a way out. If the lock could be opened from the inside…

Her pulse leapt as she touched the key that had been left in place. "It's all right, Clara," she whispered. "I'll have us out of here in no time!"

The key turned easily. She heard the click of the sliding bolt, the creak of hinges as the door released and swung inward.

Clara shrank against her leg as a familiar voice boomed out of the darkness.

"Well, Miss Gustavson! Fancy meeting you here!"

Josiah Rutledge stood in the doorway, the carriage driver behind him with a lantern. The pistol in Rutledge's hand was pointed straight at Annie's heart.

Chapter Thirteen

Rutledge's smile was a wolf's smile—wintry eyes and big yellow teeth, framed by his pomaded beard. Clara pressed close to Annie's legs.

"What a pleasant surprise," Rutledge said. "When Thomas told me he'd heard someone moving around out here, I expected it might be Mr. Seavers. But you—this is even better. You've spared me the bother of sending someone to fetch you."

Annie braced her knees to keep them from buckling. The worst thing she could do right now was show fear. "Where's Quint?" she demanded.

Rutledge chuckled. "Now that's a good question. It seems the two gentlemen I sent to meet him came back empty-handed. He was wounded, they said, and went into the bay. Until we know for sure what's become of him, I'm afraid you and Miss Clara, here, will have to remain my guests."

The blow was physical in its pain—Quint wounded, missing, possibly dead. That uncertainty, she knew, was the only reason she and Clara were still alive. Rutledge wouldn't show himself unless he planned to kill them both. As long as the chance remained that Quint had survived, he would keep at least one of them as a hostage. But as soon as they were no longer useful, they would disappear like Virginia Poole.

Clara's hand crept into hers. Fighting tears, Annie squeezed the swollen fingers. At least they had each other. If the worst happened, Clara wouldn't have to die alone.

Rutledge's gaze flicked over her costume. "I must say, I don't think much of those Chinese pajamas. You looked more attractive last night when we met at the opera. A pity you weren't there tonight. Caruso was…magnificent."

Keeping the gun leveled at Annie's chest, he reached toward her face with his left hand. The ruby in his signet ring glistened like a splash of fresh blood as he tugged the stocking off her head. Her hair tumbled free, falling over her shoulders and down her back.

Taking his time, Rutledge twined a curl around his finger. "There, that's better. Much better." He glanced back at the driver. "Tie them both up and put them in the attic."

"No!" Annie protested vehemently. "Not in the

attic! Clara won't last the night up there! Look at her!"

Rutledge lowered his hand, scowling beneath his thick, black brows.

"Leave her untied," Annie pleaded. "She's only a little girl. She's been through so much. And she needs food and water as well. Please, for the sake of common decency."

One black eyebrow slithered upward. "Now, why should I listen to your whining? You were caught trespassing on my property. You're in no position to ask for anything."

"I'm begging you! As long as the doors are locked we can't go anywhere. There's no need to keep us tied up in that dark attic!"

Rutledge smirked. "You seem quite anxious to get your way, Miss Gustavson. How far would you be willing to go?"

A nauseating fear swept over Annie as she realized what he meant. But she'd do anything to help Clara, and this might be her only chance. Trembling, she raised her chin. "As far as I have to," she said.

The smirk broadened into a leer. Reaching out, he ran his fingertips down her cheek, along her throat, then lower still to lightly circle her breast. Annie suppressed a shudder.

"Hmmm," he murmured. "Now that's what I'd call an interesting offer. Very interesting indeed. Let me—"

"Mr. Rutledge!" The young voice of the butler emerged from the darkness behind him. "Telephone call for you, sir. I believe it's Mrs. Stanhope."

"Oh." Rutledge took a step backward. "Probably concerned about that ruby earring she lost in the carriage. Tell her I'll be right there, Rogers. Mustn't keep the lady waiting." He glanced back at Annie. "We'll continue our little discussion later, Miss Gustavson. Thomas, lock the door. Make sure you take that key with you."

"Yes, sir." The driver withdrew the key from the inside lock and closed the door behind him. Enfolded by night once more, Annie heard the metallic click of the bolt.

Only then did she sink to the floor and gather Clara into her arms. They held each other, trembling in the darkness. "I'm scared, Aunt Annie," Clara whispered. "I don't like that man."

"I don't like him, either, sweetheart. But we need to be brave. Are you thirsty? If we can get to the horses, they might have some water to drink."

Clara shook her head, huddling close like a small, frightened animal. "I don't want the horses' water. I just want to go home."

"We can't go home tonight," Annie said, aching. "But I brought something for you. Look." She reached into her pocket and pulled out the seashell. "You can listen to this and think about the ocean. Remember the wonderful time we had, there on the beach?"

"That was the best day of my whole life. Even if I got sick." Clara took the shell, held it to her ear and closed her eyes. "I can hear the ocean now."

"Come on." Annie rose and lifted Clara onto the seat of the carriage, then climbed up herself. "Let's get some rest. You can lie down here with your head in my lap and let the ocean sing you to sleep."

Clara curled on her side, still clasping the shell against her ear. "Will you stay with me?"

"I'll be right here." Annie smoothed the tangled curls. She would do anything to save this precious child.

Bending down, she unlaced her high-topped shoes and removed her long stockings. "I'm going to wrap your feet in these, Clara," she said. "Then I want your promise that you'll do something for me—something very, very brave." She began wrapping a knitted cotton strip around one chubby foot. "The next time one of those men opens the door, I'll jump at him and try to fight him. When that happens, you must run out the door and get away. Run as fast as you can. Get to the street and find somebody to help you. Whatever you see or hear, don't look back. Do you understand?"

Clara nodded. "I'm scared, Aunt Annie."

"So am I. But you must get away to go home to your mama and papa."

"I want Uncle Quint to come."

"Hush." Annie knotted the wrapping on one foot

and started on the other. "Close your eyes and I'll tell you the story of Peter Rabbit."

Annie knew the story by heart. By the time she reached the part about Peter losing his jacket, Clara had fallen asleep. She lay limp with exhaustion, her head cradled between Annie's knees, her hand clasping her seashell. Overhead, the rats had reclaimed their attic. Their busy feet scurried back and forth above the ceiling.

Annie sat staring into the darkness, wondering when Josiah Rutledge would come for her. Maybe he'd been delayed or distracted. Maybe he'd decided to wait until tomorrow. It no longer mattered, she told herself. Nothing mattered except getting Clara out of this nightmare alive.

Had Quint survived the past hours or was his body already blanketed in the cold water of the bay? In her mind she tried to reach out to him. Surely if he was dead her heart would know it. But her instincts told her nothing. Wherever he might be, Quint was beyond her reach.

Her thoughts drifted back to Dutchman's Creek, to that sunny spring day he'd taught her to shoot. She remembered the scent of his skin, remembered how his arms had steadied her, how he'd leaned close to show her the workings of the sight, not the least bit aware that she was falling in love with him.

As for finding Quint tonight, her best hope lay with the man she'd sent to search for him. Chao knew the waterfront. He had eyes and ears in many places. But he wasn't a miracle worker. Miracles came from a higher source, and if ever a miracle was needed, it was now.

Gazing up into the darkness, Annie did the only thing she could. She prayed.

Quint groaned and opened his eyes. He was lying facedown on what felt like a coarse muslin sheet. From a low table, the flame of a candle cast flickering shadows around a narrow, cluttered room.

Instinctively he pushed with his arms to sit up. Pain knifed outward from his left shoulder, so intense that he almost fainted. With a grunt, he fell back onto the sheet. Only then did he remember the two men, the blade stabbing into his flesh, and his desperate plunge into the bay. Forcing his concentration deeper, he recalled the child he'd freed from the sea bag before dragging himself to safety. He remembered nothing else.

So where in Sam Hill was he now?

Clenching his teeth against the pain, he struggled to turn onto his side and move his knees forward. His damp trousers clung to his legs. His feet and upper body were bare. What had happened to his clothes? Where was the damned letter?

"No!" Strong hands seized his upper arms, pushing him gently but firmly down. "You are hurt. Do not move. Rest." The voice was a stranger's. The face that swam into his vision was that of a slim, youthful Chinese man. "Please, sir," he said in halting English. "My wife made medicine for your wound. You keep it there, rest."

Keeping his body still, Quint lifted his head and peered around him. "How the hell did I—" Then, suddenly, he understood. Peering at him from a stool was a wide-eyed little boy dressed in a flannel sleeping robe.

"My name is Wong," the man said. "You saved my son. He led us to you."

"And you brought me here." Quint finished the sentence for him. He was in Chinatown, that much was a given. But the puzzle still had a lot of missing pieces.

"We know who you are," Wong said. "Mr. Chao works for you. My brother went to find him. Long time now and he is not back."

"How long?" Quint asked. "What time is it?"

Wong fumbled in his robe, brought out a tarnished pocket watch and held it where Quint could see it. Quint stared, shaking his head.

"Ten minutes to four? That can't be right. Your watch must've stopped."

Solemn-faced, Wong held the watch close to Quint's ear. It was ticking steadily. "Soon it will be light," he said.

"This can't be…" Quint swore under his breath. How long had he lain on the dock? How long had it taken these people to find him, bring him here and dress his wound? How long before he came awake? Most puzzling of all, why couldn't he remember any of it?

"Your wound was bad." Wong answered his unspoken question. "We put in medicine to clean and stop the blood. Then we had to sew it." He made stitching motions with his hand. "We gave you medicine to make you sleep. Long sleep is good."

Long sleep is good. Quint cursed as he struggled to sit up. These well-meaning people had probably saved his life. But they'd put him out of action for hours. Lord, Annie would be frantic. And what if Chao had brought news about Clara? He had to get out of this place. He had to get home right now.

Clenching his teeth against the pain, he pushed himself to a sitting position and swung his feet to the floor. "Get me my clothes," he muttered. "I don't care if they're wet. I've got to get out of here!"

"Please, sir, I beg you." His host fluttered around him like a frantic bird. "You must rest. You'll hurt—"

His pleas broke off as the door opened and two figures emerged from the darkness outside. The one in the lead was a slender youth. Following on his heels was Chao. Quint slumped with relief.

Chao's battered face looked weary, but his eyes brightened at the sight of Quint. "I have been looking for you all night," he said. "Tell me what happened."

"It was a trap," Quint said. "The rest of the story can wait. Have you heard any more about Clara?"

Chao nodded. "My cousin found a scrap of her nightgown in Mr. Rutledge's carriage house. When you didn't come home, Miss Annie went there to look for her."

Quint's body jerked upright, triggering a flash of pain. "Annie went to Rutledge's? You let her go alone?"

"When she telephoned and found out Mr. Rutledge was at the opera, she knew he planned to have you killed. Maybe Little Miss, too. She sent me after you. I found your gun on the pier. But you were gone."

"You should have gone with her," Quint said.

"I know that now. Not then."

"Never mind. My legs are fine but my head's still foggy. Can you see me home? Maybe Annie will be there. If not, I'll be leaving to find her."

Chao nodded, then spoke in a burst of Chinese. Quint's shoes and missing clothes promptly appeared. They looked to have been carefully laid out and were damp, but wearable. The blood had been washed out of the coat, shirt and vest, but the knife slash remained. Quint found the letter where he'd left it, folded inside his vest pocket. It was soaked and perhaps ruined, but right now he had more urgent concerns. He would look at it later.

The shoulder holster would be painful to wear

with his wound. In any case, he didn't need it now. Chao rolled up the straps and tucked it into his jacket.

A short time later, with his wound bandaged and his arm in a sling, Quint was ready to leave. He thanked Wong and his family as best he could, although the shy little boy scampered off when Quint tried to shake his hand. After the farewells, he and Chao stepped outside.

"I can look for a cab," Chao offered.

Quint shook his head. "Don't bother. It's not far. Maybe the walk will clear my head."

The sky was still dark, the air cool and misty off the bay. Before long the sun would be up and the streets would be bustling with traffic. But now, in the hour before dawn, a hush lay over San Francisco. Quint had always loved this time of day, with its awakening sounds and flowing shadows. But for him, he sensed, this day would be unlike any other. By its end, he would be a changed man.

He lengthened his stride, driven by the urgency to get home. Chao trudged along beside him in silence. The two of them had plenty to discuss, but the night had drained them both.

Ahead of them, a delivery wagon, drawn by a team of tired-looking horses, creaked along Jackson Street. A black dog sniffed for tidbits in the refuse of an overturned trash can. The aroma of fresh coffee drifted from an upstairs window. A peaceful dawn. An ordinary morning.

Maybe everything would be all right, Quint thought. Maybe they would find Annie and Clara waiting in the apartment, worried but safe, and life could go on as it was meant to go on. Was that too much to ask of fate?

They had just come even with the wagon when the horses began to stamp and whinny, jerking the wagon forward. The driver, who'd been dozing, was almost thrown from his seat. He sawed at the reins to keep the team from bolting. Strangely, the dog had begun to howl, a mournful, frantic wail that was taken up by a chorus of neighboring canines. A flock of pigeons exploded from a rooftop.

Quint glanced around for what might have startled the animals. There was nothing, and in a moment the disturbance had ceased. All was quiet again.

"Odd," Chao mused, half to himself.

The darkness was beginning to fade by the time they reached the flat. Quint's anxiety mounted as he pounded up the back stairs, heedless of the jarring pain in his shoulder. If Annie and Clara were there, he would clasp them in his arms and hold them with all his strength. And he would never expose them to danger again.

The key was still in his pocket. Hoping against hope, he opened the door. His heart sank as he stepped inside to be greeted by silence. In the guest room, Annie's clothes lay strewn on the bed. He picked up her white blouse. It still carried her scent.

It was all he could do to keep from burying his face in the soft fabric.

Chao stood in the doorway, watching him. "I gave her my spare clothes," he said.

"Good idea." Quint laid the blouse on the coverlet. "I'm going after her."

"You've lost a lot of blood," Chao said. "You need food, at least. And you should change those wet clothes."

"No time. Where's that gun you found?"

"Here." Chao lifted the weapon out of his pocket. "Careful, it's still loaded."

"Fine." Quint remembered the bullets flying around him in the water. Rutledge's henchmen must have used their own guns and forgotten about his. Deciding against the shoulder strap, he clipped the holster onto his belt and thrust the small pistol into it.

"I'm going with you," Chao said. "This is my fight, too."

"Come along, then. But you've got a family. If any shooting starts, I want you to stay back."

Through the east window the sky above the bay was fading to silver. Turning, Quint glanced at the clock on the mantel. It was seven minutes after five. "Let's go," he said.

They left the building and hit the pavement, moving at a fast clip. Quint was running on adrenaline now. His brain was on full alert, his heart pumping fast. His body wouldn't hold up for long. But his strength would have to last until he could find Annie and Clara. For now he clung to the hope that they were alive. As long as the letter was a threat, it made sense that Rutledge would keep them as hostages.

But that, Quint knew, was no guarantee of their safety. If Clara and Annie were dead, then he would have nothing to lose. He wouldn't bother trying to bring Josiah Rutledge to justice. He would kill the bastard with his own hands and be hanged for it.

Dawn was stealing across the bay, brushing the city with pewter light. The streets stirred with early morning traffic—a bakery wagon bound for a downtown hotel, a trolley on its first run of the day, a newsboy picking up a bundle of morning papers.

Quint turned to Chao. "What do you know about the carriage house?" he asked. "Where would Rutledge hide a woman and a little girl?"

Before Chao could answer, a low rumble shattered the morning calm. It began softly, like the roll of distant thunder. Then, in the next instant, it was as if a monstrous freight train were barreling out of the center of the earth. The ground bucked, flinging both men to the sidewalk. Horses screamed and reared. Cracks splintered the roadway. "Earthquake!" someone shrieked.

For what seemed like an eternity the shaking continued. The ground undulated in roaring waves, toppling chimneys, shattering windows. Trolley tracks broke loose from their anchors to wave like angry serpents. Electric wires snapped and crackled. Church bells clanged crazily in their towers.

A cement cornice broke off a synagogue and crashed to the ground, taking most of a tile roof with it. A broken water main sent a fountain of spray into the air. A wood frame boardinghouse slid off its foundation to crash against the building next door. Screams came from inside the wreckage.

For the space of a breath, the quake seemed to stop, but it was only gathering strength. It began again with renewed fury. The ground buckled and twisted. Poles that carried telephone, telegraph and electric lines toppled like dominoes. Horses shrieked as a wall fell onto a wagon. Quint seized Chao's arm, jerking him out of the way as a balcony crashed onto the sidewalk, shattering pots of red geraniums.

As suddenly as it had begun, the shaking stopped. An unearthly hush fell over the city. People staggered into the street, many of them in their night clothes. They stared at the devastation in shocked disbelief.

In all, the earthquake had lasted a little over a minute.

Quint and Chao scrambled to their feet. Glancing back up Jackson Street, Quint saw that the upper story of the building where he lived had collapsed. If he and Chao had been there, they'd likely be dead by now.

Quint's throat tightened as he thought of Annie and Clara. What would he find when he reached Rutledge's place?

Chao was unhurt, but Quint could guess what he was thinking. The old brick buildings in Chinatown would crumble in a bad quake. He'd promised to go with Quint but he was desperately worried about his own family.

Quint placed a hand on his friend's shoulder. "Go home," he said. "Your people need you more than I do. I can do this alone."

"Thank you." Chao was off in a flash, threading his way through the chaos of wrecked buildings and wagons, dangling electric lines, dead horses and milling crowds. Quint watched him go, wondering if the two of them would ever meet again.

Forcing the thought aside, he pushed ahead toward Rutledge's place, to search for the two people who were all the world to him.

Chapter Fourteen

The first shock of the earthquake sent the tall brick chimney crashing onto the roof of the carriage house. Huddled on the carriage seat with Clara asleep beside her, Annie had fallen into a nervous doze. The deafening crack jolted her wide awake.

With dust and debris falling from the ceiling, she grabbed Clara, jumped to the floor and rolled underneath the carriage. The ground was shaking beneath them. Cracks were opening up in the walls. The horses were screaming. Annie covered Clara's ears with her hands to block the sound. But she had nothing to cover her own ears. The awful death cries filled her head.

A rat, squealing in panic, tumbled out of the ceiling and raced out of sight. The carriage shuddered as a heavy beam fell across the top. One front wheel groaned and splintered. As the chassis sagged, Annie feared she and Clara would be crushed. Miraculously, the vehicle held up under the weight, but chunks of wood, brick, furniture and broken shingles were falling all around them. If the shaking continued, the carriage would be buried, and they would be buried with it.

Clara was sobbing. Annie held her close, protecting her with her body. When the quake paused, the silence was startling. But then, before she had time to think or act, it began again. The ground bucked and twisted like an untamed mustang. The ceiling crashed down on them. The front wall crumbled inward, piling debris over the carriage, leaving them trapped underneath.

For now, at least, the shaking had stopped. They lay in the darkness, trembling as they clasped each other. At least they were together, Annie consoled herself. And at least Rutledge hadn't returned to collect on his bargain. But if they couldn't find a way out they would die right here.

Her groping hand closed on something in the darkness. It was Clara's seashell. She ran a finger along its thin edge. It was as delicate as a flower; yet it had been strong enough to survive the pounding ocean. Now it had survived the fury of an earthquake.

She and Clara would survive, too, Annie vowed. If she had to scrape her hands to bloody stubs, she would get them free. Clara deserved better than to have her life end at such a young age. She deserved to grow and learn, to fall in love, to marry and have children of her own.

Questions haunted Annie as she lay in the darkness. Would Quint live to watch his daughter grow up, or was it already too late for that? Was he out there somewhere, struggling to reach them, or had the bay already claimed his life?

"Is this a bad dream, Aunt Annie?" Clara whispered.

Annie hugged her niece closer. "No, it's not a dream, sweetheart," she said. "But when you get home you can tell your mama and papa that you were in a real earthquake! Think of that!"

Clara lay silent for a moment. "Is it over?"

Annie realized that several minutes had passed since the earth had shaken. "I don't know. But I'm going to start digging us out of here." She pressed the seashell into Clara's hand. "If you get frightened, hold this to your ear and listen to the ocean. Think about our wonderful day and be brave."

Without waiting for a response, Annie crawled forward. The space beneath the carriage was midnight black. Anything she could do would have to be done by touch.

Near the front of the carriage she ran into a wall of debris. It was as solid as a dam, bristling with nails, splinters and sharp edges. She would need some kind of tool to dig with. Otherwise her hands would be cut to ribbons in the first few minutes.

Her fingers probed the darkness searching for something she could pull loose—a stick of wood, a metal bar, anything. The best she could find was a spoke from the broken front carriage wheel, a smooth hickory shaft. It wouldn't work well for scooping. But maybe she would come across something better.

Gathering her strength she hacked at the barrier in front of her. Pieces of ruin loosened and tumbled around her. More chunks of wreckage slid downward to take their place, filling up the hole Annie had made. That was when the terrible truth struck her. There was nowhere for the material she was digging to go except under the carriage. If she knocked any more of it loose, the whole pile could collapse. She and Clara could be smothered.

Sick with despair, she wriggled backward and gathered Clara into her arms.

"What can we do now?" Clara whispered.

"We can wait," Annie said. "Wait and pray that someone will find us."

Quint ran, every step pounding pain into his wounded left shoulder. He had viewed the earthquake from a single vantage point. Only as he covered distance did he begin to realize how devastating it had been.

Chimneys had cracked and toppled, crushing the roofs beneath them. Houses had shifted off their foundations. Some had lost their entire fronts, opening the rooms to view like a child's dollhouse. Others had collapsed into piles of rubble with their top floors protruding from the ground. Huge chunks of pavement thrust up toward the sky. Trolley tracks were twisted and bent like playthings for a giant hand. The streets were littered with spilled belongings, crushed wagons and dead horses. Ruptured water mains spurted geysers. The smell of gas drifted like a miasma. A single spark could touch off raging fires, and there wouldn't be enough water to fight them. Chief Sullivan's worst fears had come to pass.

Everywhere there were people—crying children, frantic men and women, some hurt, some trapped. It tore at Quint to move on, leaving others to help. But he had to find Clara and Annie.

Rounding Nob Hill, he saw that the homes built on the heights, with solid rock beneath them, had survived with only minor damage. The mansions stood tall and proud as ever, including the one that belonged to Delilah Stanhope. The Fairmont Hotel looked to be in good condition, as well. Rutledge's place was just below the hill. Maybe that area hadn't suffered too much harm. He could only hope the carriage house would still be standing.

As he pushed himself faster, Quint felt the cold pressure of the pistol at his waist. If Josiah Rutledge tried to interfere with him, he knew he wouldn't hesitate to use it.

He stumbled over a chunk of cement, jarring his shoulder and jolting pain along his arm. That was when the realization hit him. Quint stifled a groan.

What had he been thinking? Left-handed he was a deadly shot. But his left shoulder was so weak and sore that he could scarcely raise his arm, let alone aim and fire a pistol. Right-handed he couldn't outgun a twelve-year-old kid.

But there was nothing he could do about that now. What mattered was finding Annie and Clara and getting them to safety. He would worry about his arm when the time came.

His strength was flagging by the time he caught sight of Rutledge's property. The house had suffered some damage. Chunks of stucco had broken off, exposing the old brick underneath. There was a wide crack down one side, and the top of the chimney was gone. But the structure was intact. No one inside would have been badly hurt. He could only hope the carriage house had fared as well.

The quake had twisted the wrought-iron fence, leaving a gap next to the gate. Glancing around to make sure no one was outside, Quint slipped through and melted into the shrubbery.

Crouching low, he took a moment to scan the house and grounds. Where would Josiah Rutledge be? Safe in the widow Stanhope's satin bed? Watching, perhaps, from an upstairs window? Or would he be at the carriage house, waiting, knowing Quint would come?

Trees hid the carriage house from view, but Quint guessed it would be at the end of the drive. Cutting a course through the tangled undergrowth, he strode up the slope. Where the trees thinned out into a clearing he froze as if the life had been drained from his body.

The carriage house was little more than a scattered heap of broken bricks and timbers.

It was plain to see what had happened. The chimney had fallen through the roof and sent the rotted beams crashing down through the floorboards of the attic. When the joists gave way, the front and back wall had collapsed inward.

Quint felt as if his world had collapsed, as well.

At the far end, the leg of a horse thrust out of the wreckage. There was no other sign of anything having been alive in the place. But Quint knew that he couldn't just walk away. If Clara and Annie had died here, he couldn't rest until he'd found their bodies and brought them home to Dutchman's Creek.

One end of the structure was still standing, supported by a stairway built against the wall. Near the foot of the stairs was a closed door. If they'd tried to get out, they'd most likely be in that area. Striding forward, he picked up a fallen roof beam and swung it to one side. Even using his good arm, the strain ripped across his back. But never mind that. If he had to, he would move every damned rock, brick and timber in the whole God-cursed place.

Grief and fury recharged his strength. Heedless of the sling on his left arm, he tore into the rubble, flinging aside what he could and dragging what was too heavy to toss. Memories swept over him— Clara running along the edge of the waves, the wonder on her face as she held the seashell to her ear. Annie in white, stepping out of the carriage like a young duchess; Annie in his arms, her skin warm satin against his, her legs opening to welcome him into her body; her trusting, passionate kisses…

Tears of rage burned his eyes. It wasn't supposed to be like this. Clara was meant to grow into a lovely young woman. Annie was meant to be the love of his life and the mother of his children. But he'd never told her, not a blasted word of what he felt. Lord, he'd give anything to undo what had happened, anything to bring them back.

What was that? It sounded like a faint cry from somewhere under the rubble. An animal, maybe a dog or cat—or more likely his own imagination.

No, there it was again. Quint froze, listening. A voice. Human. Maybe more than one. Frantically he plowed toward the sound. Nails and splinters jabbed into his hands. He barely felt them.

Suddenly there was space beyond his hand. And a cry of disbelief. "Annie!" he gasped. "Is that you?"

A scratched, bruised hand stretched to reach his.

He felt the touch of her fingertips. Her flesh was warm and solid, the contact so precious that it almost shattered him.

"Clara's here," she said. "We're all right."

There were no words for what he felt.

He widened the opening, scraping away more layers of rubble. Now he could see them, covered with grime and crammed into a coffin-size space beneath the carriage. Quint could only imagine the hell they'd been through.

Clara crawled out first. Her nightgown was torn and filthy, her small face covered with dirt. Breathing silent thanks, Quint clasped his daughter close. "Look, Uncle Quint, I've got my seashell," she said.

Dropping to his knees, he put Clara down in a safe place. Thrusting his good arm into the debris he caught Annie's hand and eased her into the open. She emerged little by little, inching through a gauntlet of nails and splinters to crumple against him. Her dirt-streaked face was etched with blood along one cheek. Her hair and clothes were coated with dust. To Quint she had never looked more beautiful.

Scooping Clara into the circle of his arm, he held them both. Annie was weeping softly, whispering his name over and over. Clara was quivering. Quint was overcome with gratitude. Fate—or a miracle—had given these two dear ones back to him. He would sacrifice his life to keep them from more harm.

His lips brushed Annie's tangled hair. There were

so many things he needed to say to her. But this was a dangerous place. He had to find safe shelter where they could get food and water. After that there'd be time to talk.

"We need to go." He eased Annie to her feet and lifted Clara with his right arm. His left arm had stiffened in its tattered sling. He could feel blood trickling down his back where his wound had opened. He clenched his teeth against the pain.

Clara hugged him around the neck and kissed his cheek. "I love you, Uncle Quint," she said.

"And I love you, princess." Quint forced the words past the lump in his throat. After a moment's hesitation, he passed her to Annie. "It's best you take her for now," he said. "I'll keep an eye out for trouble. If anything goes wrong, get her out of here. Just go. Whatever happens, don't look back. Understand?"

She nodded, her storm-colored eyes meeting his. Little Annie, so sensible and brave. He could count on her to do the right thing. Quint had never loved her more than at that moment.

"If we get separated, wait for me in Union Square. You know how to get there?"

She nodded again, eyes brimming. Quiet now, Clara clung to her.

"I'll come and find you," he said. "If I'm not there in an hour, head down Market Street, get on the ferry and leave."

"Leave? But can't we just go to your flat?"

"The flat's gone, Annie, along with everything in it. And things are going to get even worse. The gas and water mains are broken. San Francisco is a tinderbox. There'll be fires—fires like nobody's ever seen before. The whole city could go up in flames. I know you've a mind of your own, but this time you need to do exactly as I say. Whatever happens to me, I want to know that the two of you will be safe."

"I understand," she whispered. "Union Square. We'll be waiting."

Quint fumbled with his belt. His right hand drew the pistol out of its holster. Annie's gaze flickered from the gun to his injured arm. Her eyes widened. "Quint, your left hand. You can't—"

"Hush," he said. "With luck I won't have any reason to use this."

"Give me the gun," she argued. "You know I'm a decent shot. You taught me yourself. And don't think I couldn't pull the trigger. It would be a pleasure to plug Rutledge right between the eyes."

He shook his head. "I taught you to shoot a .22 rifle, not a pistol, Annie. And your job is to get Clara out of here. Mine is to bring up the rear and protect the two of you." He scanned the clearing. "Speaking of Rutledge, do you know where he might be?"

"Right here, Seavers." Josiah Rutledge stepped out from behind the standing end of the carriage shed, a cocked .38 pistol in his hand. "Drop that gun now, or you won't be the first one to die."

* * *

Annie glanced from one man to the other. Rutledge, in shirtsleeves, looked red-eyed, rumpled and mean. He held the pistol as if he knew how to use it. How could she run when Quint might not be able to stop him from shooting her and Clara?

"Go, Annie!" Quint whispered. "Go now!"

There was no time to think, only to trust and react. Cradling Clara against her chest, Annie sprinted for the trees. Every few steps she changed direction. She'd hunted enough rabbits to know that zigzagging made a target harder to hit. She hunched her shoulders, angling her body to shield her precious burden. Any second she expected to hear the shot and feel the bullet burning into her flesh.

Behind her, she could hear Quint's voice. "Pull that trigger, and you're a dead man, Rutledge. I grew up on a ranch, and I'll wager I'm a better shot than you are."

Annie knew better than to look back, but she could picture Quint standing his ground with the pistol in his right hand. While Rutledge ducked back behind the wall, Quint was bluffing for all he was worth, holding Rutledge at bay while she and Clara made their escape.

"Let them go," Quint argued. "Your quarrel is with me, not with them. I've got your letter right here. You can have it with my blessing. After today, who's going to give a damn about it?"

Annie plunged ahead. Was she leaving Quint to die? But she knew better than to ask that question. She was doing what had to be done, what he would want her to do.

A shot rang out behind her, spattering dirt on her shoes. That would be Rutledge. The answering report from Quint's pistol was almost instantaneous. Annie heard the whine as the bullet struck something solid and ricocheted off. She could imagine Quint's frustration.

"Hell, Seavers, I thought you said you could shoot!" Rutledge roared. "You want me to come closer so you can have a better chance?" He fired another shot.

By now Annie had reached the trees. The bullet nicked a trunk a few inches to her left. Clutching Clara, she dropped to her knees and crawled deeper into the undergrowth. The man had shot twice, barely missing her both times. He was proving himself a fair marksman. But now he could no longer see her. Now he would turn his gun on Quint.

Don't look back.

Keeping low she crept down the wooded slope. Through the undergrowth she glimpsed the wrought-iron fence, the broken gate and the street beyond. Behind her she heard one more pistol shot. Just one.

Annie swallowed her tears, clutched Clara tight and kept moving.

* * *

Rutledge was shooting from behind the standing end of the carriage shed. His bullet grazed a broken roof beam, missing Quint's head by an inch.

Flattened on the ground, protected by the rubble he'd dug loose to free Annie and Clara, Quint purpled the air with curses. Even firing right-handed he'd have given himself a fair chance against Rutledge. But he hadn't counted on the bastard knowing how to shoot.

With the two of them no more than a dozen paces apart, range wasn't an issue. But with Rutledge pinning him down, Quint didn't dare raise his head. And it wasn't worth risking another bad shot. His only hope would be to goad the butcher into emptying his gun.

At least Annie and Clara had made a clean escape. It would be worth his life to keep Rutledge from going after them. He would stall for as long as he could, giving them time to get away.

"Stand up, Seavers," Rutledge bellowed. "I know you're wounded. I saw the blood. And I saw the shape you're in. You haven't got a chance."

"If you're making me an offer, I'd like to hear it," Quint responded.

"I'll make it easy on you. Hand over the letter and I'll let you go. We'll forget all about this little tempest in a teapot. As you say, after today nobody's going to care about a few leaky water pipes."

"Lord, you don't know what's happening out there, do you? You just got out of bed. You haven't seen the city. You don't know what's about to happen."

"I suppose you're going to tell me." Rutledge's voice dripped sarcasm.

"You're damned right I am. The gas and water lines are broken and, thanks to you and your contractor friend, most of the cisterns are empty. Chief Sullivan knew what he was talking about. San Francisco is about to go up like a torch, and there'll be no water to fight the blaze."

"You're talking crap!" Rutledge snarled. "If the quake damage is as bad as you say, the repairs wouldn't have made any difference. The work and the money would've been wasted."

"Tell that to Virginia Poole."

Rutledge's pistol cracked. Anticipating the shot, Quint flattened himself against the earth. The bullet slammed into the rubble pile, raising a puff of dust. By Quint's count, Rutledge had fired four shots. Unless he reloaded, he should have no more than two bullets left.

Feeling light-headed, Quint struggled to focus his vision. He'd overspent his strength and lost more blood than he wanted to think about. He fought the dark mist that threatened to drag him under. Just a little longer. When Annie and Clara were safe he could rest.

The earth quivered beneath his body. The aftershock was slight, but Quint felt it. Several bricks toppled from the standing wall of the carriage house. With nothing holding it except the staircase, the crumbling structure was on the verge of collapse.

He fought back waves of dizziness. "You're not just a crook, Rutledge, you're a murderer. You killed that poor woman as surely as if you'd been there!"

"That's a lie!" Rutledge snapped. "I had nothing to do with what happened to the little fool!"

"You told me she left to take care of her sick mother. It appears to me that you're the liar."

Rutledge cursed and fired again. This time the bullet hit the ground and burrowed into the rubble. Rutledge was shooting from a low angle. To see and hit his target he would need to get to a higher vantage point.

With only one bullet left in the .38, he would want to make his last shot count. It would mean exposing himself to Quint's fire, but Quint had already shown himself to be a poor marksman. Rutledge would be angry and confident. With luck, it would make him reckless.

Quint kept low behind the piled debris, relying on his ears to tell him what was happening. Rutledge was edging around the wall, approaching the exposed staircase. "You'd better kill me now, you butcher," Quint taunted him. "Otherwise, I won't rest until I see you hang."

The stairs creaked slightly, once, then again.

Soon Rutledge would be high enough to look down at him. Quint's muscles tensed. His vision swam. He was so weak he could barely raise the pistol. But if his plan worked, he wouldn't have to hit Rutledge—just the wall.

Was it really a plan? Did it make any sense? The dark fog swirled in his mind, threatening to blot out consciousness. Quint fought against the urge to let go and sink into it. Just a few seconds more…

Rutledge had reached the top of the stairs. Quint could see him now. He was so high that the upper part of him stood out against the morning sky. He swayed lightly in the breeze.

"Die, you muckraking bastard!" Rutledge shrieked. Aiming down at Quint he pulled the trigger.

The bullet slammed into the earth where Quint's body had been an instant before. Rolling to the side, Quint felt his reflexes kick in. He fired four rapid shots in a line along the wall.

Rutledge teetered. Had he been hit, or was he just startled? Quint would never know because at that instant the wall groaned and began to disintegrate. The stairs came loose, pitching Rutledge to the floor of the carriage house. He screamed as the entire wall toppled, burying him in chunks of brick and mortar.

As the dust cleared, Quint dropped the pistol, closed his eyes and surrendered to darkness.

* * *

Annie walked through a living nightmare. Clutching Clara against her shoulder, she gazed at the twisted streets, the ruined buildings, the overturned trolley cars, the dead bodies. She covered Clara's eyes against the worst sights. But there was no hiding it all. The little girl would remember this horror for the rest of her life.

The stillness was eerie. People wandered the streets in shock. There were no rumbling wagon wheels, no clanging trolleys or auto horns. Strangest of all, despite the disaster no alarms were ringing. The city had lost all electrical power. Telephone and telegraph lines were down, as well. San Francisco, the most vibrant of cities, lay in helpless ruin, cut off from the rest of the world.

Union Square, by her calculation, should be a few blocks ahead. Quint had ordered her to wait, and she would. But she dared not hope he would come. The finality of that last gunshot had told her all she needed to know. She and Clara were alive because Quint had given his life to save them.

Quint had never told her he loved her. But his sacrifice had been the ultimate act of love. That knowledge was all she would ever have of him.

Tears blurred her eyes. Annie willed them away. Right now it was her job to make sure Quint hadn't died in vain. Whatever it took, she would get his daughter to safety.

Near the downtown area there was more activity. Crews of men were digging survivors out of collapsed buildings. Volunteers and medical workers carried the injured on stretchers. Horse-drawn ambulances raced them to first-aid stations and hospitals. Slower-moving wagons bore the dead away.

Gazing toward Market Street, Annie saw that some of the older shops and hotels had collapsed, but the newer buildings, reinforced with steel, were still standing. The Palace Hotel had been spared, as well. The huge clock had fallen from the *Chronicle* Building where Quint worked—or had worked. But Annie couldn't let herself think about that now.

Union Square swarmed with people. They sat on the grass, flocked around the marble column of the Admiral Dewey monument and crowded the steps of the St. Francis hotel. Many of them had been evacuated in their night clothes. Annie's gaze lingered on a stout, dark-haired man clad in striped silk pajamas and a fur coat. He was pacing in circles, muttering furiously in Italian. She recognized his face from the posters at the opera. It was Enrico Caruso.

As Annie gazed around her, the grimness of their situation began to sink in. She was exhausted, and Clara was in even worse condition. They had no food, no water, no shelter and no spare clothes. Quint's flat had been destroyed, everything in it lost. The only money she had was the wad of small bills she'd stuffed into her bodice for cab fare. It might not even be enough to get them onto the ferry.

Clara had been very quiet. Now she stirred in Annie's arms. "Look, Aunt Annie!" she whispered, pointing. "Smoke!"

Turning, Annie followed the direction of her gaze. To the south, where the city's poor crowded into wooden houses and tenements, a column of black smoke was rising against the sky. They watched it grow and spread, flames leaping, smoke billowing into the heavens, coming closer by the minute.

It was happening just as Quint had said it would. San Francisco was on fire.

Chapter Fifteen

Quint groaned, stirred and opened his eyes. The ground was cold grit beneath his body, the sun a bloodred blaze in the morning sky. The pistol lay a few inches from his hand. The sight of it brought back everything that had happened.

Jolted awake, he struggled to his feet. His shoulder hurt like hell, but the wound felt more stiff and sore than inflamed. Since there wasn't much he could do about it, he could only hope he was right.

The end wall of the carriage house lay crumbled where it had fallen. Still unsteady, Quint picked up the pistol and walked toward it. As he came closer, a grisly sight stopped him in his tracks.

Rutledge's dust-covered hand thrust out of the rubble, fingers clutching at the air. The signet ring, with its obscenely large ruby, glimmered in the sunlight.

Quint moved nearer, forcing his eyes to look. He hadn't wanted Josiah Rutledge dead. He'd wanted to bring him to justice, to make him answer to the people of San Francisco for his crimes. But the whole world had changed since yesterday, and this was the justice fate had decreed.

Only one thing remained to be done.

Reaching inside his vest pocket he found the folded letter. It was still damp. If he were to unfold it now he would probably find it ruined. But that no longer mattered.

Stooping, he placed the letter between Rutledge's lifeless fingers. The bloody bastard had what he wanted now. He could take it with him all the way to hell.

As he turned away, Quint saw the smoke. It was rising in huge black billows from the tinderbox of wooden dwellings south of Market Street. Here and there, leaping tongues of fire shot skyward.

Quint's heart slammed. How long had he been passed out? An hour, maybe two, judging from the height of the sun. If Annie and Clara had made it to Union Square, they might already be leaving for the ferry. He had to find them. He needed to make sure they were all right. And he didn't want Annie to leave without hearing the words he'd held back too long.

On the verge of rushing off, he stopped himself. Annie had left with nothing for herself and Clara. They would be hungry, thirsty, chilled and exhausted. There was only so much he could bring them, but he wouldn't arrive empty-handed.

The nearest source of provisions was Rutledge's house. Quint found the door open, the servants gone and the kitchen decently stocked. He chose items that would be easy to carry and keep—cheese, apples, a salami and a tin of crackers, which he dropped into an empty flour sack along with napkins and a paring knife. The water supply was down to a trickle but he coaxed enough out of the kitchen faucet to fill a mason jar. Ranging farther, he found a clean washcloth and a knitted afghan. Rolling everything into a bundle, he thrust it under his arm and set off at an urgent pace for Union Square. He was bursting with things he needed to tell Annie, things he'd been too muleheaded to say when he'd had the chance. He couldn't let her get away without hearing them.

The fire was roaring closer now, sweeping north in a relentless line toward the barrier of Market Street. Smoke blackened the air. The veiled sun cast a hellish glow over the dying city. Flames leaped skyward in a show of awful beauty.

Refugees were funneling into Market Street from all directions, lugging whatever they could salvage from their ruined homes. Seated with Clara at the base of the Dewey Monument, Annie watched them trek past. Carts, wheelbarrows, even baby buggies and toy wagons, loaded with family treasures, rolled down the street toward the ferry. One man pushed a piano on a sagging hand trolley. A woman staggered under the weight of the sewing machine slung on her back. Children too weary to cry shuffled along behind their parents. One little girl clutched a broken doll as if it were all she had in the world.

Clara stirred on Annie's lap. "I'm scared, Aunt Annie. I don't want us to burn up."

Annie hugged her. "Hush, sweetheart. I won't let us burn up. We'll be fine."

"Peter Rabbit might burn up. Why can't we go back and get him?"

"We can't go back because we have to get on the boat. I'll find you a new Peter Rabbit, I promise."

"Where's Uncle Quint? Isn't he coming?"

Annie felt the tightening, like a cold iron band squeezing her chest. "Maybe he's busy helping people," she said. "He'll get here if he can, but we might not be able to wait for him."

Annie had no view of a clock, but the sun was climbing the sky. They'd been here for at least an hour, maybe longer. Part of her had refused to believe that Quint wouldn't be coming. But it was time she accepted it as fact and moved ahead.

Clara's eyes were bloodshot. She coughed. "That smoke hurts my throat. Is it time to go yet?"

Yes, it was time to go. She had to get Clara to the ferry before the fire got any closer. But they could have a long wait to board. There would be hundreds, maybe thousands of people ahead of them. Annie knew they'd have been better off going right away. But Quint had asked her to wait. So she had waited, hoping against hope that he would come.

Laughing, passionate, danger-loving Quint. His deep brown eyes and mischievous smile flashed in her memory.

Greater love hath no man than this...

Fighting tears, she lifted Clara in her arms and joined the trudging stream of refugees.

By the time Quint reached Union Square it was almost empty. There was no sign of Annie or Clara. He could only hope they were on their way to the ferry. The fire had become a roaring monster, moving ever closer to the downtown area. The sound of it raised the hair on the back of Quint's neck.

Army units from the Presidio were patrolling the streets with fixed bayonets, herding people toward the ferry or toward open ground where camps could be set up. An official-looking sign, posted on a power pole, proclaimed that looters would be shot on sight. A mounted officer gave Quint a suspicious glance, then, distracted, galloped off in another direction.

A pump wagon, drawn by a four-horse team, stood at one corner of the square. The firefighters were connecting hoses to a hydrant. They recognized Quint as he hailed them.

"Any water down there?" Quint asked.

"There's supposed to be a cistern, but we won't know what's inside till we turn it on. Not that it'll make much difference against that." The weary-looking fireman nodded toward the moving confla-gration. "There's talk of using dynamite to blast firebreaks. But that's a dangerous business. If it's not done right, it could start more fires than it stops."

"Where's Chief Sullivan? He knows a lot about using dynamite."

The six firemen all glanced at Quint. His heart dropped as he saw the despair in their eyes. Seconds passed before one of them spoke. "The chief's dead—or dying. He was crushed in the Bush Street Firehouse. Got out of bed and fell through the floor."

"Oh, Lord…" Quint turned away, leaving the men to their work. The destruction of San Francisco was too monstrous to grasp. But the loss of Dennis Sullivan, the one man who might have known how to fight the fire, made it personal.

He strode through the stinging smoke toward Market Street, following the route Annie would most likely have taken with Clara. A river of people flowed toward the Ferry Building. Quint darted among them, searching for a slender figure in black with a tired little girl in her arms. Had they made it this far? Were they even here?

The Ferry Building was still standing. An end-less, crawling line had formed as people waited to board. Some of them clamored outside the building, shouting, demanding to go ahead. Others, knowing the wait would be long, slumped beside their possessions, dragging them by inches as the line crept forward. Abandoned furniture, loaded carts and oversize trunks crowded the ground on both sides of the line. Word had been passed back that the ferry was taking passengers free of charge, but allowing them no more baggage than they could carry in their arms.

To the south, the fire roared against the sky. Navy tug and fireboat crews fought to save the waterfront, hosing the docks and warehouses with water pumped from the bay. Farther out, private vessels milled at anchor, safe from the flames.

Quint searched along the line, growing more worried by the minute. Once he glimpsed a flash of tawny blond hair and plunged toward it—but when the woman turned her head, he found himself staring at the painted face of a streetwalker.

Asking about a woman and child had gotten him nowhere. There were too many people, most of them too wretched to pay attention. Maybe Annie hadn't waited for him at Union Square. Maybe she'd just gone on to the ferry. That would have been the smart thing to do. But what if she'd never made it this far? What if she and Clara were lost somewhere, set upon by thugs or trapped in the doomed city?

Checking with the ferry operators would be a

waste of time. They'd have no record of who'd boarded, especially not today. But Quint knew he had to keep looking. He couldn't give up until he knew what had happened.

Annie shuffled forward in the line. One hand gripped Clara's. The other hand shaded her eyes as she watched the progress of the fire. By now, the Grand Opera House would be nothing but charred timbers. Soon, if the blaze couldn't be stopped, flames would be licking at the Palace Hotel and the gleaming skyscrapers of downtown.

She swayed slightly, almost nodding off where she stood. She was dead on her feet, and poor little Clara was in even worse condition. But to rest would mean losing their place in line, and by now they were close to the front. They had to make it onto the ferry.

News of the quake would soon be racing across the country. Even in Dutchman's Creek they would hear about it. Hannah and Judd would be worried sick. She would send them a telegram from Oakland, letting them know that she and Clara were on their way.

But what would she tell them about Quint?

Would she tell them he was missing? That he was dead? That he'd given his life to save them?

Her mind was too pain-numbed to answer that question.

"Annie!"

The voice that shouted her name sounded far away.

Why should she pay attention? How many dozens of females named Annie were standing in this line?

"Annie! Clara! Over here!"

Clara yanked her hand. "It's Uncle Quint! Look!"

Steeling herself for a mistake, Annie turned around slowly. She could see him now, dodging his way through the crowd, bruised, torn and dirty. His left arm was still supported by the ragged sling. Tucked under it was a tightly rolled bundle.

Lifting Clara in her arms, she watched him come. Emotions she'd struggled to bury surged to the surface like the freshets of a spring thaw.

She shattered as he reached them. Sobs shook her body as he hooked them both with his free arm and held them close. He smelled of dust and smoke and sweat and blood. Quint, alive and safe. Annie wanted to drink him into her senses, to make him part of her and never let him go again.

With Clara pressed awkwardly between them, he kissed her cheeks, her closed eyelids. When he kissed her mouth she tasted her own tears. "Don't cry, Annie," he muttered. "It's all right. We've found each other."

"What happened?" she managed to ask. "Where's Rutledge?"

"In his grave. I'll tell you about it later. That's not why I'm here. Listen to me, there's not much time."

She stared up at him. What was he talking about? The line shifted forward. Someone nudged them from behind, and they shifted with it. Annie suddenly realized they'd be in the group for the next ferry.

"I can't let you leave without telling you I love you, Annie," he said. "You know I don't take those words lightly. When we get through this crazy mess I mean to do something about it. So don't you dare go home and marry Frank Robinson. Hear?"

Her eyes widened. "You mean you're staying here? That's crazy! You don't even have a place to live!"

He stepped back, thrusting the bundle under her arm. "Here. Some things for the trip. It was the best I could do on short notice. The railroad is taking people for free, but just in case you need it—" He fished a handful of soggy bills out of his pocket and pressed them into her hand. "San Francisco is my home, Annie. I'm needed here. I have a job to do, and I can't just walk away. You and Clara are safe now. We'll both be fine."

"Quint, this is insane!" The line was sweeping her into the building like a river in flood. "Come with us!"

He had stepped aside and was already beyond her reach. "I'll write!" he shouted over the crowd. "I love you, Annie! I love you!"

In the next instant the double doors closed behind her. Choking on tears, Annie clasped Clara tight and moved toward the gangplank.

As the ferry pushed across the bay she stood at the rail, gazing back at the burning city. Above the horizon, the blazing sky cast a hellish glow over the water. Blistering hues of yellow, crimson and amber rose into soot-black clouds that blotted out the sun. She and Clara were safe, headed for home. But somewhere back there in that horror was Quint, who'd finally said he loved her.

If he really loved her, why wasn't he here, standing at her side? She could live a hundred years and never understand the man.

The fire had reached the skyscrapers in the center of downtown. Burning from the inside, they glowed like giant candles as the flames crept upward.

Heartsick, Annie turned away.

Dutchman's Creek, Colorado
May 7, 1906

Annie's knees went liquid as the postmaster handed her the battered envelope. She had haunted the Dutchman's Creek post office for the past two weeks, hoping for some word from Quint. At last, here it was, addressed to her in Quint's familiar, sprawling hand.

Giddy with relief, she walked outside to the hitching rail where she'd left the buggy. Her first impulse was to rip the envelope open and read the letter on the spot. But with her emotions so raw, that could prove to be a mistake. She would do the prudent thing and wait until she was alone.

Climbing into the buggy, she took the road that led across the open pastureland to the Seavers ranch. Although she usually boarded in town, Annie had been staying at the ranch to help out. With Hannah bedridden and Clara still fragile, she knew she was needed there.

A mile out of Dutchman's Creek, she pulled the buggy off the road and into the shade of a big cottonwood tree. There in the dappled shade, with meadowlarks calling and sunlight streaming through the branches, she opened Quint's letter. The single page was crammed with writing on both sides.

San Francisco
April 29, 1906
Dearest Annie,
Finally a chance to write! I've been camping with a crew of newspaper folks in a half-ruined mansion on Pierce Street. There's no electricity or water, and we have to do our cooking on the sidewalk, but the pantry's well stocked and, yes, we do have the owner's permission to be here. We're gathering stories from all over town and ferrying the news to Oakland for printing. Newspapers are the lifeblood of a city. We're doing our best to keep that lifeblood flowing.

Annie glanced up from the letter. Her eyes followed the flight of a red-tailed hawk along the willow-lined path of the creek. Quint had said he needed to stay and do his job. She understood how important that job was. But she and Clara had needed him, too. The trip home had been exhausting, with Clara feverish most of the way. And telling Judd and Hannah about the kidnapping had been one of the hardest things she'd ever done.

I don't need to tell you how bad it was here. You saw that for yourself. It took three days to bring the fires under control. By the time we were able to stop and count the cost, two-thirds of the city had been destroyed. To be here and see it has been unimaginable. I hope, by now, you understand why I couldn't leave.

Did she understand? Heaven knows, she was trying. But this was so typical of Quint, rushing into danger, heedless of the anguish he was causing the people who loved him. Annie read on.

Chao says hello. He and his family are living at a camp set up for Chinese in the Presidio. And Clara will be happy to hear that the bear and the other animals in the park are fine. You can also tell her that I went back to what was left of the flat and found Peter Rabbit. He'll need some cleaning up and a bit of mending. Maybe you can do that when I come to Colorado early next month.

When I come to Colorado...

Annie's heart slammed. Quint was coming home at last. But for how long? Did he actually mean to stay? Hands shaking, she turned the page over.

I won't have much time to spend at the ranch—which brings me to my real reason for writing. I want you to come back to San Francisco with me, Annie, as my wife. Granted, I haven't given you much of a courtship—not like Frank Robinson would. But I love you and I've discovered that I can't be happy without you. You are my safe harbor, my rock and my anchor. You know the best and worst of me. I've made my share of mistakes and I'm far from perfect husband material. All I can offer you is what I have and who I am. It's less than you deserve, but I hope it will be enough.

I know better than to assume you'll have me. It's not an easy life I'd be bringing you to. But San Francisco is rising from its ashes, and we'd have the chance to rise with it. Housing is scarce, but I've put a deposit on a small flat in North Beach where the fire didn't reach. My investments are safe, so before long we'd be able to move to a better place, maybe a fine house. I want the best for you, and it will be the best. San Francisco is going to be everything it was, and more.

Take your time. You can give me your answer when I arrive. If it's no, I'll understand. But I hope you'll make me the luckiest man on earth. Think what a wonderful life we could have together...

Tears blurred Annie's eyes. She had wanted Quint for years. But wanting was simple. Having was a lot more complicated. Quint's footloose ways had broken her sister's heart. Would they break hers, as well?

Rousing the horses, she guided the buggy back onto the road. Quint was as restless as a wild mustang, ready to rush off at the slightest whiff of adventure. How could she tie him down with a family and expect him to be happy? How could she be dependent on him when he might not be there for her?

How could she say no when she loved him so much?

Annie gazed at the far mountains, still glittering with unmelted snow. A flock of blackbirds swooped low over a newly planted field. Next to a clapboard farmhouse, an apple tree quivered with white blossoms.

Quint had given her plenty of time. But with her heart and head at war, how could she trust herself to make a decision?

She needed to talk with the one person who understood and loved them both.

* * *

Annie found her sister sitting up in bed, propped against the pillows. Her hands cradled her enormous belly. Daniel chugged a toy train over her feet. Clara sat cross-legged, drawing pictures in a notebook. Toy animals and wax crayons littered the patchwork quilt.

"I don't know how you manage it," Annie said. "Less than two weeks to go, and you still look beautiful."

"As beautiful as a bloated cow," Hannah responded with a strained laugh. "I see you have a letter. Judging by the look on your face, I'd guess it's from Quint."

Annie nodded. "He's fine. I'll let you read it when you have some peace and quiet."

"I could use some peace and quiet right now." Hannah shooed her children off the bed. "Take your brother out to play with the puppy, Clara. Tell Rosa where you're going, and don't let Daniel get in the mud, all right?"

Annie closed the bedroom door as the youngsters scampered down the stairs. "Read it all," she said, taking a seat and handing Hannah the letter. "Then you can help me decide what to do."

Hannah unfolded the letter. Annie watched her face as she read it, studying her response. When she turned the paper over, Hannah's eyes lit up. Her smile widened as she read down the page to the end.

"Why, Annie, this is wonderful! You and Quint— I've been hoping it would happen! You're the perfect woman for him! We can have the wedding—" She broke off, staring at Annie's distressed face. "What on earth's the matter?"

Annie stared down at her hands. "I'm scared, Hannah. What if Quint doesn't really love me? What if it's you he's wanted all along, and I'm just the consolation prize?"

Hannah refolded the letter. "That's foolishness. Quint and I were childhood sweethearts. And that's all we were—just children. Even when Clara was conceived, we were just two kids who barely knew what we were doing. Then Quint went off to try his wings and I fell in love with Judd. Looking back, I know I was meant to be with him—just as Quint was meant to be with you."

"But what if I tie him down? What if he gets tired of having a wife and wants to be free?"

Hannah reached out and captured Annie's hand, cradling it in her own. "My sensible, cautious little sister! Don't you know how many brides-to-be have asked themselves that same question? Marriage is about risking your heart. It's about loving someone enough to take that chance." Her grip tightened. "Do you love Quint?"

Tears welled in Annie's eyes. "Oh, I do. I love

him so much I can hardly stand it. That's why I'm afraid."

Hannah brushed a kiss onto her sister's cheek. "Then listen, my dear one," she said, "not to your fear but to your heart."

Epilogue

⁘☙∞☙⁘

Dutchman's Creek
June 8, 1906

The Gustavson family wedding gown was out of style and yellowed with age. One sleeve bore a tiny burgundy stain from the wine that Mary and Soren Gustavson had drunk to toast their wedding in Norway. The hem was slightly grass-stained from the game of tag Hannah had played with the children after her wedding to Judd. Because the lace was too fragile to hold a tight seam, Annie hadn't attempted to take in the waist. Instead she had fashioned a rose satin cummerbund with a trailing bow to fit the dress to her slender middle. Only the veil was new—a plain circle of tulle gathered and pinned to Annie's upswept hair with one of Hannah's precious pink roses.

Her widowed mother and her sister Emma, who'd just become engaged to a boy from town, had helped Annie dress. Now they'd gone to take their seats, leaving her alone in the downstairs bedroom where Quint's mother had spent her last days. Standing before the mirror, Annie smiled at her reflection. Once she'd dreamed of walking down the aisle in elegant ivory silk. A kidnapping and an earthquake had taught her how little such things mattered. She was about to marry the only man she would ever love. Their families and friends were here to share their joy. The timeworn gown was perfect.

"Hurry, Aunt Annie! Everybody's waiting!" Clara darted into the room, her cheeks as pink as the ribbons on her new dress. One arm clutched a cleaned and mended Peter Rabbit, looking smart in his new red jacket.

"I'm coming." Annie picked up her bouquet of freshly picked roses and baby's breath and followed her niece out onto the porch. There her ten-year-old brother Samuel was waiting to escort her across the lawn to the blooming snowball bushes that would serve as a backdrop for the ceremony.

Her eyes swept over the people who'd gathered to celebrate. Her landlady and some friends from town were there, as well as Rosa and her family. Annie's mother sat with her younger children, all of them scrubbed and beaming. Next to them, Hannah sat in the soft armchair Judd had carried outside for her. In her arms, she cradled her new daughter, Mary Kate, to be called Katy. Three-year-old Daniel, never still, darted among the chairs until corralled by his grandmother.

Waiting by the snowball bushes, clad in ministerial black stood Annie's twenty-one-year-old brother Ephraim. Newly ordained, he was thrilled to be officiating at his first wedding ceremony. On his left, Quint stood beside Judd. His impossibly handsome face broke into a smile as Annie glided toward him.

His lips shaped the words *I love you*—words that were reflected in his adoring eyes. Annie knew those words were true. Quint would give his life for her. He very nearly had.

"I love you, too," she whispered, her eyes misting as the ceremony began that would make them man and wife.

Marriage to Quint wouldn't be easy. Annie had come to accept that. But it would never be dull. There would always be new places to see, new adventures and new challenges. But through it all, she knew he would take care of her and their children. He would be a loving husband and father, and she would always be there for him.

Her hand trembled as he slipped the finely worked gold band on her finger. She would never take it off, Annie vowed. She was Quint's wife now.

* * * * *

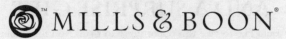

2 FREE BOOKS
AND A SURPRISE GIFT

We would like to take this opportunity to thank you for reading this Mills & Boon® book by offering you the chance to take TWO more specially selected books from the Historical series absolutely FREE! We're also making this offer to introduce you to the benefits of the Mills & Boon® Book Club™—

- **FREE home delivery**
- **FREE gifts and competitions**
- **FREE monthly Newsletter**
- **Exclusive Mills & Boon Book Club offers**
- **Books available before they're in the shops**

Accepting these FREE books and gift places you under no obligation to buy, you may cancel at any time, even after receiving your free books. Simply complete your details below and return the entire page to the address below. You don't even need a stamp!

YES Please send me 2 free Historical books and a surprise gift. I understand that unless you hear from me, I will receive 4 superb new books every month for just £3.79 each, postage and packing free. I am under no obligation to purchase any books and may cancel my subscription at any time. The free books and gift will be mine to keep in any case.

Ms/Mrs/Miss/Mr ——————— Initials ———————

Surname ————————————————————

Address ————————————————————

——————————————— Postcode ———————

E-mail ————————————————————

Send this whole page to: Mills & Boon Book Club, Free Book Offer, FREEPOST NAT 10298, Richmond, TW9 1BR